THE APOCALYPSE PARABLE

A Novel By

Brian Kaufman

This book is a work of fiction. Names, characters, place and incidence either are the product of the author's imagination or are used fictitiously and any resemblance to actual persona, living or dead, business establishments, events or locals are purely coincidental.

The Apocalypse Parable: A Conspiracy of Weeds
A Last Knight Publishing Company book
Copyright 2006 Last Knight Publishing Company
All Rights Reserved

No part of this book may be reproduced or transmitted in any form or any means, electronic or mechanical, including photocopying, recording or by any information storage and retrieval system, without the written permission of the publisher.

ISBN # 0-9720442-5-6

Cover Illustration by Waldek Kaminski
Cover design and text formatting by New Renaissance Studios

Printed by Colorado Printing
Grand Junction, CO 81520
USA

For my Mom and Dad
- Brian

"A hypothesis is always more believable than the truth, for it has been tailored to resemble our ideas of the truth, whereas the truth is just its own clumsy self."

— Machiavelli

I

The old man sat up a little, held back by wires and tubes that pinned him to the bed like a shriveled Gulliver.

"Ninety-five hundred dollars," he said. "That's more than your usual retainer, isn't it?"

Daniel nodded, staring at the check on the night stand, wondering how high the check would bounce if it slipped out from under the prescription bottle and hit the floor. He needed the money. The car insurance was about to lapse and the rent had emptied his checking account. But if the check was bad, what good would it do? And if the check was good, the job would be bad.

"When you finish the assignment, I'll pay you the balance," the old man croaked. "One hundred thousand dollars. You probably don't make that much in three years."

The tick of the machine beside the bed marked the silence. Daniel closed his eyes and chewed the inside of his cheek. The air in the old man's office was stiff with the odor of disinfectant and alcohol. Mordecai Ryan rustled under the covers, dry skin sliding around on crisp sheets. "I'm not sure what you have in mind," Daniel said at last. "I'm a skip-tracer. I find people that are hiding from creditors."

"And I want you to find someone," the old man said.

"I'm not a hit man."

Ryan drew back, sending shivers along the wires taped to his arms and face. He opened his mouth, papery lips pulled back, a tiny wet tongue pushing against his teeth. He was laughing. "I don't want you to kill anybody, Mr. Bain."

"Ninety-five hundred dollars is a lot of money. Who do you want me to find?"

"A hundred thousand dollars," he corrected. "The ninety-five hundred is a retainer, meant to convince you of my sincerity. You seem indifferent, Mr. Bain."

"I'm not a demonstrative person."

"Take the check to the bank and cash it. Perhaps you'll discover your enthusiasm when you have cash money in your hand."

Daniel shook his head. "We haven't discussed the details of the job. Who is it you want me to find?"

"The retainer is yours whether you succeed or fail," the old man said. "All you need do is make a good faith effort, and I'll be satisfied. You have a fine reputation for integrity."

"I haven't given you any references," Daniel said. "I do most of my work for finance companies, and I wouldn't value their moral judgement." He glanced at the check again. "Is there some reason you don't want to tell me who you want me to find?"

The old man smiled again. His moist eyes narrowed. "I'm wondering if you'll take the check, or if you'll leave." The square bandage on his cheek had a tiny brown blood stain in the middle of it. He slipped a hand out from under the sheets, and tapped his chin with a pointed finger. "I think you're curious. I think you could use the money. And I think you're wondering if I've lost my mind. Old people have diminished capacities, or so I'm told."

"Jimmy Hoffa's corpse is buried inside a support beam in the Jersey Giant's football stadium," Daniel said. "They'll never find him. Who else is worth a hundred thousand?"

The laugh came again in a sudden rush, followed by a wheeze and the shaking of wires. "You're a very funny man, Mr. Bain. I like you, I really do. I won't play with you any more. I want you to find Jesus Christ."

The micro-drip connected to the old man's wrist clicked again. "I want you to find him, and bring him to me," Ryan continued. "I have a question I want to ask him. He may take some convincing. We haven't spoken, not in a long time, and I don't think he wants to see me."

"You've spoken with Jesus Christ?"

"Oh yes. He and I go way back."

"And how am I supposed to convince him to talk to you if he doesn't want to see you?"

"That's your problem," the old man snapped. "Reason with him, trick him, I don't care. Just bring him here. Did you think you wouldn't have to work for the money?"

Daniel shoved his hands in his pockets, and shrugged. "Thanks for the interview," he said. "I don't think I'm the right man for this job. I could recommend someone, if you like."

The old man nodded, a smile softening his face. He slumped back into his pillow. "No, you're the right man. I'm sure of it now." His withered hand fumbled for the edge of the blanket, and then slipped back underneath. "I'm certain you could recommend some-one to me, someone who would take my retainer and meet with me once a week, to patronize me or lie to me." He was not smiling now, and his face had hardened into a mask. "It's an ugly world. Integrity is rare. Why haven't you picked up the check?"

"Because I don't believe I'll be able to find Jesus for you."

"You see? You're the right man after all. Now take the check, and cash it. We'll meet again tomorrow." He sighed. "I'm tired now. I've enjoyed our conversation, Mr. Bain." Then he closed his eyes by way of dismissal.

Daniel waited. The old man's eyelids were wrinkled parchment. Could he already be asleep?

A whisper: "Take the check, Mr. Bain."

The call requesting an interview had come from the old man's personal secretary, Winthrop. "I'm calling on behalf of Mordecai Ryan. He would appreciate your assistance concerning the location of an associate. I understand that you find missing persons?"

Mordecai Ryan was bedridden and wanted to be attended personally in his office, which also served as his residence. Daniel worked from his home and was relieved not to have to give his usual speech. "Some agencies put their money into a nice office with wood paneling," he would explain. "I put my money into equipment." If Daniel needed to meet a client, he went to Brian's Diner, a neighborhood restaurant. The waitresses were pretty and a tip was easier to pay than office rent.

What was left of Daniel's money was tied up in a computer, fax, scanner, and copier. His one-room apartment looked like an office cubicle, equipped, as an after-thought, with a bed. He'd been in business for a year, building a tiny customer base, watching what was left of his savings disappear. Daniel owned his old Hyundai free and clear, and the rent was covered, but the cupboards were empty, and there wasn't much money coming in. A new client would be a blessing.

When the interview was over, though, Daniel left, check in hand, baffled by the extent to which the old man had controlled the meeting. Daniel had an objective, but no information. Jesus Christ? Back on earth? What made Ryan think so?

Daniel knew he should return, give Winthrop the check and leave. He did not care to be a part of a hoax. But there was another way to test the old man, and Daniel found himself two blocks from Mordecai Ryan's offices, standing in front of the Western Community Bank of Fort Collins. The sun had already slipped behind the mountains that rose up just to the west of the Colorado town. November wind whistled through his jacket and into his bones. He folded his arms and shivered, staring at the bank entrance. "Well, I don't like being laughed at," Daniel whispered, "but I am curious."

Afternoon tellers waited inside for him, and for the first time in memory, he had no line to stand in. He placed the check on the counter. Before he could explain that he simply wanted to see if the check would clear, the teller pushed it back at him. "You need to endorse this," she said, smiling. "I also need to see some identification." As he reached for his wallet, she pushed a form at him and held out a pen. "And I need you to fill this out."

The wallet wouldn't come out of his pocket. He grinned at her, still fumbling, but she looked away, setting the pen on the counter. When the wallet came free, he hurried to sign everything in front of him.

After comparing the signature on his driver's license to the endorsement, she ran the check through a scanner. Daniel stared off to the side, pretending to be engrossed in the Christmas tree next to the "new accounts" desk. Thanksgiving was three weeks away. Wasn't it too early for Christmas decorations?

"How do you want this?" the teller asked.

"Pardon?"

"Will hundreds be all right?" She seemed tired or irritated, and he was not paying attention, which made her more of whatever she was.

"Hundreds will be fine," he answered. He stood transfixed as she began counting stacks of hundred dollar bills, nine piles of ten each, and one smaller pile of five. Her manicured fingernails clicked over the stacks as she counted.

"Do you have a bag to carry this in?"

He shook his head, imagining a Santa bag full of bills slung over his shoulder. She pulled a blue plastic zipper bag from her drawer and handed it to him. He stared at the bag, his mouth open, suddenly dry.

No longer smiling, she pushed a pile of hundreds across the counter and asked, "Can I do anything else for you sir?"

Daniel stared at the money. "That's a lot of cash."

"Sure is," she said with a hint of sarcasm, as if to say, "I handle two hundred thousand dollars a day, mister, and your little pile of bills doesn't amount to much in my world." She stared over his shoulder to the next customer.

Daniel shoveled the money into the bag.

Ninety-five hundred dollars! He had to buy something. He stopped at a liquor store and purchased a six-pack, selecting one of the local micro-brews, breaking a hundred dollar bill to pay for the beer.

He was hungry, but he didn't feel like spending the rest of the night shopping for groceries. A to-go sandwich from Brian's sounded better.

The outside of Brian's Diner was tasteful, red brick encircled by evergreens, but the interior was a clutter of mismatched tables and booths, with wall decorations that looked as if they'd been cobbled together from a dozen different restaurants. Old traffic signs hung next to color prints of mountain lakes. The menu was scattered as well, with everything from spaghetti to burritos.

Veronica was on duty, which was a bonus. She stopped to flirt with Daniel for a moment before moving on. She was a pretty woman in her late twenties, with straight brown hair pulled back behind her, always tied off with a ribbon. "Gonna party tonight, huh?" she asked, peeking inside the shopping bag to see what kind of beer he'd bought.

"I'm celebrating," he said. "New client. Big job, lots of bucks."

"Really?" she asked. "Congratulations. That's marvelous."

Brian noticed him too, and waved him over. "You come in for a sandwich?" he asked. Daniel nodded. "Let me guess," Brian said. "An Italian Sub. Am I right?"

Daniel shrugged. "Yeah, I like those."

"I knew it!" he cried, slapping the counter with his meaty hand. His belly jiggled, held in check by his apron strings and cook's shirt. "I have it ready to go. I knew we'd need it."

"What a coincidence," Daniel said, staring at the foil-wrapped sandwich sitting under the heat lamps.

"There are no coincidences," Brian assured him. "Everything happens for a reason." He grabbed the sandwich and stuffed it in a bag. "Fastest service in town, huh? Anything else for you?"

Behind them, the cook set hot plates in the food window and called for Veronica. She let out an angry groan. "They're not done with their salads, Brian," she complained. "I told you to slow it down."

"I can't stop time for you," he replied. "Serve the food while it's hot."

"You can stop time," she growled. "Put your face next to the clock."

Daniel paid for his sandwich. As he turned to leave, a woman joined him at the counter. "I had an Italian Sub to go," she said. "I got held up at work, and I'm really late. . ." Daniel looked down at his sandwich and shook his head.

Driving down College Avenue, the main strip that ran through the middle of Fort Collins, he thought about Veronica. She had a quick, smart mouth. He liked watching her argue with Brian. She had a boyfriend, but she always had a boyfriend, and she seemed to change one for the other like clothing.

"I ought to go back and ask her out," Daniel muttered to the steering wheel. He practiced. "I have something to celebrate, and I don't want to celebrate alone. Why don't we go drink some beers?"

He could take her back to his apartment. She could sit at his computer desk, and he could sit on a box of files. It would be swell.

A familiar ache of despair cut him short. Daniel had not dated anyone since Marianne's death. Perhaps it was still too soon. Veronica would never go out with him anyway. She was nice to him (after all, he was a big tipper) but she had other customers she seemed to like more, guys who ate dinner every night she worked. She would greet Daniel with a smile, and others with a squeal, and Daniel thought that a squeal was definitely worth more than a smile.

The car had pointed itself home, and he had work to do. His new client might appreciate getting something for his money.

Home then. Daniel wound his way through the neighborhood streets, grinding his teeth, listening to the radio, pausing in the parking lot to hear the end of a song he didn't like. At his door, key in hand, he paused again. Tree branches, stripped of their leaves, shivered in the wind, scratching the side of the apartment building. A Halloween pumpkin, caved in at the face and crumbling to pulp, guarded the neighbor's porch.

Inside, he began to relax. The dread was always worse than being home, he reminded himself. When his stomach settled, he went to the kitchen to eat his sandwich, avoiding the computer. If he checked his e-mail too early in the evening, he would check again and again, wondering if a new message had arrived just after he signed off. Besides, he had a bank bag full of money to distract him. He managed to stay away from the computer for the first two beers.

Standing at the kitchen counter, he made notes for the following day. The retainer had been an effective way of getting his attention, proving how serious Mordecai Ryan was about finding Jesus. The old man might be crazy, but he was a man of substance. Daniel began to list questions for the next meeting. He wrote, "What makes you certain that Jesus has come again?" Then, "Can you describe the man you spoke to? Where did you see him last? What were the circumstances? Do you know of an alias he might be using?"

Daniel stopped, and rubbed his eyes. What did the old man want to ask Jesus anyway? He added that to the question list.

The retainer made him uneasy. It was just short of ten thousand dollars. Daniel tried to recall what he knew about bank regulations. Wasn't the IRS supposed to be notified on transactions over ten thousand dollars? Perhaps Mordecai Ryan wanted to avoid a paper trail.

The hundred-thousand dollar fee was absurd, of course. There had to be more involved than a simple trace. How had Ryan selected him anyway? Daniel searched his memory, trying to think of a connection between himself and Ryan that would explain the old man's interest. One thing was certain– Mordecai Ryan didn't hire him for his skip-tracing ability. Daniel had been in the business for less than a year, and he was going broke. Now someone wanted to drop a small fortune in his lap. It made no sense.

He wrote down another question. "Why me?"

Then he started a second list. Where would Jesus hide? A monastery? Were there still places like that around? How about a church? The Vatican? Daniel would talk to Thomas, of course. His jogging partner was a bona fide church pastor. "If he can't tell me where to find Jesus, then who can?"

Daniel stopped. It was wrong, the whole thing was wrong. Taking the fee would be like stealing. Jesus Christ was not back on earth. The old man was a nut case, and the whole thing would end badly. Daniel finished his beer, washing the back of his throat with frost. "To oblivion," he whispered. No pain. No thoughts. He opened the refrigerator and grabbed another bottle. He would have to return the money.

Three beers into the evening, he went on-line. He had two emails waiting. The first was from his sister, reminding him of dinner at his mother's apartment the following evening. He sent off a quick reply. "I'll be there," he promised.

The second email was from Rayleen. Though she usually answered his letters within a day, she almost never wrote him first. The letter was a nice surprise. He filed it, unopened, and went onto the Internet, using a search engine to surf. Most sites linked to other pages, and riding the links took him from a site that sold rare first-edition books, to a book reviewer, and finally to a web page that featured captions from the Bible.

When his fourth beer was empty, Daniel decided to go to bed. He would save Rayleen's letter until the morning.

He stripped off his clothes and slid under the comforter on his bed. The lights were still on, but he could turn them off later. He would be up again. He rarely fell asleep on the first try.

Tonight, he would think of the money and of the letter waiting for him. He might keep the cash after all, and the letter could be something urgent and personal. Possibilities, so nice to savor. Perhaps he wouldn't spend the night twisting in the sheets. No trips to the sink for a sip of water. No listening to traffic sounds as the night crawled into the morning.

But the memory of Marianne's accident lurked at the periphery of his thoughts, darting in and out like something half-seen in a mirror. He began dredging for images. The cloying scent of funeral flowers, lilacs and daffodils stacked in the parlor. His mother-in-law's tears running furrows through her caked-powder face. . .his own mother Louise, gripping his arm— "You can't serve the food! None of her family is here yet!"

By the time he thought of his daughter's casket, her remains boxed like a Barbie doll in a toy store, he was fully awake, curled in a painful ball.

A fifth beer might put him under. He considered it for several minutes before going to the refrigerator for another bottle. Groggy, he reached for the opener on the counter by the empties, tipping one bottle over. The jarring sound triggered him. He swept the bottles off the counter, flinging them against the wall, shattering glass, leaving a hole the size of a quarter in the plaster just above the baseboard.

He stared at the glass shards, shifting weight from one bare foot to the other. When his head cleared, he went for a broom and dustpan.

II

Http://www.truthzhammer.com

But the Samaritans did not welcome him
because he traveled to Jerusalem.
When the disciples James and John saw this,
they asked, "Will you call down fire from heaven
to devour those who would not welcome us?"
Jesus turned and rebuked them both,
and they went on to another village.

As they walked a man said to him, "I would
follow you wherever you choose to go."
Jesus answered, "The foxes have their holes,
the birds of the air have their nests, but the
Son of Adam has no place to lay his head."
Another man said, "I would follow you,

the road to Jerusalem my new home,
but first let me go and bury my father."
Jesus said, "Let the dead bury their own!
Go now! and announce the kingdom of God!"
Another man said, "I would follow you Lord,

*and forsake my filial pledge, but first
let me say goodby to friends and neighbors."
Jesus then answered, "I tell you now— your
neighbors await you in Jerusalem."*

*And of those who heard, seventy were sent
to every city where he was to go. . .*

III

The alarm rang at five-thirty. Daniel spilled from the bed, his left leg caught in the comforter. He kicked himself free and stumbled to the window. The first snow of the season had painted the cars in the parking lot with two inches of white.

He gave a brief thought to breakfast. He had eggs, fruit, vegetables, and some sliced turkey in the refrigerator. What he wanted was sausage and biscuits, or a slice of cold pizza. He decided not to eat. Better no breakfast at all than rabbit food.

He argued with himself for a moment about his morning laps. Pastor Thomas met him every day for three miles around the Oval, a paved quarter-mile lined with trees on the Colorado State University campus. It was cold, but Thomas would be there, waiting to run him into the pavement. Daniel couldn't let him down.

He shaved and then put on his sweats and shoes with his back to the bathroom mirror. Some mornings, the reflection showed him someone trying to lose weight, someone who worked out. Other days, he could only see the belly. Either way, he could not relate to the person in the mirror. One quick glance told him that today was a fat day. "I don't know about Christ," he muttered, "but Buddha's here in the bathroom. . ."

Then he remembered the money. He had a decision to make, and he had to make it in the next hour or two. He could use the cash, but the job troubled him. He finished dressing, glancing again at the face in the mirror. The blue eyes were piercing and angry. Surprised, he turned away.

The Hyundai started, not the parting of the Red Sea, but certainly a minor miracle. It was still dark, and there was no traffic. In a few minutes the sun would bring on the cars. Until then, the little blue Hyundai could slide safely through the streets of Fort Collins, fish-tailing over the ice, leaving a serpent's trail in the fresh powder.

Daniel parked his car near the entrance to the Oval. Thomas arrived less than a minute later, gliding up in his Saturn. The pastor was a tall, stoop-shouldered man, thin at the waist, with long runner's legs. In his jogging suit, he could have passed for a businessman were it not for the beard, a graying, slightly unkept growth that covered much of his face. "My beard is an aesthetic prop," he'd explained. "A little bit of the 'voice in the wilderness' image helps sell the tougher messages." They'd met at a running clinic a year earlier and had been jogging in the morning ever since.

Thomas climbed from the Saturn, gloved hands tucked under his armpits. "Sorry I'm late. Have you been waiting long?"

"Less than an hour," Daniel said. "Do your stretches. I have something to ask you."

Thomas bent to touch his toes. Behind him, hundred year-old elms lined the Oval's inner curb. The trunks stood like the pillars of Stonehenge, ancient and mysterious in the yellow glow of the streetlights. Some of the original campus buildings, used now for administration offices, lined the outer curb. A century's worth of students had walked the path they were about to run. It was the oldest and most beautiful part of the campus.

"Ready," Thomas pronounced. He took off with the easy side-to-side motion of a distance runner. Daniel pounded after him. "Do you have a question for me?"

"It's a weird question," Daniel said. Halfway through the first lap, Daniel had already begun to breathe through his mouth. "Where would I look to find Jesus Christ?"

Thomas glanced at Daniel, eyes narrowed. "Are you kidding?"

"No, I'm serious."

16

"If you want to find Jesus, Daniel, all you have to do is open up your heart. I know you've been searching for some answers. . ."

"No, no," Daniel said, sucking air. "Not like that. I mean. . .where would I find Jesus the man? What if he came back? Where would he be?"

Thomas looked back to the pavement, and slowed his pace just a little. "When Christ returns, he will go where he needs to go. Anywhere, I suppose." They ran on, keeping cadence to the rhythm of Daniel's breathing. "Why do you ask?"

"I've been hired by a client to find Jesus. I was wondering where to look."

Thomas frowned. "You are kidding."

"No, I'm serious." Daniel gave him a brief account of his meeting with Mordecai Ryan. "The check cleared," he concluded, "so I have to make an effort to find Jesus, or I have to return the money."

"I'm going to assume you're not pulling my leg," Thomas said. "You're a skip-tracer. Why would Jesus be hiding? Trying to duck an ex-wife? Tax troubles? Not likely, my friend."

Daniel nodded, huffing. The sun hinted at the morning, crouched behind the row of buildings that lined the east side of the Oval. Snow clouds overhead caught the first rays, glowing pink at the tips. He tried to enjoy the view, to force himself to appreciate the sky, but he was breathing too hard, and his ankles hurt.

"I don't know if I can keep that money."

"The case sounds very dubious," Thomas nodded.

"How's your wife doing?"

"She's busy with the women's worship group." Thomas's denomination considered church pastorship a team effort, and insisted on the participation of wives. Margaret had invested her energies in activities to divert her attention from a full measure of personal sorrow. Daniel did not know the whole story, since Thomas was a reserved man, friendly on the surface, adept at the small touches of human contact like a touch on the sleeve or an attentive eye, but distant on closer inspection, slow to share personal details, more apt to listen than to speak. In bits of conversation, a reference here, an aside there, Thomas had related the disappearance of his teenage daughter. The girl spent her time with unsavory friends. She had become withdrawn, and Thomas suspected that she used drugs. Communication had broken down, and then one day, she was gone.

"Margaret was devastated," Thomas said, never talking about his own pain, always regarding it from a distance through the misery of his wife. "The church here is very small. We took this assignment with an eye toward moving to a larger congregation, but Margaret won't think of leaving now. She still hopes that someday. . ." Daniel had suggested a computer search. He was, after all, a skip-tracer. Thomas rejected the offer. "We're here if she wants to find us," he said.

To fill her time, Margaret threw herself into all aspects of the church operation. There was a great deal of work to keep her attention. The church building was little more than a barn in an older part of town. Thomas was good with his hands, and the work in progress was evident. There was fresh paint in the entryway and the roof was patched, waiting for shingles. The nursery smelled of new carpet. Daniel envied them. Their lives had been shattered, and they had responded by rebuilding. They had courage, and they had each other. Daniel thought that his own life stood in contrast to theirs. The contrast was not flattering.

The sun was up, gleaming over the horizon when they finished their final lap around the Oval. "Twenty-seven minutes," Thomas said.

"How fast could you do this if you weren't dragging me around behind you?" Daniel asked, walking in a circle, holding his side.

Thomas shook his head, wagging his beard. "I could go faster, but I'd never do it alone, not on a regular basis. I need the company."

"Well, I appreciate your patience. And some day, I am going to beat you." Thomas smiled. It was a daily boast for Daniel.

"I'm curious. What are you going to do about the money?"

Daniel shrugged. "I guess I'm going to turn down the job. I don't know what the old guy has in mind, but the job isn't as simple or as silly as it sounds. I just wish I could figure out what he really wants."

After the run, Daniel went straight to the gym to complete his morning routine. While buying a sandwich at a bagel shop a few months earlier, he'd entered a drawing for a health club membership and "won" a free month with the purchase of a limited membership. He knew his way around a weight room, and the idea of adding to his workout routine appealed to him. His life seemed dull and flavorless now, but any day might bring an unexpected opportunity, and he needed to be ready. So he ran, lifted weights, took self-defense classes through the gym, and hiked the nearby mountains. (He hadn't been camping since Marianne died, but he would again someday. He was certain of it.)

Today was "leg day," his most dreaded of all weight-lifting days. His legs were already stiff from the morning run, and when he was done lifting, he would ache.

He went to the squat rack and loaded two forty-five pound plates on each end of the bar, locking them into place with clamps. It was not a lot of weight, not for him, but it would be enough to hurt. He lifted the bar and positioned himself by checking the mirrors that lined the walls of the weight room. His reflection vexed him. He was a sloppy, sweat-soaked mess. Knees parallel, his head thrown back, the bar balanced on the back of his shoulders, he began the squats, driving the weight up from his heels, through his spine, until his legs quivered. When he thought he might quit, he stared into the mirror and let anger take him another rep.

Thin jazz trickled from ceiling speakers as he lifted. Between sets, he thought about the case, wondering how he'd proceed if he kept the money. He was not a religious man. Thomas said that Daniel was "searching." Perhaps he was, but religion seemed long on commandments and short on answers.

The idea of a search for Jesus was intriguing, though. If he really found him, Daniel might have a few questions of his own to ask. He thought of Marianne and Courtney, and began to lift again, hammering out rep after rep until his face flushed purple.

On the other side of the room, a woman in pink sweats struggled with the lat pull-down machine. She should have been sitting still, pulling the bar down from above until it touched the top of her chest, using the muscles under her armpits to pull. Instead, she was jerking the bar down behind her head, using her ample body weight to move the stack of weights, snapping her neck back with the effort.

Mind your own business, Daniel thought. Don't bother that woman. She doesn't want any interruptions.

Then he crossed over, smiling hello as he went. The woman watched him approach in the mirror, like a housewife regarding a salesman through a cracked door.

"Hi," Daniel said. "Say, I was watching you work that machine there, and I spotted something that might help you. Mind if I show you a trick?"

The woman turned in her seat, but did not meet his eyes. "Sure," she said, not sounding sure at all.

Daniel hoped that she would step aside, so he could demonstrate. She didn't move. He crouched down next to her, and mimed the proper motion. "You want to keep your body still, and pull straight down. You should feel it in your sides, right here." He gave her a gentle touch, just below her shoulders. She moved away. "Pull down in front, not behind. That will prevent neck injuries. You should probably be working a lower weight, too. The form is much more important than how many bricks you're moving."

She nodded, frowning. "Those are common mistakes," he continued. "I'm having a little trouble with my shoulders because I tried to do a military press with too much weight, and the next thing I know, I'm doing rehab with two-pound dumb bells."

He paused, hoping for a smile. "Well anyway, I thought I'd just pass on a little tip."

"Thanks." She glared at him.

"No problem. Only the serious lifters work this early, and we have to stick together, right?" He went back across the room to the squat rack, muttering. "We have to stick together? Shut up, shut up!"

The woman was back at the machine, pulling down a smaller stack. Her form was still rough, but it was better, and she probably wouldn't hurt herself. She looked over at him. "Excellent!" he called. She scowled.

No good deed goes unpunished, he decided.

Later that morning, he showed up at Mordecai Ryan's building carrying the bank bag. He replaced the money he'd spent with a personal check. "Don't cash the check for a week," he said, setting the bag on the foot of the bed.

The old man stared. At first he said nothing. The sound of muted traffic seeped through the window. "Hot check? Well, I won't ask if you need the money." His head dropped back into his pillow, buried like a bowling ball in a pile of blankets.

Mordecai Ryan waved to Winthrop. "Please leave us alone for a minute, would you?" Ryan's personal secretary was a short, rumpled little man in a tan shirt and brown tie. He smiled, a grimace full of little round teeth, and left the room. Ryan turned his attention back to Daniel. "Now, tell me why you don't want the job."

Daniel shrugged. "I went to the bank to see if the check was good. Curious, I guess. I never really meant to take the money."

"I asked you why you don't want the job." The old man's voice had sharpened, pointed and precise.

There was no avoiding an answer. "I don't think Jesus has come back," Daniel said. "Nothing comes free. If I took the job, I'd be stealing from you. That, or in some way I don't understand yet, I'd be selling my soul. Either way, someone would be getting taken."

The old man quivered, and made a staccato sound like a series of coughs. It took a moment for Daniel to remember Mordecai Ryan's unusual laugh.

The old man pulled a small hand from under the covers, dragging tubes and wires along with it, and dabbed at the corner of his eyes. "Ah, pardon me, pardon me please."

"I'm glad I was able to entertain you," Daniel said, his lips pressed together with a forced smile. "I wish you luck with your search."

"Don't go," Ryan said. The words were an order, but the tone of voice was a plea. "I gave you the check so you would take the job seriously. I see that I have your attention. I would not expect you to pursue the job without a starting point. Can we proceed?"

Daniel stood, shifting his weight from one foot to the other.

"Is something wrong?"

"I just told you I didn't want the job," Daniel said.

"Yes, I heard you. I take your reluctance as a sign of integrity. Now let's move on. Do you have some questions for me?"

Daniel's face colored, a sudden flush of red to the cheeks and neck. He'd brought back the money, but he had also brought the list of questions he'd written the night before.

"Sit down, please," Ryan said. "I will tell you what I know, and if, when I'm finished, you don't want the job, then you can leave and I'll give this money to someone else. All I ask is that you show a little professional courtesy and promise me that our conversation will be confidential."

Daniel frowned. "Of course it's confidential. I don't discuss my cases with anyone." Then he blushed again, remembering his conversation with Thomas earlier in the day.

"Will you sit? Will you listen to what I have to say?"

Put in such a way, Daniel could not refuse. He pulled a chair from the corner, and sat. He took the list of questions from his shirt pocket. "These are tentative questions," he explained. "I wrote them up before I decided to turn down the job."

The old man began coughing again, hiding his face with spindle fingers. "Go ahead," he said at last. "Ask me whatever you want."

"Does Jesus go by that name, or does he use a different name?"

"Derek Becker."

The answer was quick and final. Daniel stared, disoriented again. Perhaps there was a person, a real person to be tracked down. Perhaps he could do the job after all. "Do you know his last whereabouts?"

"Austin. That's in Texas." The old man was grinning. The thin tendons on his neck stood out from the effort.

"When did you last speak to him?"

"More than a year ago."

"Describe him for me."

The old man squinted, closing one eye, as if he were closely examining a memory. "Tall, thin, with shoulder-length hair. I think they call the style a "mullet." Caucasian, sparse beard. More than a touch of gray. Soft voice, thin-timbered. He's young, but he's not aging gracefully."

Daniel folded his list of questions, and tucked it back in his shirt. "We're talking about a real person here."

Ryan nodded, his eyes wet and glistening. "Of course we are."

"And what do I do when I find him?"

"Bring him to me," Ryan said. "I have a question for him."

"What question?"

The old man's face drained, and he turned away. When he spoke again, his voice was flat and weak. "In general, I want to ask why he presides over an unjust world." He took a shallow breath. "Specifically, I wonder at the arbitrary nature of grace. Do you know what happened to Judas Iscariot?"

"Judas, who betrayed Christ in the garden at Gethsemane?"

"It was an orchard, not a garden," Ryan said. "Yes, that Judas. Do you know what happened to him?"

"I'm remembering that he killed himself."

"True," Ryan agreed. "And what do you suppose happened then?"

"I wouldn't hazard a guess," Daniel said. "I'm not big on heaven and hell."

"Pope Benedict XIII, the second of the Avignon popes during the Great Schism, preached that Judas tried to reach Christ while he hung on the cross, and beg his forgiveness. The crowd was dense, clustered around the three crucified prisoners, taunting and laughing. Judas couldn't make his way, or perhaps the crowd was an excuse. Perhaps he was in no hurry. A crucifixion could take days."

The old man stopped to catch his breath, and dab at the corners of his mouth with the edge of the blanket. "The movies are quite wrong, you know. They didn't put nails through his palms. They nailed them just below the wrist." He tapped his bony wrist with a finger.

"What does this have to do with Judas?" Daniel asked.

"I'm getting there," Ryan said. He licked his lips. "Christ was spared the full agony of the cross by a centurion who pierced his side with a spear, killing him. Suddenly, with no warning, Judas lost his opportunity to ask for forgiveness. He went back to Gethsemane and sat in the orchard, wondering what to do."

Daniel found himself taken in by the old man's story, though he had no idea what it had to do with hiring him to find Christ.

"Imagine it. Can you? The orchard was full of fruit. Not what you would find at a grocery store. Fruit was smaller then, bruised, more flavorful, and sweeter than you can imagine. I think Judas probably took an apple from a branch, and sat nibbling."

"He wanted to make amends," he continued. "He reasoned, 'I couldn't reach him because of the crowd. I must find a way to reach his soul.' And so, full of humble piety, or so Pope Benedict XIII would have us believe, Judas slipped a rope over the apple tree branch and hung himself." The old man stopped to cough, a wet rattle that ended in a hiss. "Pardon me, I am not used to talking."

"I can come back if you need to rest."

"No, I'll finish," the old man said. He closed his eyes and lay still for a moment. "All right then. The soul of Judas departed, floating through the orchard, finding its way to Mount Calvary. There, Judas asked Christ for forgiveness, and it was granted. When Christ ascended to Heaven, the soul of Judas went with him, sitting at Christ's side, the Prodigal Disciple, so to speak."

"Lovely story," Daniel said.

Mordecai Ryan stared, his eyes narrowing. "I've paid you for your time, skip-tracer. Go looking. If you need to, start with me. I've left a paper trail. Everyone does. If I told you my story, you'd never believe me. Find out for yourself. When you know enough to ask me some intelligent questions, come back. I'll be waiting."

IV

TO: Daniel Bain

FROM: Rayleen

SUBJECT: No reason. . .

Dear Daniel,

I know you like to hear stories about my adventures. Here's one I haven't told you yet.

I'd been hired to do a little entertaining at a college-dorm birthday party— someone turned the big two-one. I went in wearing a coat, and nothing underneath. I was so nervous! There were two guys and two girls, drinking beer and laughing. Some of the guys tried to hit on me before I even took off the coat. (No one asked, "What's your sign?" thank God!)

Someone put on a record, and it was music I could dance to. Believe me, I had everyone's attention very soon! The guys were clever enough to catch on. By the time I had the buttons open down to my waist, conversation had pretty much stopped!

One of the girls was pissed! I think she couldn't stand the competition! She was out of there by the time my coat hit the floor!

The other girl was different. She had long, straight hair, pulled back and tied behind her. She was slender, and pretty, and she was staring at me like the boys were. I found myself dancing for her, more than for the guys! We ended up dancing together, which was a little strange, since she was dressed, and I was naked, but it was nice!

And was she ever nervous! "We're driving them crazy," I said. "Let's give them a show."

They say a picture is worth a thousand words, so a video must be worth a whole book! One of the guys had a camera going, and everything that happened is on tape! I've seen a copy, and it's hot-Hot-HOT!

If you'd like to see me and my new friend make love while two horny guys watch (I'll let you guess if they join in!), then let me know. I don't try to make a lot of money on these tapes (I'm not in business, I'm in heat!) so just send me thirty-five dollars (enough to cover shipping, the cost of the tape, and a little for the rent!) and I'll send you a copy. It will be just like you were there with me, watching my every move. Be sure to ask for tape VI.

By the way, how's your business going?

Love and Wild Times,

Rayleen

V

After he deposited the money in his checking account, Daniel wrote a check for four month's rent and stuck it in the box by the manager's office. The retainer was a windfall. It was a small amount that would slip away quickly enough, but he would enjoy the thought of it for a while.

Then again, there was the hundred thousand. Perhaps he could collect the full fee. All he had to was find Jesus Christ. Or Derek Becker. He dropped into his desk chair, and called up his unopened e-mail. If the letter from Rayleen was a disappointment, he would think about the money instead.

He'd never met Rayleen, not in person. He had been surfing the Internet one night, six empty beer bottles lined across the desk, when he rode a pop-up link to a page called "Rayleen's Room." He almost backed out, double-clicked the button and returned to pictures of movie stars in lingerie, because hardcore photos didn't interest him, but there was something about the girl in the pictures that caught his eye.

She looked young, just eighteen according to the text. He had visited hardcore sites before, half in curiosity, half for the sheer pleasure of doing something wrong in the privacy of his home. He had been disturbed and disappointed by the photos he'd seen. Most were shoddy teases, promising a better payoff for a credit card payment. Some sites were pathetic, with tired women and soft, aging men. The prettier models were waxed fruit, staged and posed, shiny faces rigid with smiles.

Rayleen was different. She had the face of a sprite, fresh and natural, as if she were surprised by the camera at every turn. Her smile was a sudden breath caught, her brown eyes a moment of recognition, a wink and a whisper of joy. She was sweet, he was sure of it.

The photos were not the usual dark tangle of legs and sweat. They were bright, clear shots of nearly every sex act imaginable, uninhibited fun between a close circle of friends, delivered with candid commentary. "I love to do this," read one of the captions. "Some girls don't like it, but I could do this all day long."

One picture caught his eye, because Rayleen was dressed, looking quite lovely in a simple black dress and dark stockings. She was glancing to the side as if lost in thought, both hands clutching a purse. She had nice taste in clothing.

There had been an e-mail address at the bottom of the page. "Write me, and tell me about yourself," it said. He decided to write to her. Why not? There was still beer in the refrigerator, his work was done for the day, and he had no one to answer to and nothing to lose. He would send a letter, and it would either go unanswered or he would end up on a hundred mailing lists for adult products.

He sat down to write:

Dear Rayleen,

I visited your web page tonight. I have gone to other pages, and been disappointed by what I've seen. Not so with your page. You are really quite pretty, and your photos are not the usual rip-off. Your web page said to mail you a letter and tell something about myself. I am single, in my thirties, and I don't own a damned thing except my computer

Daniel frowned at the screen. "That's not very attractive," he whispered. He erased the last sentence and tried again.

I'm a single guy in my early thirties. I am a skip-tracer. That's someone who hunts down people who are on the run, trying not to pay their bills

He stopped again. How would she picture him? A bill collector who hunts down people? Some fat guy, probably losing his hair, with a pickup truck and a gun collection. Someone who hadn't had a date in a year. He erased again.

I'm single. I'm in my thirties. I own my own business— a high-tech version of private investigation, finding missing persons, etc. I work out in my spare time. I enjoy camping, and

". . .long, romantic walks on the beach," he moaned. He sounded like a single's ad. He slapped his forehead, and took another sip of beer before erasing.

"What the hell do I care what she thinks?" he muttered. He took a breath, and started typing again.

I'm a single guy in my thirties. I try to keep in shape, but I drink too much beer, and some of it came to rest around my waist. I work as a skip-tracer. The money stinks, but I can pick my own hours. I don't own much, so I'm not what people call a success, but I'm a nice guy and I don't hurt other people if I can help it.

I liked your pictures, even the one with you dressed— you have legs to die for. Love, Daniel

He thought about erasing the word "love," but in the end, he kept it. The word was an onion, layers wrapped around other layers, peeling back to nothing. It was amusing to deliberately misuse the word, to spend it on someone he'd never met.

He queued up the message and sent it, before he could change his mind. Then he dumped the letter from his out-box, so that he wouldn't have to read it and wince when he sobered up.

Rayleen returned the letter the next morning.

Dear Daniel,

Thank you so much for your kind letter. I'm glad you liked the pictures. I also enjoyed getting to know you.

He sat dumbfounded, touched that she took a moment from her busy day, doing whatever successful models do, to write him.

He wrote back, not often, and every letter was answered within a day. There were mentions of products, thanks for the interest in the web site, and always a personal note. "How's the new business? How's your love life?" When a new e-mail arrived, he would keep it in the file unread, a savings account of anticipation.

When he wrote her, he agonized over the wording. He was a fan, but he did not want to seem like one. Fans were a vacuum, filling their empty places with tumbling images of the beautiful people. Fans pieced the shards of their own lives together, fashioning celebrity photos— that's me, right behind that famous face, that famous hair! That's me waving. I shared space with an actress, a ballplayer, a gangster.

He didn't want to seem like a loser. Losers were anonymous laborers, sad gerbils on the wheel of life, forty times around— now give me my food pellet— Thanks! Back to work!

He didn't want to seem lonely. Lonely people latched onto celebrities like leeches in a pond, content to drink, never worrying if the host needed the blood, or if the host was repulsed by the sight of a bloated leech anchored to the skin, sucking.

On the other hand, he didn't want to lie. Honesty was his preference. There was no logic behind his stubborn insistence on the truth. After all, the Internet was full of lies, distortions, and illusions. That included Rayleen. She wasn't a person. She was a web site, a marketing scheme, a set of images for him to build a person around. She wasn't real. So it didn't matter, he reasoned. He could tell the truth. He could afford to be himself, because if she rejected him— no!— she would never reject him. He was a customer, a valued customer. He had five of her video tapes in his desk drawer, three of them unopened. He would be welcome until his credit card was maxed.

Despite his windfall and an inclination to go shopping (he really did love camping, and now he could afford better equipment), Daniel forced himself to work until early evening. There were no easy answers. He looked for Derek Becker in Austin, searching for a paper trail, finding nothing. If Becker lived there, he did not have utilities registered in his name. No driver's license, no apartment leases.

A background check on Mordecai Ryan was easier. Ryan listed his home address as the office building where Daniel first met him. The old man had other Colorado land holdings, including a bookstore in Fort Collins and a church in Wellington. A duplex in Loveland had a lien against it, strange given Ryan's obvious resources.

Ryan's link to Ryan Enterprises was easy to discover. The company had additional assets in Colorado, New York, Austin, Dallas, and an office in Israel. The New York properties seemed to be rentals, but the overseas operation had something to do with antiques and exporting. Daniel pulled up an investment profile on Ryan Enterprises. The company history was a single paragraph— ad copy, nothing of substance.

As he typed, he made notes in pencil on a legal pad. Every step of his search brought a different step to mind. Investigating a person was like piecing together the image on a picture puzzle. If he was inept, he would force pieces together that didn't fit, and he would discover nothing. If he was good, then he still had just a picture, a representation, not the real thing.

When Daniel first began skip-tracing, he'd been hired to find a husband who had deserted his wife and three children. The man had been a restaurant manager, working in the same pub and deli for years, quietly supporting his family. He attended church and coached his son's football team. When he left, he took exactly half of the savings account. The stocks were sold and a cashier's check was forwarded for half of the proceeds. The mail service that handled the transaction gave him away— he'd moved to Cleveland. An application had been made for a liquor handling license. Daniel searched for new hires in Cleveland pubs but came up empty. It made no sense. Surely the man would repeat himself and find a job in the service industry.

Instead, Daniel found the man hiding in plain sight, a popular disc jockey on late night radio. The radio station had a five-state range at night, and a friend Daniel contacted had recognized the voice.

The case bothered him. A man with a family and a secure job escapes to become an all-night disc jockey? How could Daniel have guessed? He changed his technique with subsequent clients, asking personal questions that could provide insight to complex cases. And in the end, most of them were complex cases.

People who ran away were escapees, prisoners. Each pictured freedom differently. For a convict in maximum security, freedom might be a green pasture with fat, lazy flies and the smell of ragweed. For a man drowning in debt, freedom might be a job waiting tables downtown, tips in his pocket, in a city with too many faces to care about just one.

Daniel began approaching the picture-puzzle process different-ly. People didn't see themselves as others perceived them. If Dan-iel could gather the puzzle-pieces of someone's self-image, and put them together correctly, the resulting picture could help solve even the most difficult case.

Daniel began to ask a different kind of question of his clients. What were the missing person's hobbies? What dreams did they have? Did they ever express regrets? Who did they admire? What were their childhood obsessions? What did they want to be when they grew up? An sstronaut? Fireman? Nurse?

Mordecai Ryan was a different problem. There was a wealth of information to be had, but none of it fit together. There was the church in Wellington, for example. Ryan was listed as the pastor, be-ginning in 1980. Daniel noted the denomination, and traced church records, looking for a history of affiliation, but there was no record of a Mordecai Ryan in any of the church roles prior to the purchase of the Wellington church itself. It was as if Ryan had bought a building, and then gone looking for a denomination.

Daniel went back, looking for Mordecai Ryan the child. Ryan's name yielded a link to immigration records, and Daniel discovered that Ryan had come to the United States in 1904 at the age of nine, emigrating from Wales. Daniel tried to remember the old man's voice. There had been no trace of the Isles in his speech, though there might have been a hint of the Bronx in the back of his throat.

Daniel searched for any other records of Ryan's childhood, but the search was fruitless. No public schooling, no record of graduation, and no record of college. There was no work record, no police record, nothing. Mordecai Ryan disappeared for sixteen years. Daniel found him again at the age of twenty-five, still in New York, working at the docks as a longshoreman. The gap was a bad sign. He made a note on the legal pad and moved on.

After the war, Ryan worked for customs, overseeing imports at the New York shipyards. Next came a small import business, Ryan, Wilkins and Company. Daniel traced Robert Wilkins, the partner. Wilkins was born in 1902 and died overseas in Jordan during the second World War. He never married, and his substantial estate stayed in his partner's hands. Ryan-Wilkins became Ryan Enterprises.

Robert Wilkins was born into money, the only son of a foundry owner. Daniel supposed that Wilkins had befriended Ryan, and helped to bankroll the import business. Most of the company records had Ryan's signature. Was Wilkins a passive partner? Why no wife, no children? Surely Wilkins's father would have enjoyed an heir. The thought came without invitation— was Wilkins gay? Daniel shook his head. He'd crossed the line of sensible conjecture into useless speculation.

Neither Wilkins nor Ryan served in the military. They spent the war doing business as usual, and the United States Government became a customer, using Ryan's middle-east contacts for one purpose or another. Working backwards, Daniel discovered that Ryan-

35

Wilkins had done business with the Germans before the war. He printed off the records he could find, and moved on.

By the sixties, Ryan Enterprises had millions in assets. Real estate became the main business, with overseas offices closing one by one, until only the office in Israel remained. In the early sixties, Ryan married a twenty-two year old divorcee named Margaret Hagan. Still tracing real estate holdings, Daniel found that the company had shifted west, buying property in Colorado beginning in 1969.

Something changed in 1980. Ryan bought the church in Wellington and installed himself as pastor. Daniel noted the date on his pad. People found God in times of stress or tragedy. Ryan had apparently taken that process one step further. What had transformed the old man from an importer to a preacher?

The church lasted less than three years, closed for service in 1983. The building was maintained by Ryan Enterprises. The church reopened in the late nineties, but again, service was short-lived, and the doors were closed after ten months. Daniel made a note to check news files to see if there was a reason for the failure to build a congregation.

Having traced the business from imports to real estate, Daniel tried a different track. On a whim, he refined the search with the keyword "spiritualism," and came up with a single hit. He clicked and found himself on a new-age web site, touting mysticism and Zen aphorisms. He was about to write off the link as one of those inexplicable mysteries of web search-engines when he spotted a link to "Occultism and the Third Reich." He clicked again and scrolled down the page. There he found an old photo of Hitler holding an artifact. The caption read, "Hitler takes possession of the Spear— 1938." In the background, staff officers smiled at the Fuhrer and his prize. To the right, at the edge of the picture, Mordecai Ryan stared at the camera, grinning. Daniel felt a sudden chill. Ryan was just forty-three in 1938, but the picture showed an old man, thin and wrinkled. Other than being bedridden, the old man had not visibly changed in sixty years.

"That's not possible," he whispered. The text mentioned "Mordecai Ryan, expert in Christian artifacts. . . ." There was no other information connecting Hitler and Ryan. Daniel opened a new file in his case records, and copied the picture into it. Then he set the pencil down and closed his eyes. The apartment was quiet, except for the rush of air from the heat ducts.

He ground his teeth, chewing a hunch. He thought he knew what Ryan wanted him to find. He would need a little more research.

First, he e-mailed an associate in Boston.

> *I need you to look for a Mordecai Ryan, early nineteen hundreds. The burial would have been 1904 or later. I think within the first two years. Somewhere in New York. I can pay you for this one, but I need the answer quick. I have a meeting with the client tomorrow.*

Then he contacted the F.B.I., asking for information on Mordecai Ryan's activities during World War II. It was probably an exercise in futility. There would be the usual dragging of feet, the filing of forms, and the information would trickle in, cut and pasted, long after the case was over.

No matter. He already knew the answer to most of his questions. The government was aware of Ryan's pre-war connection to the Nazis. The early expansion of Nazi Germany saw the plunder of a great deal of art. Some of it was sold, and a way of getting contraband to interested buyers had to be found. Mordecai Ryan had an import company. Later, when the United States entered the war, anyone with a connection to the Nazis was a traitor or an information source. Mordecai Ryan became a source.

Daniel made another note on the legal pad, and went back to researching the Spear itself. A goth-rock web site, complete with thrash-metal background music, retold the legend of the Spear with the names of conquerors who possessed the icon. There was a picture of the Spear, or rather, the head of the Spear, now in three parts, old and corroded, wrapped in fragile silver and gold thread.

Some of the pages were no help, straying too far into mystic babble. Daniel was more interested in the historical background. He printed off the best of the articles, a short feature from a mythology site, and added it to his pile of research.

One last web page mentioned the fate of Longinus the Centurion. Daniel printed the page, and underlined a single paragraph.

> *According to legend, the Centurion Longinus was doomed to wander the earth forever, unable to die, until the Day of Judgement, when he would be called to answer for the death of the Savior.*

Who was Mordecai Ryan, really? The sun was fading, leaving the room a sullen gray. Daniel turned on the desk lamp, but the light did nothing to chase away the vague feeling of dread that suddenly threatened the room.

VI

http://www.mythspot/xtian/spear

The Spear of Longinus is purported to be the weapon used by the centurion Longinus to pierce the side of Jesus at the Crucifixion.

The piercing of the Saviorwas considered an act of mercy, hastening his death and his subsequent ascension into Heaven.
Death by crucifixion was slow and cruel.

The weight of the victim was distributed so as to restrictbreathing. The chest cavity was extended, unable to facilitate exhalation. Death came through suffocation. Arms and legs were traditionally bound with rope. Nails, when used, were a blessing, because blood loss resulted in a quicker death.

Contrary to artistic depiction, it is believed that nails were placed below the wrist, between the radius and ulna. (Nails through the palms would be anchored in soft flesh, not bone, and a crucifixion victim would tear free in minutes.)

Recent archaeological discoveries support this theory, including the discovery of the skeleton of a crucifixion victim, intact, complete with bone damage below the wrist. Should a victim's tormentors decide in favor of mercy, clemency took the form of breaking the victim's legs, for broken legs cannot support body weight, and suffocation would be hastened.

According to Biblical prophecy, the bones of the Messiah could never be broken. (John 19: 34-37) Death by the Spear fulfilled the letter of the prophecy, and lent credence to the claim that Jesus was the Messiah promised in the Davidic Covenant. A subsequent legend arose around the Spear itself.

Whoever had possession of the Spear would have an advantage in battle.

The Spear thought to be the actual spear of the centurion presently resides in the Hoffburg museum in Vienna.

The Spear's history can be traced backward to a number of notable owners, conquerors all, beginning with Constantine the Great, the Roman Emperor.

Others include Alaric, King of the Visigoths and sacker of Rome, Attila the Hun, and Charles Martel, "The Hammer," who halted theadvance of the Moors into Europe in 732 A.D.

Charlemagne allegedly carried the Spear with him through forty-seven battles, never losing, until he accidently dropped the weapon while crossing a river. He died shortly thereafter.

Adolf Hitler was fascinated by the Spear, and took personal possession of it in 1938 after declaring Austria to be a part of Germany. Accompanied by Heinrich Himmler,the Fuhrer visited the Treasure House of the Hapsburgs the very day German troops entered Vienna, securing control of the icon. The Spear was guarded by handpicked SS troopsthroughout the war. It is said that Hitler died in his bunker within minutes of the capture of the Spear by United States soldiers in 1945.

VII

Daniel arrived at his mother's house fifteen minutes late. He regretted not being able to continue his research, but he had canceled two previous "family gatherings," and he could not avoid this one.

His mother's small house sat at the end of a cul-de-sac. The November chill had killed most of the vegetation, but the straw bones of the summer's growth clung to the chain-link fence in front. Wet brown piles of leaves squatted in rows along the walkway. Daniel's sister Penny sat shivering on the front step, waiting for him. "The Bad Seed. . ." she called.

"...returns to the House of Weeds," he finished. Their mother's yard had always been poorly kept, even before their father left. A neighbor's insult, overheard by the children, became Penny and Daniel's private name for the house.

"It's a little cold to be sitting out on the steps, isn't it?" Daniel asked.

"I wanted to let you know that Christine is here for dinner."

"Thanks for the warning."

"I want you to be nice."

"I'm always nice," Daniel scoffed.

Penny stood, blocking his way up the steps. "Daniel. I know you're having trouble accepting the way things are. I'm really sorry, but I have a right to be who I am."

"I don't have any trouble accepting who you are," Daniel said. "I have trouble with Christine. She's not a person, she's an agenda. If you want us all to get along, tell her to stop talking politics."

"Everything's political," Penny said, her thin face pinched and sour.

"So you tell me," Daniel said. "Let's go in and have meatloaf. Is that political too?"

"No," she said, swallowing a laugh. She stepped aside. "At least don't pick a fight. Okay?"

Daniel opened the door. "I'll be a saint."

Christine was Penny's live-in girlfriend. She sat at the kitchen table in a floppy bib overall and a knit top pulled tight against her chunky torso, waving a single finger like a baton. Her blond hair was chopped in the shape of a helmet. Louise Bain stood listening at the stove, stirring mashed potatoes with a wire whip, nodding in Christine's direction. Christine stopped when she saw Daniel, her finger suddenly still, floating in the air.

"Hello, Daniel," she said.

"Hello, Christine. Hello, Mom."

Louise turned her full attention on Daniel, concerned eyes searching him. "How are you doing, Daniel?"

"Fine. Excellent. I got a new client this week that is paying me a fortune. Things might be coming around for my business."

"That's right, you're a private detective of some sort," Christine said.

"I'm a skip-tracer," Daniel corrected her. "I look for missing people, people who have gone into hiding."

"That's right," Christine said. She leaned back in her chair, folding her hands behind her head, stretching, her thick arms bunched and muscled. "So, is your new client a collection agency?"

"No, private party," he said. Turning back to his mother, he sniffed the air. "Meat loaf. Smells wonderful." He frowned, and sniffed again. "New recipe?"

"Oh no, I wouldn't change my recipe," his mother assured him.

Daniel walked toward the sink for a glass. As he passed by Penny, he whispered, "I smell oregano and politics." Penny jabbed him with an elbow.

"What's that? Did I miss something?" Christine asked.

"No, he's just being funny," Penny said. She pushed a strand of sandy hair to the side, and then stared at the ground. Her hair fell forward, covering her face.

"Please, let me join in the fun," Christine said, her cheeks reddening as she smiled.

"I was making a political joke," Daniel explained.

"About meatloaf?" Christine scoffed.

"I know, it's hard to believe, but everything's political..."

"Is there something wrong with my meatloaf?" Louise asked. "I thought you liked it, Daniel. I suppose I could have made spaghetti. . ."

"I love your meatloaf, Mom," Daniel said, glancing at his wristwatch.

"Actually, you're right. For once, hah-hah. Everything is political." Christine slid back from the table, scraping the legs of the folding chair on the vinyl floor. Then she sat forward, elbows on the table, the bib of her jeans falling forward. "If you think of meatloaf, you think of women in kitchens with aprons on. If you think of grilled steaks, you think of men. Food is gendered. The act of cooking is political, because it either reinforces or challenges cultural norms."

Here is where I shut up, Daniel thought. I'm not going to allow anyone to stage a debate. I'm here for dinner.

Penny stepped in front of Daniel, led by her smile. "Can I get anything on the table for you Mom?" she asked. Her left eyelid drooped, leaving one eye half-closed.

Daniel sat at the table, directly across from Christine. She leaned forward even more, sprawling over the tabletop, gazing directly at him, waiting for a response. He put his hands in his lap and put his feet and knees together. I'll say just one thing, he thought. "Everything may have a political explanation, but that doesn't make everything political. There are other aspects of a culture. Religion. Education."

"Yes, yes, but any 'independent state apparatus' reinforces the ruling class's authority. If you accept cultural norms, you are submitting." The finger jumped out again. "An independent state apparatus is. . ."

"I'm familiar with the jargon," Daniel said. "And you're wrong. Different aspects of our culture are not only independent, but contradictory."

"How so?" Christine gave him a gracious smile, and waited for him to speak.

Daniel tucked his elbows in, and stared off to the side. "For example, market economies reward individual behavior, and religion encourages collective behavior. They don't mix. Have you ever listened to a Christian conservative apologizing for capitalism?"

"I have no idea what you kids are talking about!" Louise interrupted gaily. "Isn't anyone hungry?" She set a platter with a ketchup-topped meatloaf on the table.

"Looks great Mom," Penny said. Her left eye twitched.

"No one can apologize for capitalism without sounding like an idiot," Christine declared.

"No one who derives their individual subjectivity from group affiliations can explain a system that promotes individuality," Daniel answered. The meatloaf was small, brown, and probably overcooked. He reached for the carving knife.

"By all means, you're the man at the table," Christine observed. "Carve away."

"We could sing Kumbaya and wait for the meatloaf to carve itself," Daniel muttered. He had to push to get the blade through the loaf.

"I think I overcooked it," Louise worried.

"No, it looks fine." The meat crunched when he cut it. "Besides, I like meat cooked all the way through."

"I thought you'd be a medium-rare kind of guy," Christine said.

"Not at all," he lied. Daniel put a slice on Christine's plate. "Here you go. You might think twice about eating this, though. It might be an act of submission."

"Have I irritated you?" Christine asked.

"No, I'm enjoying the conversation," Daniel lied again.

"Are you seeing anyone?" Penny asked, ushering in a sudden silence. Daniel continued to cut the loaf, sawing through the meat, scraping the blade on the platter. He waited for Louise to interrupt and save him, and when she didn't, he shook his head, much too late to be graceful or casual.

"No, not really." He put a slice of dried loaf on Penny's plate. She stared down, her eyelid jumping. The nervous eye had begun bothering her during her marriage and had continued after the separation and divorce.

"I thought you were seeing that waitress," Louise said. She took a bite of meatloaf, and then stopped. She stared at her plate in horror, a tiny ball of meat still half-chewed in her mouth.

"This is great, Mom," Penny said.

"Yes, wonderful," Christine agreed, though she hadn't tried the food yet.

Daniel noticed his mother's expression, her mouth full of food, and launched into a sudden confession. No, he wasn't dating anyone. No, he had no one in mind. He didn't date clients, and he didn't meet eligible women in his line of work. Dating and relationships were a miserable way to eat time. Being alone was sometimes a good thing, even preferable.

"Have you tried the Internet?" Christine suggested. She placed a serving of mashed potatoes on top of her meatloaf, chopped and stirred the pile, and began to eat with apparent gusto, waving the fork as she talked between bites. "Lots of lonely people meet on the Internet these days."

"It's not much different than a singles bar," Daniel said.

"I heard there's a lot of pornography on the Internet," Louise said. She had eaten all of her potatoes, but the slab of meat sat with just one bite missing.

"The Internet is all about pornography," Christine declared. "The information superhighway is a red light district, set up for the display of porn and the collection of fees. And— surprise!— women and children are the victims. Not just the women and children who pose, but the women and children who find the porn, and the women and children who live with the men who want the porn."

"I use the Internet for my business," Daniel said.

"Do you ever visit porn sites?"

Daniel paused. He felt his face flush and then flush harder with anger at being an open book. He did not like being in the wrong, being caught at something he was ashamed of, or being forced to lie. He blinked, and in that moment, became an aggressive opponent of censorship. "Yes, actually, I have seen some porn sites. Most of them are all tease and promise, and the chumps who pay to go there get what they deserve."

"And exactly what would constitute a porn site that delivered the goods?" Christine asked.

Daniel paused again. "I can't define that, any more than you can define what obscenity is."

"Obscenity is the use of human beings for prurient ends."

"Restated, not defined. You can't tell the difference between art and porn with that as a guidepost."

"That's because so much of art is all about posing women for the object pleasure of men." Christine slapped the table with her palm. Penny's eyes glistened, and the twitch threatened to squeeze a tear onto her cheek.

"See, you didn't answer the question. How do you define obscenity? You can't do it. You can't set guidelines that will help you decide if any particular picture is pornographic or not. That's because it's not about porn, it's about control. People who want to censor porn aren't concerned about porn, they're concerned about a target group that can't control itself in the presence of porn."

"First, I can define pornography— I did define it. Second, I'm concerned about the victims, the women who make porn. . ." Louise stepped away from the table, staring at Christine, and then at Daniel. Her face was a block of chalk.

"They get paid," Daniel said. "How are they victims?"

"How are they victims?" she exploded. "Are you aware of the connection between pornography and sex crimes?"

"Sure," Daniel said. He could feel anger burn its way up from his stomach to his face. "There's a correlation between porn use and sex crimes. Are you saying that men are animals who can't control themselves in the face of porn?"

"I spent an evening last month with a girl who earned her living taking off her clothes," Christine said. Her voice had lowered, slowed, and her lip was beginning to tremble. Penny put an hand on Christine's shoulder, fingers caressing her. "She was beaten to a pulp, a pulp!" Christine's fist struck the table. "And she sat there. . .trying to decide. . .if she wanted. . .to live. . . ." The last words were accompanied by a broken voice.

Daniel decided that the combination of tears and haircut made Christine look like a chunky Joan of Arc. Good manners demanded that he be silent, despite his certainty that Christine's emotional response was a performance tactic. "I'm trying to understand," he said finally, "how your friend's misery is connected to porn."

"She strips for a living, Daniel," Christine sputtered. "You just admitted that porn causes sex crime. . ."

"I said there was a correlation," Daniel said. "There's also a correlation between tomatoes and crime. Ninety-seven percent of all criminals eat tomatoes. It doesn't follow that tomatoes cause crime."

"Oh, fucking swell," Christine said. "Good thing we have a man here to explain reason and logic to the emotional women-folk." Now Penny burst into tears, and Louise wrapped motherly arms around both of them, calming them with nursery words and cooing.

Daniel sat with his hands in his lap. "My concern is. . ."

"Stop, Daniel. Just stop it!" Penny's voice was shrill and raw.

Daniel tried a joke. "I don't think anyone's enjoying the conversation anymore. . ." The room was silent, and Daniel closed his eyes. Get me out of here, he thought, get me out now. He felt the door calling to him from behind. He knew that to just leave would be unforgivably rude. To stay would be unimaginably uncomfortable. He had no course of action past invisibility. He tried to shrink. He imagined himself folding in on himself, closing off to the sound of a full and angry kitchen.

He waited for enough minutes to crawl by to allow a less obvious exit, minutes filled with the clattering of pots, scraping of plates, crisp meatloaf tumbling into the disposal and wastebasket, and bits of conversation— "What time is the meeting on Wednesday?" and "I wish people could just talk to Leslie. I was so impressed with her, so very impressed."

"I have to go," Daniel mumbled. "Work to do. Sorry things got so unpleasant."

"Sorry you have to leave so soon," Louise said. Christine and Penny were silent.

Daniel wanted to express his anger at the stupidity of a culture that refused to acknowledge the work of women, leaving slim choices that made pornography an attractive option for too many women.

He wanted to express his misgivings at the implied consent that occurred whenever the shutter snapped, or a porn web page was accessed. (Rayleen! he thought.) He hadn't really considered what that consent meant until now. He wanted them to know that he'd gotten food for thought.

More, he wanted them to know that he knew it was an unjust world that let men physically hurt women, that it caused him shame and sorrow when he thought of it. More, he was glad that Penny had Christine, because Christine cared about his sister, and everyone deserves someone to care about them.

Instead he nodded a silent goodby to the two women sitting huddled at the kitchen table, leaning into each other for support. Then he kissed his mother's cheek, and went to his car.

Outside, the sight of a mottled patch of weeds pasted to the chain-link fence reminded him of the hole he'd made in his apartment wall. He groaned, and kicked at the sidewalk. "Fucking Christine," he muttered. He climbed into the Hyundai and headed for the nearest McDonald's.

There was an e-mail waiting for him when he got back to the apartment. The associate in Boston had an answer for him.

Mordecai was a surprisingly common name back then.

But I found what you wanted. He was buried in Greenwood Cemetery in old Brooklyn. The marker said 1905, ten years old. Hope that helps. Usual fee will suffice, but send it quick. I have rent due.

Daniel stared at the monitor and then called up the picture of Mordecai Ryan, 1938, aged forty-three. He stared at the grinning old man, Ryan's wrinkled skull-face leering in the direction of the Fuhrer and his newly acquired Spear. The easiest way to assume a new identity was to take one from someone that had died. Mordecai Ryan might have assumed the name of a young boy in an east coast cemetery. That would explain the gap years in Ryan's childhood. But why take a child's identity? What was wrong with his own?

Daniel decided to take an evening drive. Ryan listed the office building as his home. Daniel would pay him a visit.

The door to the office building was locked. Daniel walked to a pay phone and called. Winthrop answered, his voice fogged with sleep. "Mr. Ryan told me to get back to him as soon as I had some focused questions for him."

The phone clicked, and the line went dead.

Daniel stood in front of the office building. The night winds drove ice into the back of his neck. He ducked down inside his coat, ears under the collar, hands in his pockets, like a turtle pulling into its shell. As he waited, he became angry. He had to go to the bathroom, and the cold was cutting through his pants legs.

"So why am I here?" he demanded. The money? He wanted the money. But that wasn't all of it. The case was intriguing, and he was curious. Why had he been chosen for the commission? Who was Mordecai Ryan?

And what about the come-again Jesus? If Daniel confronted Jesus the man, what would he have to say about Marianne? About Courtney? Daniel wanted answers. He would stay with the case until he had the truth firmly in hand.

The door latch popped, and Winthrop shoved the glass door open, startling Daniel. The secretary was in his robe.

Daniel was ushered upstairs. He found Ryan in the same bed, connected to his wires and tubes, a fragile marionette, blanket tucked up under his wrinkled chin. He was wide awake. "What can I do for you, Mr. Bain?"

"You told me to come back when I had some focused questions," Daniel said.

"I said, come back when you have intelligent questions," the old man corrected. The room light was off and the blinds were shut. A single desk lamp lit a small yellow circle around the old man's face. When he spoke, reflections of light flickered on his teeth.

"How did Ryan-Wilkins make its money?" Daniel led with a pointed question to demonstrate that he knew something about the old man's past.

A grin, teeth flashing in the light. "Sit down, Mr. Bain. You look cold. I can hear the wind through the window."

Daniel moved closer, and grabbed the chair from the foot of the bed, dragging it with him. "I don't bite," the old man said.

"Imports," Daniel said. "Some of them were illegal."

The old man shrugged, and then lay still.

"I'm guessing the real estate purchases were financed by the illegal imports. After a while, you had all the money you could need, and the risk wasn't worth it. So you went legit."

"You make it sound very exciting," Ryan said. "Like something from a gangster movie. Tell me, Mr. Bain, have you done any searching for the party I hired you to find, or are you content to dig through the past of a sick old man?" His words were a ploy, designed to control the conversation, but his voice told a different story. His tone was unmistakable— he was disappointed. And bored.

"I know about the Spear," Daniel said.

The old man's eyes widened slightly. "Tell me."

"I found your picture. 1938, in Vienna. You haven't aged much since then. I wonder if your congregation in Wellington knew that you were pals with Hitler?"

The old man beamed. "You are a clever fellow after all, aren't you? A picture? How did you find such a thing? No matter, it's wonderful. You know everything then?"

Daniel shifted in his chair, his hands resting uselessly in his lap. "I don't know everything," he said. "Tell me what's going on."

The old man's eyes narrowed. "I pay you," he said. "You report to me."

"Mr. Ryan, I've done what you asked," Daniel said. He slumped in the chair, exasperated. "Can you please answer some questions?"

The old man drew breath, a long, raw wheeze, and nodded. "What do you want to know?"

Daniel nodded, and pulled out a pad and pen. "I need some information about Derek Becker. First, what were his hobbies?"

"Hobbies!" the old man sputtered, his sudden laugh turning into a fit of coughing. "What waste of time is this?"

"Look, people disappear, but they don't change. They like the same things. They have a new identity, but they're the same person. What did Derek Becker like to do in his spare time? What magazines did he read?"

"What, do you think that Jesus reads Maxim?" Ryan asked, flecks of spit flying as he spoke. "Do you imagine that he collects bottle caps? Are you an idiot?" His fingertips crept over the lip of the blanket, like the legs of a hermit crab, scrambling and scraping at the edge of the cloth. He gripped the blanket and pulled it up over his chin. "You don't believe a word of it, do you? It's all a joke, isn't it?"

Daniel collected his thoughts, and tried again. "You hired me to find a person. People have interests. I once traced a person who liked model railroads. He left his wife and kids, and he got away with it. Then he subscribed to the model railroading magazines, because he had the same interests, and he was still the same guy. The new-subscriber lists are small, comparatively. I had an idea which state the guy went to, and when I traced the new subscribers, one of them was him."

Mordecai Ryan blinked. "Do you know what an aesthetic is?" Daniel shrugged. "An aesthetic is someone who has turned his back on material things. A holy man. Jesus Christ doesn't have hobbies, unless you think the salvation of the world is a hobby."

"I need a list of Derek's friends," Daniel said.

"Jesus has followers, not friends," Ryan croaked.

"I need a list of his followers."

The old man groaned in frustration. His breathing was a tiny, scratching sound. He fumbled for the button that regulated the flow of medicine to his right arm. Morphine, Daniel thought. The old man is in pain.

"Look, can I get you anything?"

"A real detective," the old man muttered.

"Pardon?"

Ryan bit his papery lip and glared at Daniel.

The interview was pointless. Daniel had no idea what the old man was getting at. He wondered how to tactfully excuse himself.

"What do you think this case is about?" Ryan asked.

Daniel blinked and sat back. He knew what the old man wanted him to say. "Well, I'm sure of this much. You're not Mordecai Ryan. Mordecai Ryan died in 1905 outside of New York City. Whoever you are, you took his name. It's a lot harder now, with social security numbers, but it can still be done. You use a birth certificate to get the social security card, and you go from there. Back then, I imagine you just took a name and ran with it."

Ryan stared, his mouth open. "Go on."

Careful now, Daniel thought. "Why change names? To duck the law? Why bother? You could leave town and start over. They didn't trace everything from phone calls to bowel movements back then." The old man chortled.

"The picture called you an expert on artifacts. Now the Spear of Longinus is an interesting artifact. And the story of the centurion is also interesting. Longinus stabs Christ, and is doomed to walk the earth forever. I imagine he never changes much in appearance."

The old man sank back into his pillows. His face was a death mask, stripped of expression. He did not move, and for a horrible moment, Daniel thought he'd stopped breathing. Then the old man let out another raspy wheeze. He frowned, still staring, studying Daniel. Then he smiled. His paper lips pulled back, a thin sneer with teeth. "What do you believe?" he asked.

"I'm a little short on belief these days."

"You don't believe?" the old man asked. "You don't even trust your eyes?"

"My eyes are good," Daniel said.

"But you don't believe."

"I don't believe," Daniel said.

The old man popped his claw out from under the blanket and motioned him forward with his bent finger. "Come here," he grinned, his tiny little teeth glinting in the light of the lamp. Daniel didn't move. "Come on, you aren't afraid are you? Fear would indicate a certain amount of belief. You're not one of those fellows who believes in ghosts at night, and disbelieves during the day, are you?"

Daniel stood up. "I don't like being played."

"Come closer," Ryan whispered. His voice was a kitten on a counter top, soft clicks and wet mewing. Daniel went halfway to the bed, his face flushed. He was uneasy, and it angered him.

"All the way, Mr. Bain. I want to show you something." Daniel stepped next to the bed, glancing to the side, noting the prescription bottle on the table.

The old man's claw hands pulled down the blanket, revealing his torso, or what had once been a torso. The chest was open at the sternum. The skin around the cavity was grey and papery. The rib cage was gone, replaced by a protective wire apparatus. The few organs that were left were dry, shriveled bulbs, bits of viscera, dusty webs of old sinew. A strip of red-stained gauze hung from one of the steel wires, trailing off into the bowels. Mordecai Ryan was open and gutted, crumbling into ruin.

"Pretty, isn't it?" the old man said, his lips and teeth in rictus, the grimace of death.

VIII

TO: Daniel Bain

FROM: Victor Sharpe

SUBJECT: RE: Dream Analysis

Dear Daniel,

Thank you so much for you kind words. I worry about my dream, because it imparts a violent subtext to a seemingly innocent surface. I can't tell you how disturbing the rocking horse image has become. Suffice it to say that I sold my daughter's rocker at a garage sale last weekend.

Freud called dreams "desires" clothed in the "residue of the day." Yet the particulars of my dream are dredged from my childhood. There is nothing contemporary in the imagery. I have hinted at my ghosts— what if ghosts are fears clothed in the residue of the past?

I do take issue, however, with your rather straight-forward account. Though I've been known to "over-analyze," I think the dream must have greater import than any anger I might feel towards my mother.

Your dream, of course, would appear to render everything I just said into nonsense. Still, I think there are insights to be gleaned from the proper analysis of even so straight-forward a dream as yours.

First, did you notice that your wife and daughter, the focus of the dream, are never present? You run from room to room, looking for signs of absence, clothes missing, etc. Yet as dream characters, they are indeed absent. Perhaps the thing you can't accept, the fact that they were gone, is the thing that structures the dream.

Second, the dream ends with the knock on the door, a knock you never answer. But the incident didn't end there. You did answer the door. Why only dream half of the story? Perhaps you can bear the separation, but cannot bear the rest of it.

The sequence with the goodby note tucked under the covers in the baby's crib (you called it a "paper changeling" — how appropriate!) was horrifying. I hope it was metaphorical. Surely your wife had the good sense and compassion to leave the note on the table.

At any rate, my friend, there are my humble insights into these matters. I hope that reading my meager response will help diffuse the potency of this sad nightmare of yours.

Nothing new on campus. Rumors of more cutbacks, (as is always so), thus everyone not tenured is on their best behavior. Except perhaps Rhodes, who is, as you recall, without personal restraint.

Take care. Victor

P.S. I often think of your abandoned career, and wonder if you regret your decision. Perhaps enough time has passed to give teaching another try. I would be honored to put a word in for you. We're not hiring now, of course, (I mentioned the cutbacks!) but it's always good to keep your name floating around so that they don't forget you. Also, Anne Gagne mentioned you this week. She organized a concert at the student center this Friday to raise money for the famine-fund (Given the famine and various diseases, is there anyone left alive in Africa?) and she thought you might show up. I know she's wound a little tight, but she likes you, and she has a brain. Just a thought.

IX

He woke up sobbing, wracked with tears, his chest aching. The dream had been pure, distilled grief, and his body shook from the memory of it. The sun was a hint through the window. It would be morning soon. Daniel's head throbbed, but he pulled himself from bed and stumbled into the bathroom. No more sleep, no more dreams.

He stood by the sink, shivering on the cold tile. Gradually, the hammering in his chest slowed, replaced by a familiar distance, as if watching himself from across a room, then across a street, finally from so far away that he was just a speck, a fleck on the horizon. He was awake.

Daniel washed his face and took two aspirin. Sunday, he thought. He would go to church. Thomas would be happy to see him. Perhaps his friend could spare a moment from his busiest day to talk about the hole in Mordecai Ryan's chest.

The shower washed away everything but the dream. Daniel put on his dress shirt and tie and his only pair of dress slacks. His closet was nearly bare, just a few pairs of jeans and tee-shirts along with the polo shirts he used for transacting business. He had one sweater, a nice one that his mother had given him for Christmas. He thought of it as his date sweater, though he was not dating.

The kitchen sink was littered with beer bottles. Seven. Had he finished seven beers? He couldn't remember.

Driving to church, the car stalled twice. Daniel couldn't decide if the engine was cold or if the car really needed repairs. He didn't know enough about cars to know the difference, and every encounter with a garage left him feeling suckered and helpless. He usually ignored repair problems until a tow-truck had to be called.

He stalled a third time when he pulled into the church parking space, lurching to a stop a few feet shy of the curb. Daniel put the car in neutral and pushed it forward until the front wheels touched concrete. Then he reached in, set the parking break, and closed the door.

His first kick surprised him. He felt the pain in his foot and saw the dent in the door. He kicked again, harder this time. In a sudden flash of rage, he slammed against the side of the car, driving a knee into the door panel. He felt the metal buckle.

"What is that man doing?"

A church-bound family had stopped to watch Daniel. He gave them a small wave and a weak smile. "Car repairs," he explained. He brushed car dirt from his pants and straightened his tie while they walked on.

He winced, both from the pain in his knee and from a glance at the damage to his car. What the hell was wrong with him? Perhaps he needed to visit church more than he'd imagined.

Thomas's church looked like a converted barn, washed with white paint and laid open with windows. Recent changes were evident. The wooden entry doors had been stripped, stained, and rehung. The old gable above the doors, built as a canopy, styled as a turret in a medieval castle, had been torn out and replaced with a smaller, less intrusive pediment, a triangle frame graced with a wooden cross made of weathered aspen. The roof was freshly shingled, and the crack in the cement steps was patched. (Thomas had been trying to budget the removal of the cement, hoping to replace it with a redwood stairway to match the pediment. "Some day soon, my friend," he'd promised.)

The grounds were beautifully kept. During the spring and summer, the flower beds were a shock of color. Margaret, Thomas's wife, invested her energies in the church, and the flower beds took a fair share of her attention. In the winter, the rectangular beds were picked clean to remove the wet swatches of leaves that hugged the street curbs and molded themselves to the corners of every house in the neighborhood.

But the church was also made in the image of its congregation. The front lawn had a new marquee with the message, "Eternity– Have You Made Your Reservation?" The storage garage to the rear of the church was covered from the base to the lip of the roof with a fresco, painted in oranges and purples by the church's teen-club. Margaret called the shed, "Thomas's graffiti barn." Thomas noted that, "The church belongs to the teenagers too."

Two church "greeters" blocked the door. Daniel had been introduced to the couple, but he could not remember their names. They recognized him and beamed as he approached the steps. "Good morning! How are you!" The man, a bent willow with graying hair, grabbed Daniel's hand and pumped it. "So glad you could make it!" The woman wore a huge turquoise cross on a silver chain that drew attention away from her small eyes, too close together. "Hello!" she chirped. Her voice was the sound of insect legs rubbing together.

Daniel offered up a smile and pushed his way into the church. Teenagers playing a piano, two guitars and a drum galloped through a contemporary hymn. Scattered voices of the congregation stumbled over the words posted on an overhead projector. The room was more than half full. On one visit to the church the previous summer, the room had been three-quarters empty. "Everyone's on vacation," Thomas had explained.

Daniel slid into a pew near the back of the room, bumping his sore knee as he sat. Thomas saw him from the pulpit and smiled. Daniel looked around the room to see if there was anyone else he recognized and was surprised to spot Veronica, the waitress at Brian's Diner, sitting in the second row. Her hair was down, draped over her shoulders, and she looked lovely. There was a man sitting next to her, but it was not clear if they were together.

The music stopped. Thomas stood waiting for the chattering to die down, his eyes hardened in anticipation of the sermon. He gripped the pulpit, an old school podium, and stared straight ahead until the room went silent. Then he began to speak, his voice calm, reasoned, sweetened with a hint of gentleness.

"We are mindful," he began, "of the tragedy last month. We live in a nice town, not too large, still small enough to recognize the people we meet on the streets. We live peaceful lives, and then something happens that makes us question our peace, our safety, ourselves."

A few weeks earlier, a man had entered the Fort Collins Post Office with a handgun tucked in the back of his pants, hidden by his overcoat. He took the elevator to the Federal IRS office on the second floor. There, he signed in on the appointment clipboard and sat with a handful of other taxpayers, waiting for an appointment. When his turn came, he went back into the conference rooms, pulled his gun out and began shooting, killing two account managers, the receptionist and a filing clerk before turning the gun on himself. The man was in arrears for less than three thousand dollars. Surely no one would kill four human beings for a debt so small, so manageable! Perhaps his divorce, a year earlier, contributed to the attack.

The town was paralyzed with shock. The national media spent two weeks interviewing anyone in Fort Collins with an opinion that could be delivered in a single sound byte or a prose-worthy sentence. Metal detectors were installed at the IRS office entrance, and donation cups were set on counter-tops in liquor and convenience stores to collect money for the families of the victims.

"I don't know what demons chased the unfortunate man who chose violence and chaos last month. That is precisely the point— we don't know what anyone else is feeling or thinking. I believe that he was a profoundly tortured soul. My faith tells me that he could have been ministered to by the word of God. Instead, he chose to commit a horrible crime, and the lives of four others were cut short."

"And now we look at each other and we ask, 'How can we be safe?' But we can't. We know that. We are all vulnerable to the hand of evil."

"But that isn't the worst of it. The worst is the realization that we are alone, that we are born marked with the sins of Adam and Eve. We live alone, we die alone, and we never really know what those around us are thinking."

"Or do we?" Thomas paused. His eyes hardened, and he picked up the pace of his words. "We can guess some things about the man who committed these horrible murders. We can see the hand of Satan, can we not? And we know that anyone can be tempted. Any one of us can fall into despair."

"Through sin, we are separated from one another. But are we really alone? No."

"Praise Jesus." The call came from the front. Heads nodded in affirmation. The old woman next to Daniel smiled at him. He managed a grin, nodded, and looked away.

"You know, people come to church for different reasons." Thomas stepped away from the podium, waving a hand in time with his words. His tone was suddenly casual. "Ask yourself. Why did you come to church today? Some of you came to meet and share fellowship with other Christians. Some of you are searching, not quite sure what's missing in your life, and you came looking here." Daniel looked down and stared at the braided hair of the little girl sitting directly in front of him.

"In one way or another, we're all looking for the same thing. We don't want to be alone. We are cut off from one another, and from God, by sin. We feel the loss, and we spend our lives searching, searching for something to fill the void."

"But it need not be that way. Jesus is waiting for a personal relationship with each and every one of you. You do not need to be alone. All you have to do is ask, ask Jesus to come into your heart."

Now the people in the pews began to stir. The calls of "Praise God," and "Praise Jesus" bubbled up while Daniel stewed in his seat.

"Why then don't we ask Jesus to be a part of our lives? What holds us back? Why do we procrastinate and postpone the thing we all search for, the thing we all crave? Pride? False, ugly pride? Or are we too busy with the search to recognize its end?"

Thomas looked down at the podium, opened the Bible, and pulled his reading glasses from his shirt pocket. "Today's scripture is from the Gospel of Luke, chapter nine, verse fifty-three to verse sixty-two." He began to read.

"But the Samaritans did not make him welcome, because he was determined to go to Jerusalem. When the disciples James and John saw this, they said, 'Lord, do you wish for us to bring fire from the heavens to consume them?' Jesus turned and rebuked them, and they traveled to another village."

"As they went along the road, someone said,'I will follow you wherever you go.' Jesus answered, 'Foxes have holes, and the birds of the sky have nests, but the Son of man has no where to lay his head.'"

"To another, he said, 'Follow me." But he answered, 'Lord, let me first bury my father.' And Jesus answered, 'Let the dead bury the dead. But you go and proclaim the kingdom of God.'"

"And another said, 'I will follow you, Lord, but first let me say goodby to my family at home.' Jesus answered, No one who first sets a hand to the plow and looks back is fit for the kingdom of God.'"

Daniel sat, his head tilted to the side, puzzled. I wonder what translation of the Bible they're using? he thought.

Thomas closed the book, and looked up, tucking the glasses back in his pocket. "You see, then as now, people have a thousand excuses for maintaining the separation between themselves and Jesus. And his answer is always the same. 'Come now. No excuses. Come to me now.' The people in the scripture are busy with their lives, their tragedies, their families. But Jesus says, 'No excuses. Come now.'"

"What are your excuses? What holds you back? In the scripture, Jesus demanded that a man leave his father unburied. Are we not supposed to 'honor thy father and mother'? Think about that. What a bizarre demand! 'Come to me now.' Do any of us here today have such a compelling reason to put off a personal relationship with Jesus? Perhaps you are suffering from the loss of a loved one. Perhaps you are going through a divorce. Good reasons, all. What would Jesus say? 'Come to me now.'"

"What are your reasons? 'I'm in debt.'— 'Come to me now!'" He slapped an open palm on the podium for emphasis, and half of the crowd jumped.

"'I don't know if I believe. I can't be sure.'— 'Come to me now!'" He slammed his fist into the wood, like the crack of a rifle, and Daniel slid down in the pew, searching for cover.

Thomas stood hunched over the podium, his voiced wired with fury. Daniel closed his eyes, but Thomas' dark stare drilled through his eyelids. He could picture the pastor's beard sizzling, his hands gripping the podium, crushing it to splinters.

And then the sermon ended, quietly. The hush was a relief. Thomas bowed, hands folded in front. "To remind us that we can never be alone, not when we are gathered in his name, in Christian fellowship, I would like for you to turn to the person next to you and hug them. Put your arms around them, and let them know that Jesus loves them." Daniel froze, his skin crawling with the ice of apprehension. The old woman next to him had turned, waiting. Her perfume would cling to his shirt and tie when the hug was finished. Days later, when he went to take his sweater from the closet, he would find that the perfume was still imbedded in the shirt's fibers.

Then a prayer.

"Lord, there are those here who are reluctant to ask you into their lives. We pray that they can find the courage, the love, the faith to ask. Only to ask. Because if they ask, Lord, you will answer, and the blessings will leave them breathless. Give them the courage, Lord, the love, the faith. Let them come to you now. Amen." Silence, then, "If there is anyone here who would receive the blessings of Jesus Christ today, then come forward now."

No one moved. Daniel sank into the pew. He means me, he thought. Why did I come here? What did I want? He closed his eyes. I want the truth. I want to know what's going on. Thomas is a smart man. I will speak to Thomas. After the service.

Mordecai Ryan was a mystery. At first, Daniel had believed that Ryan was running a scam. Then he saw the hole in the old man's chest. He still suspected Ryan was playing games, but what was the point? What did he hope to gain?

Daniel opened his eyes. A little boy had approached the podium wearing a tight-fitting red sports coat and a clip-on tie. He was no more that twelve years old. He pushed his glasses back up on his nose and said, "I want to accept Jesus."

Thomas leaned down, and said, not too loudly, "Gregory, you accepted Jesus into your life last month."

"I know," the boy said, panicked, "but I've sinned."

Thomas didn't laugh. "We all sin, Gregory. If you're sorry for the sin and ask forgiveness, then it will be forgiven. And you don't have to ask Jesus twice. He's already with you. I promise."

The little boy nodded and went back to his seat. Thomas was alone, but only for a moment. A man stood and walked to the front of the church. He was in his mid-twenties, overweight, with coarse black hair that covered the collar of his sweater. His jeans had a hole in the back pocket.

Daniel watched as Thomas said a few words to the man. The old woman next to him leaned forward, drew in a breath, and held it. The man at the podium muttered something, and then Thomas put his hand on the man's head.

Suddenly, the man in the torn jeans shuddered and pitched backward, nearly banging his head on the front pew. He arched his back in a convulsion, thrashing like a fish on a taut line. A collective gasp went up from the congregation. Thomas, caught by surprise, stepped off the alter landing and knelt by the quivering man. A woman in the third pew stood and called out: "Robert! Robert!"

Robert stopped shaking and tried to sit, pushing himself off the floor with an elbow, then rolling up on his forearm, and finally sitting, his back to Daniel. Thomas steadied the man with a hand to the shoulder while the man's wife rushed forward, her fingers in her mouth, frightened. The congregation burst into excited chatter. "What happened? It was the divine hand of God. . .he's all right now. . .he's lucky he didn't break his skull. . .a miracle, a genuine, solid-gold miracle. . .thank you, Jesus. . ."

Thomas had Robert on his feet. Robert's wife stood sobbing behind him, her face pressed into his back, her arms wrapped as far around her husband as his ample waist would allow. Robert shook his head, tossing his shaggy black hair. "It was like a bolt of lightning. . ."

The congregation was on its feet, hovering, asking questions, turning to one another in wonder. Daniel stayed in the pew.

At the end of the service, Daniel stopped to say a word to Robert, who was flushed with the excitement and the attention. "Congratulations on finding God," Daniel said, repeating what he had heard others say.

"It was like a bolt of lightning. God's hand touched me through Pastor Thomas, and it was like a bolt, right through the body." He paused. "A bolt of lightning."

"Lightning. That's good."

"It was a miracle," Robert said, frowning, as if Daniel didn't understand. "A terrible, wonderful miracle. I'll never be the same."

Robert's wife tugged at his arm. "Robert? Come on, Honey! We need to be on the road if we're going to make New Mexico by dinner." Robert nodded and explained, "We're going on vacation. Two weeks. We're going down to east Texas to see my parents. Then on to Kentucky." Thomas joined them, shaking Robert's hand one last time.

"I'm so excited," Robert's wife gushed, pulling him toward the door. "I haven't seen my sister in two years!"

"Drive carefully," Thomas said. "They're having pretty rough weather in the Midwest. Lots of snow."

"None of that in Texas, that's for sure!" Robert laughed, waving as his wife dragged him backwards. "See you in a few weeks, Pastor Thomas. I'll bring you pictures. Maybe we'll go to the beach!" They slipped out, only Robert's waving hand remained for a moment, and then it was gone, swallowed by the door.

Daniel stood staring at Thomas.

"What?" the Pastor asked.

"If I was touched by the hand of God, I'd never miss another church service. I'd be the first one here on Sunday. I'd camp out on the steps to make sure I didn't miss it."

"Ahhh." Thomas tugged at his beard. "Before you pass judgement, my friend, let me suggest an alternate possibility. Perhaps God's presence is already so much a part of their lives, that Robert and his wife are not shocked by miracles. Perhaps the idea of being touched by God isn't so revolutionary to them."

"But didn't they hear your sermon? What about the gospel you read? Jesus said, 'Come to me,' and they answered, 'I'll join you in Jerusalem, but first I'm going to Texas. I'll bring pictures. Maybe I'll go to the beach.'"

Thomas frowned. "I think you're being unfair."

"Maybe. Probably." Daniel shoved his hands in his pockets, suddenly ashamed of himself. What did he know about Robert's life? How could he judge? He tried to change the subject. "I was a little surprised by the passage you read. I've read it before, but it seemed like the translation was completely different from the one I've seen. I remember one line; 'You're neighbors are in Jerusalem.' Are all Bibles so different?"

Thomas shook his head. "The language varies from translation to translation. I use several, including the original Greek, when I'm preparing a sermon. I don't recall anything like that."

"It came right after the guy said he needed to say goodby to his friends and family. Your translation says something about a plow. It was different."

Thomas shrugged. "I couldn't say." He paused. "I was pleased to see you here today. It's been several weeks."

What could he say? Of course I came to your service. We're friends, aren't we? If you were a baker, I'd buy your doughnuts, wouldn't I?

Instead, he blurted, "I saw something that scared me. It was like a lightning bolt, and I'm here."

Thomas stared at him for a moment and then pointed to a door behind the altar. "I'll meet you in the office in a few minutes. I have to say goodby to the rest of the congregation."

Daniel stood waiting in the office. He couldn't sit, he had been sitting too long. The room was not much more than a closet with bookshelves. There were no family pictures, no picture of Thomas's wife. The walls were light green. Prison green, he thought with a laugh. There was no touch of the personal beyond the cross on the wall, a plaster rendition of a stone cross, and the rows of books on the back wall.

A multi-volume, annotated Bible caught his eye, along with various books of Biblical criticism. There was also a row of philosophy books, the works of Aristotle, Plato, Descartes and Nietzsche, even a few modern volumes, including Foucault and Cavell. Thomas was a knowledgeable man. He was a professional, an intellectual. What was he doing cloistered in this small church, hidden away in the oldest part of town?

"Thank you for waiting," Thomas said, stepping into the room. "Tell me what's going on."

Daniel sat down. He stared at the plaster cross and tried to think of how not to sound like a fool. He kept his voice low, serious, and did not look over at his friend. "Do you know who Longinus was?"

"Tell me."

"The centurion who pierced Christ's side with a lance."

"Ahhh. I remember now. Why do you ask?"

"According to the legend, he can't die. He keeps on going forever, like the battery bunny."

"Until the Second Coming," Thomas said. "He waits for Christ's return."

Daniel turned to Thomas. The look in his eyes seemed to warn the pastor. Thomas leaned forward, elbows on the desk, his hands cupping his chin. "What did you see?"

Daniel told him about Mordecai Ryan and the hole where his chest should have been. He told him about the Internet picture with Hitler and the Spear. Thomas sat motionless, hardly blinking, his dark eyes pinning Daniel. When the story was done, he sat back, and stared at the ceiling.

Daniel cleared his throat. "I don't think he's Longinus."

"Oh, I agree." Thomas closed his eyes and sighed, stroking his beard. He seemed to be considering something. Finally he asked, "Did I tell you that I did missionary work in New Zealand when I was younger?"

"No."

"Backward country. A lot like the old west. I did my errands on horseback. That's the way everyone traveled. One day, I was coming back from a baptism, and a storm kicked up. The sky turned yellow, pudding yellow. My horse was a good old mare, steady as a rock, but the wind made her nervous. I was anxious to get home. As I rode, I passed a bundle of blankets, and I thought I heard a child."

"I stopped and tied off the mare," he continued. "She was going crazy, and I almost went on rather than leave her tied. I thought she might pull free and leave me. But there was the bundle, and if a child had been abandoned. . ."

He paused again and looked straight at Daniel. His face had the same sense of urgency it had during the sermon. "I walked over to the pile of blankets and peeled back the flaps, one blanket, then two, and there was the baby. It little thing, perhaps two weeks old. No more than that. I reached out to touch its cheek, and it opened its eyes. It had crimson-red eyes. It smiled, and I saw two neat little rows of sharp, pointy teeth, like tiny needles. Then it spoke. It said, 'How do you like my teeth?' I must have fallen back, because I found myself scrambling away, crawling in the dirt. I got to my horse somehow, and I got out of there."

Thomas tapped the desk with his finger. "I don't know what I saw. And I don't know who your Mr. Ryan is. Is he a two-thousand year old centurion? Not likely. Is he dangerous? Very possibly."

"You see," he continued, leaning closer, his beard shaking, "I believe in evil incarnate. I believe the devil and his minions battle the good and the not-so-good every day. I've seen the face of evil, and I know it exists. And I have a bad feeling about your Mr. Ryan."

Daniel frowned. "What's to gain? Why fool with me?"

"A soul is a soul," Thomas said. "Yours is troubled. You are easy pickings, my friend."

Daniel started to protest, and then sat back. "True enough," he admitted. Then an idea came. "I'm wondering. What if Jesus has come back, and the old man is trying to track him down to stop him. Could that happen?"

"There is palpable evil in the world," Thomas said. "If Christ returned and that evil decided to stop him, then there wouldn't be many places to hide. Sanctified places, perhaps. A Monastery? In the wilderness? I don't know. I don't think there's anywhere safe from evil. Not in this world."

"You don't think Christ has returned, do you?"

"I don't know," Thomas said, smiling. "I don't suppose so."

"Why not?" Daniel asked. "It seems pretty easy for you to believe in the devil. . ." Thomas started to protest, so Daniel amended himself. "Or some sort of evil being. Why is it hard to believe that Christ has come back?"

Thomas sat back, his mouth open. For a moment, it looked as if he had forgotten what he was going to say. His eyes shone in the dim light of the office. "That's not. . .I'm not. . . ." He blinked. "You're right, of course. There's no reason not to think Christ has returned. I just find it easier, personally, to believe in evil than to believe. . . ."

Daniel flushed with a sudden realization. "You're having a crisis of faith." He said it softly, without malice, but it came out as an accusation. Thomas stared, his face blank, and Daniel took the silence as an affirmation.

"It's true, isn't it? You're questioning your faith."

"Faith is acting as if you believe," Thomas said. "I can't bear to think of the world without the possibility of a God, a loving God. So I will act as if I believe." He exhaled, a sudden convulsion of breath. His eyes reddened, and he couldn't meet Daniel's gaze. "I've told no one," he said. "Not even my wife. She couldn't bear it." He grimaced, fighting any further display of emotion. When Daniel reached out to touch his hand, Thomas pulled away.

X

C:\MyFiles\Truth\Nov

I am invisible. I walk through people, past people, and they do not notice me. I make no impression. I have no reflection. Even a duck in a pond leaves a wake, but I have had no impact on this world.

I can't live like this. I must have an impact, I must find my part in God's plan. I am certain he has a plan for me. A God without a plan would be an abomination, a helpless, impotent sputter, a quasar in some corner of the galaxy, all energy and bluster. My God has a plan, and I will find my small place in it, and it will be my place, my place, mine.

Somehow, my fate links to hers. I am certain of it because I know her. I feel as if I know her. I have risen each morning, alone, walked mountain paths alone, tasting the sweet air alone, waiting for someone to share my life, my part in God's battle. I yearn, not like an animal, but like a father, a brother, a friend; yearning for someone to join me in my quest. I will not be alone. She is the one, I can see it in her eyes. Her pictures scream out to me and the cry is for help. She will be the one to help me find my place.

She may even be my first task. I may be required to save her. I am ready.

I have been preparing, making myself into the perfect instrument. I have purified myself, emptying myself of wants. I am hollow, ready to receive the blessings of my part in the plan. I am hardened, like steel, like tempered steel, forged in the fire, hammered into the shape you desire, oh Lord, hammered and ready for your instructions.

And I know your plans include the girl, for you are merciful and would not leave her to rot in the world in which she is trapped. She will rise with me, to me, and together, we will become visible, and those who see us together will know that we are to be acknowledged. We are to be reckoned with. We will be His emissaries, and His wrath will be terrible and beautiful.

We will assert ourselves, and together, we will be as one, because one plus one is more than two, and one plus one plus God is infinite, and unstoppable against the forces that (backspace) forces of darkness (backspace) forces that oppose (backspace) forces that would (backspace) evil (backspace) unstoppable.

But first, I will announce myself to her, and she must recognize me. She must acknowledge me. I will not be invisible. Not to her. I will not allow it.

XI

Driving away from the church, Daniel remembered Veronica. He had hoped to say hello and make a little contact, perhaps even invite her out for brunch or a cup of coffee. She was long gone, though. She might be headed to Brian's for a shift. Daniel was hungry. He decided to drive over to the diner and get some lunch. If she was scheduled, he would sit in her section and give her a huge tip.

But she was not working. Daniel sat at the counter and ordered his usual Sunday fare— scrambled eggs, sausage, hash browns, bacon, toast, and a biscuit and gravy. The rest of the week he ate healthy. Sunday was a reprieve that was always regretted, from the moment that it was ordered. He ordered it anyway.

"Do you have a thing for her?" Brian asked. "Veronica's got a boyfriend. He's an asshole. Hell, none of my girls date nice guys. I think it's against the waitress-club bylaws to date anyone who treats them well."

"Ahhh," Daniel said, doing his best Thomas impression.

"She was off late last night, Saturday night for Christ's sake, what the hell does he expect? She served him coffee and told him to be patient, be nice, she'll be done soon, and he just sat there sulking. They got into an argument, and she wasn't worth a damn at the tables for the rest of the night. I'd kick the bastard out if I wasn't afraid of losing a good waitress over it."

"It's a mystery," Daniel said.

"Nah, it's no mystery, it's predictable. A nice girl like Veronica is too smart to wait tables for a living. Not that this is a bad job. It's honest work. She could do better, that's all. But she doesn't think much of herself, so she earns her living as a waitress. It's a job she thinks she deserves. Same with that guy. She thinks she deserves a jerk, so she goes and finds herself one, time after time. Later, when she's older, and the sag sets in, she'll either be married to a jerk, or settle on the biggest wallet she can find."

"That's quite unflattering," Daniel said. The gravy was pasty, and the taste of butter-fat coated everything on his plate like a glaze. It was wonderful.

"It's the truth," Brian declared, planting his elbows on the counter. Grill burns marked his forearms like crosshatching in an ink sketch. "It's all anthropological. Women need protection. They look for someone with power. In the dinosaur days, that meant a guy who could swing a club. Now it means a guy with money. Money is power, see? Power means the woman can have a baby, and it'll survive. That's all it boils down to." Daniel didn't respond. Talking to Brian was like listening to the radio.

"Now, men are just looking to spread the seed," Brian continued. "That's why we look for physical beauty, because that means healthy babies, in an anthropological sort of way."

The diner was nearly empty. It was not a popular spot for the church crowd, and Brian was free to lecture without interruption. "It gets complicated when you look at who cheats on who with who. Or whom. Which is it? Oh, hell, I never did get that straight. Anyway, when a woman cheats on her husband, she goes for a kid with sad eyes, no butt, and an empty head. Why? Because the watcha' call your 'biological imperative' is already taken care of. She can raise a litter, and they're protected while she finds herself a boy-toy. Now when a guy cheats. . ." He paused, for extra significance, ". . .a guy looks for someone he can talk to." He snorted, and his nose-hair rustled. "Go figure."

"There doesn't seem to be room for love in your scheme."

"Love?" Brian snorted. "We all want what we can't have. We want to own each other, and we only respect those who reject us. Love? Love is wanting to own what you don't deserve."

Just then, another customer entered the diner, a short man in his thirties, wearing a poorly-fitted sports coat. Brian frowned, and shook his head. "This place just got a little too 'Hebrew' for my taste," he whispered.

Daniel glanced at the man who was seating himself in a booth on the other side of the diner. "What do you mean?" he asked.

Brian nodded in the other customer's direction. "You know, Hebrew. Jewish. That guy sits there all day, getting his coffee refilled about a thousand times, and he doesn't tip for shit. He never orders dinner. He just comes in and does his work at my table, like the Sabbath doesn't mean anything. Is this a diner, or is it a branch office? Am I right, or am I right?"

"You're open on Sunday," Daniel said.

Brian scowled. "I have to be. It's a fucking diner." He grabbed a coffee cup from the shelf, and turned, his back to the new customer, in full view of Daniel. Shoving a pudgy finger into his nose, he pulled a bit of phlegm free and wiped it on the inside of the cup. "One coffee, coming up!" Smirking, he delivered the coffee to the guest.

Daniel sat frozen to the seat. He wanted to pay his check and leave. He wanted to warn the man, "Don't drink the coffee!" but Brian was back at the counter before he could move. The last of Daniel's runny eggs sat on the plate. Suddenly, they didn't look appetizing. "Remind me not to get you mad," Daniel said, trying to joke. "I sure don't want to cook for myself on Sunday."

Brian frowned. "We're both white, and we're both Christian. Why would I be mad at you?" Daniel stared, silent. Brian looked away, muttered something, and walked off, waving behind him.

The bill was on the counter. Daniel debated the gratuity, his disgust with Brian's behavior battling the loyalty Daniel owed to the diner. It was like his second home.

He left a tip. He immediately regretted it.

Daniel enjoyed listening to Brian spout his street-theories. It had been somehow comforting to imagine that one of the wise minds of the world was at his disposal, working in a diner. But the wisdom was tainted with bigotry, a discovery that made him feel naive and simple-minded, especially after a morning of group-hugs and questionable miracles.

And Daniel was no better, really. He ought to have warned the customer, and he didn't. He ought to call the health department, and he wouldn't.

He slapped the steering wheel as he drove. "Why am I so upset? Why didn't I say something? Because the diner is my home, that's why. I like it there. I'm not just a customer, I'm family. . ."

He pulled the car over and stopped next to the curb. "Crap," he whispered. He slapped the steering wheel again, and then drew back his fist for still another blow, harder this time. It took all of his self-control not to swing. He found himself breathing heavily, and his face flushed hot. He sat still for a long time before driving on.

With nowhere else to go, Daniel went back to his apartment. Perhaps if he focused on work, he could earn the money he'd already collected. Work was clean. People hired you, and you worked hard for them, and you both got what was agreed upon. If he concentrated on the job, he might forget about the dirty business at the diner.

He returned to his computer. Daniel had taken the doctor's name from Ryan's prescription bottles. It took him two minutes to find the doctor's email address on Yahoo-search. He sent a short note, asking about the hole in Mordecai Ryan's chest. There had to be a medical explanation for what he'd seen.

Then Daniel searched for Derek Becker. There were probably hundreds of Derek Beckers in the world. He could eliminate some, concentrating on likely candidates. Becker was in his early thirties. And of course, Ryan had said that his Jesus was white. "Hah," Daniel said, banging away at the keyboard. "Always white." He thought of his sister, and her girlfriend. "And male," he whispered. "Always male." He shook his head. In his mind, he had just stepped over a trap, a snare designed to catch the self-righteous. He couldn't focus on one kind of bigotry to the exclusion of another. If he did, he was more dangerous than a bigot, because he would perpetuate bigotry under the guise of righteousness. And he was a sexist, was he not? "No I'm not," he whispered. Then he thought of Rayleen's web page, and his mind took a sudden left turn.

He typed in the address. The server was slow, and he had time to reconsider while the main page downloaded. He nearly shut down the connection and returned to his work. Then the header for "Rayleen's Room" popped up, and thoughts of work disappeared.

Daniel clicked on the "NEW!" banner, and was pleased to see that two new pictures had been added. One was a shot of Rayleen at a barbecue, laughing and shoving a hamburger into her face. The background was beautiful, lined with mountains, and suddenly, Daniel thought, I know those mountains. That's near Boulder! I camp near there! Where exactly does Rayleen live? He studied the photo, as if the silhouette of the range behind her would give him directions. If I knew where she lived, he thought, I might go there, just drive by, and see if I can meet her.

Then he sat back in his chair, and slapped his forehead. "I'm a skip-tracer, for God's sake! I can find her myself!" He backed out of the site and went to work.

He went into the Linux operating system of his Windows program to run a "who-is" command on the web address. Every web site had to register with Internic to avoid address duplication, similar to registering a trademark. The actual physical address of the web page was available to anyone who could use a terminal emulation system. Five minutes later, he had her address. As he had suspected, she lived in Boulder. Forty minutes away.

He copied the address on a sheet of paper, and stuck it in his wallet. Like a check from the old man, the address was an exciting possibility, a break from the gray sameness of every day. It was a blank canvas, an un-scratched lottery ticket, an unopened e-mail letter. In that sense, the address was more valuable hidden in his wallet. An actual visit would be a certain disappointment.

By evening, he was disgusted with his lack of progress in locating Becker. The man that Ryan wanted him to find left no paper-trail, at least nothing easily discovered. Daniel decided he needed a break, so he headed for his car, remembering to warm it up before he took off. *I won't go to Boulder*, he thought. *I'll just drive and get some air.*

Before long, he found himself on the highway to Boulder. He spent the next thirty minutes trying to decide if he would turn around before arriving. He weighed the alternatives but could not decide. Meanwhile, his car made the decision for him.

The city of Boulder sat nestled in a pocket of the Rocky Mountains, in the shadow of a stretch of jagged peaks called the Flatirons, surrounded by rural plains. The Boulder highway ran end-to-end through the town. Daniel stopped at a gas station at the south end, and asked for directions. Rayleen's address was less than two minutes from the station. He drove several blocks into a nice residential area, streets bordered with huge elms and oaks, houses with wind chimes and porch lights, and nice cars lining the curbs. The sun had gone down. An early winter frost had glazed the windshields and leaves with ice.

The right street was easy to find. He stopped to look for a house number. He noticed the girl running toward the car, but did not recognize her until she banged on the passenger side window.

"Mister! Open up, please!" she shouted. Her hair hung over her face so it took him a moment to realize that the girl was Rayleen.

Daniel popped the lock and pushed the door open. Rayleen glanced back. A man ran to the Hyundai from the front door of the house where Daniel had stopped. Rayleen threw herself into the front seat and shrieked, "Go! Please!" Daniel put the car in drive and stepped on the gas.

The car lurched once and stalled. Daniel turned the key to start the car again. Rayleen hit the door lock, and the running man slammed into the side of the car. "I just want to talk!" he shouted. He wore a bright blue jogging suit and a grey sweat jacked. The hood of the jacket was pulled up over his head, and Daniel could only glimpse his face. A mustache. An agonized grimace.

"Fucker!" Rayleen shrieked. She turned to Daniel and began to plead. "Can't you go? He's a stalker. . ."

The jogger slammed his palms against the passenger's side window. Rayleen jumped, and covered her head.

Daniel put the car in park, and opened the door. "No!" she shouted. The girl was clearly frightened.

Daniel walked around the front of the car, his eyes on the jogger. "You're way out of line." The jogger stared at him as if he'd been invisible until that moment. Daniel stopped just a few feet away. The man crouched, poised to attack. Daniel threw out his chest, and folded his arms. "Decide what you want to do."

"Stay out of this!" Dark hair tumbled from under the jogger's hood. He balled his fists. "This is none of your business!"

Daniel smiled. "Get away from my car."

The jogger stared at him, measuring him, calculating the odds. Then he unleashed a torrent of angry words. Daniel relaxed a bit, though he kept his eyes on the center of the man's chest, watching for a sudden attack. When the jogger took a breath, interrupting the tirade, Daniel stepped closer. The jogger flinched.

"I told you to get away from my car," Daniel said. "And leave the girl alone."

Again, the jogger hesitated, and for a brief moment his eyes widened. He looked as if he might swing. Then he backed away, eyes on Daniel, nodding. "Fine. I know you. I know you now. You just made the worst mistake of your life." He turned, and trotted off.

"Thank you. Thank you so much," the girl said when he stepped back behind the wheel.

"He won't bother you now," Daniel promised. "Do you want to go inside and call the police?"

Rayleen pulled her hair back from her face. Her cheeks were wet with angry tears. She shook her head. "I can't go back in there. Not tonight. That bastard was in my house."

"The police. . ."

"The Boulder police are a national joke," she said. "And I don't want them in my house."

He stared at her. In the faint light, he could recognize the subject of his fantasies, but she looked different. Her pictures were flat, two-dimensional. Her videos were grainy and hollow sounding. In his car she was alive, breathing, real. And she was in trouble.

"Do you have friends you can stay with?" he asked. "I can drive you there."

"Will this thing start?"

He laughed. "Sure, now that I don't need it to." He turned the key. The engine coughed, and then roared. The stink of oil seeped in through the window. "Where to?"

She sighed. "Just go," she said. "I want to get out of here. I'll think about where we're going while you're driving." She paused, and added, "Do you have plans? If you do, I can get off at the gas station up the road."

Daniel shook his head. "No, I'll get you to some place safe. Will your house be okay? The door's open. Do you want me to lock up?"

She bit her lip. "Yes, would you? But hurry, okay?" He shut the Hyundai down again. As he stepped from the car, he heard her groan. "Oh hell. I need my wallet, and I need some clothes. Will you go in with me?"

"Of course," Daniel said. He led her up the walk. Huge shrubs bracketed the front door. Trees at the front walk blocked the street lights. It was dark, and Daniel had a sudden premonition that he would be attacked. He stopped.

The man in the jogging suit had backed down, but he was a tire iron or a knife away from shifting the advantage. Perhaps he had a car parked a block away, and a gun in the glove compartment He'd been inside the house. Could he get in again? Or was he waiting on the street, planning to do something to Daniel's car?

And if Daniel felt vulnerable, how did Rayleen feel?

The inside of the house was tidy, though a little Spartan in its decor. A pillow-couch and chair cornered a television. Hanging plants spilled out of their pots, and a print of one of Monet's haystacks added a splash of color to the wall. The rest of the living room was office space, packed with file cabinets, a computer desk, and a pair of metal shelves stacked with video tapes and packing materials. "This is where she runs her business," he thought. The desk had a pair of wire baskets for in and out mail, and a pencil holder. It was clean. "Do you run a business here?" he asked.

"Yeah," she snorted. She stood at the stairway, looking up.

"What?"

"Look, would you go upstairs with me? I don't want to go up alone." She winced. The words cost her something.

"Of course I would." He went first, stopping her at the top of the stairs. He heard a muffled sound, like a footfall, or something bumping a wall. The bedroom? He paused, the chill of danger creeping along the back of his neck. "Stay here," he ordered.

He opened the bedroom door, and reached in for the light switch, fumbling for long moments, finally finding it. The room looked empty. He went straight to the closet and then to the bathroom.

Finally, he took a quick glance under the bed. "Okay, it's clear," he called. Rayleen peered through the door.

"Don't be afraid," he said.

"Why not? You are."

He nodded. "Yes, but that's my job." It sounded cheerful and stupid, and he tried to think of some way to amend it, but he couldn't, so he kept quiet. She took a gym bag from the closet and stuffed it with clothes from the dresser. Daniel looked out the bedroom window, wondering if he could spot his car. He could see the left front fender through the leaves of a tree. That was all.

He looked around the room while she packed. There was another Monet print over the bed and a Raggedy Ann doll on top of the pillows.

"I've got what I need," she said. "Let's go." He followed her back down the stairs. She was wearing gray sweat pants, a tee-shirt, and tennis shoes, and he decided that she looked cute in a floppy, casual sort of way. Then a sound in the kitchen stopped him dead on the stairs.

She looked back, clearly frightened, her eyes wide, her lips pressed tight. He moved past her and walked through the living room to the kitchen.

No one. The back door was slightly ajar. Had he heard the wind? Is this where the jogger had come in? He shivered.

"Can we get out of here?" she asked.

He closed the door and turned the deadbolt. Then he retraced his steps through the kitchen and living room, Rayleen at his heels. They paused at the computer desk. "Are you sure you don't want to call the police? You have a lot of expensive equipment here. The computer alone could set you back a bundle." She was using a top-of-the-line Sony. If the jogger decided to break something, it would cost her dearly.

She stared at the computer. "Let me burn a backup," she said. "The files are what can't be replaced. The computer just costs money." She popped a blank cd into the slot, and downloaded her files. Reaching up into the overhead cabinet, she pulled out her purse and a spiral notebook and stuffed them into her duffle bag. When the backup was safely inside the bag, she headed for the door. "Let's go."

"We should lock up," Daniel said. "Do you have your key?"

She patted the side pocket of the duffle bag. Just then, they heard the kitchen door rattle. They both stopped still, not breathing. The door rattled again.

Rayleen grabbed his arm, holding him back. "Let's just get out of here. What if he's got a gun?"

"I can end this nonsense right now. Then you won't have to worry."

She looked into his eyes, and shook her head. "Let's just go." He didn't bother to argue, she was already heading for the door, pulling him along, key in hand.

Outside, she stopped to lock up while Daniel stood in the wind, wondering which side of the house the jogger would come from. A gust blew ice into the air, swirling and cutting like powdered glass. In the distance, he could hear a door or a shutter banging in the wind.

They went down the walk to the waiting car, past black trees and shrubs crouching in the storm. Daniel's nerves were splayed open, wired to the wind. He glanced around as they walked and noticed that the girl was doing the same thing.

The car appeared untouched. Daniel looked into the back seat before he opened the door for her. As he circled back around to the driver's side, he looked for a sudden burst of dark motion. Another gust bowed the trees, otherwise, there was nothing.

The first turn of the key failed, and it occurred to Daniel that the car might strand them, an embarrassing and frustrating thought that dissolved with the second turn and the firing engine. Rayleen whispered something, and Daniel laughed.

A glance in the side mirror brought a hint of motion. He turned and saw nothing. Go, he thought, and the car pulled away from the curb.

"Where to?"

"There's a breakfast place near here," she said. "They have a phone. I can make some calls."

With the help of her directions, he found the restaurant, open all night. He kept his eyes on the rearview mirror the whole way. No one was following them. When they reached the parking lot, she started to speak, perhaps to say thanks and goodby. She would be out of the car and gone. He threw open his door, interrupting her. "I'll go in and get us a table. We can eat something while we wait for someone to come and get you."

"Great," she said. "I was hoping you wanted to eat, because I'm starving." She paused and laughed. "Fear makes me hungry."

Rayleen went to the payphone in the lobby, promising to join him in a few minutes. No one was at the front register, so Daniel headed for a booth. As he sat, a waitress spotted him, and notified him that the booth was closed. She took him to another empty booth nearby and left him with two menus and pot of coffee he didn't want.

He glanced at his reflection in the window and patted his hair back into place. He looked tired. His eyes were ringed with dark circles, and the faint reflection made his skin look gray. He frowned and turned away.

The menu boasted the usual late night fare, breakfast and greasy sandwiches. The waitress tried to rush an order out of him. "I'm waiting for a friend," he explained.

Daniel struggled through six pages of entrees, finally deciding on biscuits and sausage. He wondered if they were better than the ones at Brian's Diner. The thought of Brian brought back the unpleasant memory of lunch after church, which in turn made him wonder if he was really hungry, but he had to eat something, after all, or she wouldn't eat, and then there would be no excuse to stay and talk. He put down the menu and looked around for Rayleen.

After he had waited quite a while, anxious to talk, he went looking for her. The pay phone was unattended. She was gone.

He returned to his seat, wondering if he could leave without ordering. He would probably give the waitress a heart attack. If he tried to explain that he was alone after all, she would smile knowingly, and he would leave feeling like an old weed.

Then Rayleen bounced up and pitched into the booth, laying her head on the table. She groaned. "No one's answering. I mean, no one. It's Sunday night. Everyone I know is passed-out or out of town." She tilted her head and looked at him out of one eye. "My roommates went skiing, and they took my car. I was actually looking forward to a weekend alone. Then I got a stalker, for God's sake!"

"When do your roommates come back?"

"Tuesday, I think." She sat up, and pulled her hair back. She had the soft, dark hair of a child, and it slipped through her fingers like silk. He had not really had a chance to look at her yet. They had been busy running away. Now he drank her in, and went helpless with the sight of her. Her brown eyes were laced with greens and grays; sharp, piercing eyes that pinned him to the booth. "What's wrong?" she asked.

It was clear that she did not photograph well, web site or no. She was much more beautiful in person than in her pictures.

He shook his head. "Nothing." (I want you to come home with me, he thought.) "So, what will you do?"

She shrugged. He had lost an opportunity. He saw it slip away in her eyes. "I don't know. I think I'll get a motel room."

The waitress arrived, again, and took their order. Rayleen selected a fruit and yogurt cup. Daniel reconsidered his sausage and biscuits, and asked for the fruit and yogurt cup as well. He ordered a diet pop, and Rayleen ordered water. The waitress rolled her eyes when she left.

She stuck out a hand. "My name's Rayleen, by the way."

"Hi Rayleen. My name's Daniel." He shook her hand. "Do you know the guy who was after you?"

"Maybe," Rayleen said. "I correspond with a lot of people in my business and he might be one of them. I've had stalkers before, but they were the harmless, pathetic kind. This guy was in my fucking house, you know? He scared the crap out of me." She glanced at her watch. "I wish I hadn't ordered anything. I don't like eating so late."

"Want me to cancel?"

"No, no," she moaned. "I'm so damned hungry."

He liked her. He was sorry the night had to end. "When we're done eating, I can drive you to a motel," he said.

She frowned slightly, and tapped the table with her fingertips. "I don't especially feel like being alone, even in a motel." She sighed. "I must be losing my touch. I was hoping you'd take me to your place."

"Sure," he said. He fumbled with his napkin. He wanted to say more, but his tongue was fat in his mouth, and he could barely breathe.

"Thanks," she said. She wet her lips and smiled. "That guy really freaked me out."

"Do you have any idea how he got in?"

Rayleen's face darkened. "I don't know. That part worries me. I was about to head for the shower, too. That would have been swell."

"Good thing I showed up."

"Yes it was. What were you doing there, anyway?"

Mistake. Daniel looked away, his face flushed. I'm giving her a straight answer, he thought. "I was in town on business," he said, starting with a lie, despite his resolve. "And. . .I drove past your house, hoping I could catch a glimpse of you." She colored, and shrank in her seat. "I'd seen your web page, and. . ." He shrugged. "I guess I'm a stalker, too, only not the dangerous kind. I'm more of the harmless, pathetic kind."

She laughed, a nervous cough of a laugh, but a laugh nonetheless.

"I'm a skip-tracer," he said, rushing his words now, so she couldn't excuse herself and leave. "That's a kind of private investigator. I was hired on a really weird case. . ." He stopped again.

"Really? Who are you supposed to find?"

Another mistake. She would think he was lying, or that he was out of his mind. "It's confidential," he said. She rolled her eyes, and he could see that she was losing patience with him. He winced and leaned forward, whispering. "Okay. I was hired by a rich old man to find Jesus Christ. I know that sounds crazy. But I've been doing the research, and there's a lot of strange aspects to this case. He may be pulling a scam, but I'm getting paid a lot of money to do the work, so I'm going to stick with it until I find out what the truth is."

She sat back, measuring him with her eyes. "Jesus?"

"I know," Daniel said. "It sounds like nonsense."

The waitress returned with the meal, a check, and a faint thank-you. Rayleen frowned at the woman's back as she left. "Friendly old bat."

Daniel shrugged. "Waiting tables is a tough living."

"I've waited tables," she said. She was staring at her fruit cup.

"Hey, listen," he said. "If you changed your mind about staying with me, I understand. But I'm a nice guy. I know they're not supposed to exist, but you're safe with me. I'd understand if you felt nervous. If you'd rather go to a motel, I could take you there, or if you'd rather get a cab and go to the motel alone, I could call you a cab. . ."

She giggled. "You're a dork."

He flinched. "Yeah, I guess that's true."

She reached over the table and grabbed his hand. "I mean it in a nice way," she said. She sat back. "If you don't mind, I'd still like to go home with you."

"I'd like the company," he said. He took a bite of his meal, and nodded. "Try your fruit and yogurt."

She took a bite, and stared off into space as she chewed. Then another bite, and another. Then she put the spoon down. "I wonder if it's delivered from the factory this way, or if they extract the flavor in the back?"

He burst out laughing.

On the way to the car, she said, "I'll sleep on the couch, okay?" Her voice was casual, but her eyes were locked on his.

"I don't have a couch," he told her.

XII

C:\MyFiles\Truth\Nov

I should not be angry. I will not be angry. I
have prayed for this, prayed for a sign, and now I
have it. I KNOW WHAT I MUST DO. I was right, my
instincts were right. I am to save the girl. But
the battle for her soul will not be uncontested.
Someone has taken her away.

I went to see her tonight. I wanted to talk to
her, to tell her about her part in HIS plan. She
wouldn't let me speak, she was afraid. What did
I expect? That she would give up the life she'd
chosen and accept her part without a struggle?

A man joined her. There are no accidents, no
coincidences. Everything that happens, happens for
a reason. Someone directed the man, assigned him
to the girl, to make my task more difficult. They
left her house together. I will deal with the man
eventually. I know where he lives— I followed them.

Then, I went back to her house and left her a
message. I was angry, but the anger focused me.
She will be shocked. She will hear me. She must
hear me.

Despite the setback, and the appearance of an
interloper, I am elated. The headaches are worse
(that is to be expected) but everything I have
predicted is coming to pass. I am vindicated in my
beliefs. I am justified. The critical moments of my
life are aligned like notches on a staff, like the

staff that our Lord, the shepherd of men's souls, uses to tally his flock.

From the beginning, I have been singled out. My mother's death could not prevent my birth. Doctors plucked me from her womb, saving me. In black, sightless dreams, the beating of her heart stops, and I can't breathe. I wake, gasping for air. My survival was a miracle. God saved me for a reason.

My education was rigorous, demanding, and I was equal to the task. I was well-prepared to join, perhaps even lead others with ordinary lives. I could have shared the worn path of the average. That path has its charms- one is never without company. But a conventional path was not what God had in mind. I could feel that, even then.

I waited for a sign.

The wait has been taxing. I have been alone, and loneliness is the brutal burden of the chosen. But the Lord is merciful, and he has seen fit to choose for me a partner, a mate. He will not ask me to face the tasks set before me on my own. But His will does not go uncontested, and if she does not recognize the path she must take, then I will act as His FLAMING SWORD. I will shine through the windows of her soul with the fierce fire of a billion candles, and THE LAST THING she will see is the white, phosphorescent light of God's FURY, and my enemies will be SLAIN, and their bodies will be STACKED LIKE CORDWOOD, and I will do His bidding, etc., etc.

I am tired (but I will not sleep).

XIII

"Nice place," she said. "Great decor."

"You've got no room to talk. I saw your house. You live like a monk."

"I'm in business."

"So am I." He pointed at the computer desk. "That's where I do most of my work."

She turned on the desk lamp, and sat down at the computer. "Nice. This is top of the line, isn't it?" She reached for the mouse. "May I?"

"My business files are in there. You probably shouldn't muck around."

She glared at him. "I think you can trust me. I'm trusting you, aren't I?"

He nodded. He wanted her to trust him. But he didn't trust her, not really.

She was into his files in a moment. After a few clicks, she said, "Well, you are a private eye after all."

"A skip-tracer," he corrected. "Didn't you believe me?"

She let go of the mouse and turned to face him, serious and even a little sad. "You won't go terribly wrong in life assuming that everything you hear is a lie."

"That's pleasant."

"No. But it's true." She turned back to the files. She was running through his financial records. "This billing software is about a thousand years old. Doesn't it drive you nuts? I mean, it's so slow." She grabbed his pencil and made a note on his notepad. "I have a much better program at the house. I'll download it for you if you like. Very user friendly. You need to get out of the dark ages."

"I like the program I have," he protested. "I'm used to it."

"Can you call up all past-due bills with a keystroke? Can you print off a list of payables? Thirty day accounts? Sixty? Your files are a mess, I can see that just poking around." She clicked her way through a few more screens. "You need a secretary or a bookkeeper."

"Are you volunteering?" he joked.

She turned to him again. "You couldn't afford me," she said.

He shrugged, and went to the kitchen. He needed a beer. "You want something to drink?" he called.

"I'm sorry."

He poked his head back around the corner. "I have beer and pop."

"That was uncalled for. I get carried away."

"I didn't take offense," he lied. "Truth is, I'm a pretty lousy businessman. I make ends meet. That's about all."

"I can show you some things. It would take about an hour. I won't bug you about it, but it would help your business."

"I'd appreciate that," he said. "I put this business together on the fly, and I never stopped to evaluate how effective my systems were."

"I understand," she said. "Look here. . ." She began listing changes. Some of them seemed minor, hardly worth the effort to change. Others were first-rate suggestions. "I can't believe you don't have a web page," she said, shaking her head, tossing her hair in waves. "You could do a lot of Internet business, finding old friends and relatives. You could bill them at your site, and never leave the apartment. How long does it take you to find someone?"

"If they're not trying to hide, less than an hour."

She laughed, the sound of a child being tickled. "See, silly? Bill them thirty bucks, no, forty. That's lawyer money. They don't have to go to an office and you don't have to break a sweat. You won't even need a credit card capture system. You use a payment service. It doesn't cost much at all."

"Where did you learn this?" he asked.

She shrugged. "Books. Fooling around on-line. I have a mind for business." She pulled up the picture of Mordecai Ryan, and scrolled back and forth between Ryan and Hitler. "Who is this?"

"That's the old guy who hired me. He's paying me a bundle, too."

"How much?"

"I got a retainer for ninety-five hundred dollars."

"Oh, that's a lot," she said. Her voice softened around the lie.

He stared at her for a moment and then smiled. "You probably make a lot of money in your business. Ninety-five hundred dollars doesn't impress you much, does it?"

"You're just starting out," she answered. "Don't feel bad. You could make a lot of money at this."

He swallowed a laugh. She was wonderful. Charming, clever, and full of shit. "How much do you make a year?"

"Last year was a good year," she said. Her voice had dropped, and he could barely hear her. "There are a lot of lonely guys out there." She opened another file, and found pictures of herself, downloaded from her web site.

Daniel's stomach dropped. He had to turn away. He should never have let her into his computer. Trust be damned. He went into the kitchen, opened a beer, took a huge swallow, and then leaned his head against the cabinet where he kept his water glasses. If he'd been alone, he'd have banged his head against the wood panel.

"Can I ask you something?" she called.

He went back into the room. "What?"

"You have four pictures of me in this file, and two of them are the ones I posted where I'm wearing clothes. Why is that?"

"I like the portrait. You have beautiful eyes. The other is funny. I like your grin."

She frowned and closed the file. "Tell me about the case you're working on."

He sat on the edge of the bed, and began with his initial contact with Mordecai Ryan. He had no intention of telling her about the last encounter, and how he saw the old man's gaping chest, but by then he was on his third beer, and she seemed so intent on his story. "I don't know what to think," he finished. "I haven't had any luck at all finding Derek Becker, whoever that is. He's well-hidden."

Rayleen sat still, her eyes dark brown and hot with sudden intensity. "Why would he hide?"

"What do you mean?"

"Jesus. Why would he hide?"

Daniel thought of Thomas. "My friend is a pastor for a church here in town. He thinks there are 'dark forces' after him. He thinks there's nowhere safe."

Rayleen nodded. "Maybe. Or maybe no one's after him, and he's hiding in plain sight."

"What do you mean?"

"I have a friend who got in trouble with the law over a drug deal," she said. "It wasn't her fault, but she was involved, and they were going to squeeze her to get to the guy she was seeing. Anyway, she couldn't afford to leave the state, and she couldn't stay, since they were after her. So she checked into a homeless shelter." She laughed, and blinked. "She went to the administrators and asked for help. She said she had been abused, and had a drug problem, and needed counseling. Poof! She was a just another non-person, someone needing assistance. She stayed there for three months, asking for help, being ignored. She was invisible, get it?"

"What does that have to do with Jesus?" he asked.

"You're assuming that Jesus is hiding," she said. "What if he isn't?"

Daniel lay back on the bed, and covered his eyes. After a moment, he said, "Why hasn't anyone heard from him? I mean, if Christ came back, he'd be on the television news, wouldn't he? Giving interviews, doing miracles for the Fox network, that sort of thing."

"Maybe he thinks network news is bullshit. Maybe he chose a different medium." Daniel glanced over. She was patting the computer monitor. "Maybe he's on the Net."

He sat up. "That's interesting." He considered it some more. "Oh my God. . ."

"So to speak." She was giggling again.

"Get up," he said. "Sit on the bed."

"Like there are a lot of choices," she laughed. She sat on the corner of the bed, but in just a few moments, she returned to the computer to watch.

He did a series of searches, focusing on personal web pages. He started with references to the Second Coming and Jesus, and pared down the thousands of responses with modifiers. "How do you know what words to plug in?" she asked.

"I make a guess," he said. He could smell her hair. What was that smell? Coconut? Almonds? He tried to focus on the screen. He needed a new modifier. Something that would make a claim, separate the interpretive and critical web pages from the kind of site he was looking for. Then it came to him, with a chuckle. Truth. He modified the search again, and cut the number of remaining sites in half.

"Why did you do that?" she asked.

He shrugged. "Truth. It's what I'm after. It's the claim every religion makes. It's the thing that modern philosophers make fun of. And it's the territory Jesus would stake out for his own if he returned."

He began visiting the remaining sites, noting the dead ends on his pad. One site featured a young Latino man who claimed to be both the direct descendent of Buddha and an avatar for Vishnu, a human receptacle for the God's force. Despite the strange juxtaposition of the Hindu and Buddhist faiths, the avatar suggested Mexico City, overwhelmingly Catholic, as a holy city for a new faith. The man called himself La Verdad, and demanded, among other things, a strict adherence to a vegetarian diet, worldwide sharing of income, and an end to United States involvement in the Middle East.

A second site called for the end of the Jewish conspiracy to control the world through international banking, while promoting the Truth, an "Afrikan-centered" view of history. This version of the truth included the possession of whites by demons, and the racial superiority of the "sun people." The site advocated a "coordinated effort, working together with brothers and sisters to destroy oppression." It further advised visitors that the community is "more important than any one individual," and that the way to serve one's community is to "follow the decisions of our leaders."

Another site predicted the end of the world in October, more than two thousand years after a "super-nova announced the birth of Jesus." The page claimed that the true Christ had come again, and was living in seclusion in London, England, waiting for the proper time to announce the end of the ages. Daniel wrote the web site address down on his pad, and moved on.

Another site featured quotes from scripture, apparently selected at random. "I've seen this before," he told her. "I think I was drinking and surfing." He showed her a passage similar to the one Thomas had quoted that morning. "Look here. This part isn't in all Biblical translations, at least not the ones I've seen. It's like someone is rewriting the Bible."

"Iambic pentameter," she said. "Blank verse. Shakespeare used it. This is a poem."

He studied the lines again, tracing line to line over the screen. "How did you know that?" he asked.

"I like Shakespeare," she said. "The men are all shallow, and the women are all victims. It's very realistic."

"Hah." He noted the address on the pad, and scrolled down to the bottom of the page. There was a button for e-mail correspondence, and a single quote:

". . .the Truth has stumbled in the streets— Isaiah 59:14"

"That's weird," Rayleen said. A yawn followed a shiver.

"You're tired."

"I guess so," she admitted.

"You sleep on the bed," he said. "I've got a sleeping bag. I'll sleep on the floor." She nodded with visible relief.

Rayleen used the bathroom first. "I'm going to shower, okay?" He heard the door close, followed by the click of the lock.

He decided to check his e-mail while he waited. There was a single letter from his colleague in Boston, the one who had searched for the grave of the real Mordecai Ryan:

Dear Daniel,

Here's one I can't quite figure out. I sent out queries on the grave you requested, and something new turned up. It seems you get four for the price of one. There are four separate graves for boys named Mordecai Ryan dated 1905. Three are for ten-year olds. One is for a twelve-year old.

What the hell are you into, buddy? By the way, no charge for the extra graves. . .

101

Daniel read it twice, unable to comprehend. "What the hell does this mean?" he whispered. He saved the letter, and sat back, rubbing his aching eyes. He yawned and tried to stretch. His body was tight with exhaustion and wouldn't unwind.

"Okay, you're next," Rayleen called, walking into the room. She wore a floppy, oversized dress shirt for bed clothes. Her hair was pulled back in a pony tail. Her face was scrubbed clean, makeup stripped away. She seemed lovelier (and younger) than she had before.

"You look nice," he mumbled as he headed for the bathroom.

He showered and changed into a fresh pair of sweats. The mirror pointed at him like a handgun, but he refused a glance down the barrel. Now that he was preparing for sleep, he found himself worrying about being able to do so. He suddenly wished that she'd taken a motel room.

When he came back into the room, she was already in bed, facing the wall. He whispered "goodnight," more to himself than to her, and shut off the light. He tried to lay still in the sleeping bag, not wanting to be noisy. He wanted her to have a good night's sleep.

His leg itched. He snaked a hand down to scratch, and the back of his hand made a sound on the sleeping bag fabric. He found that he was holding his breath, and that made him angry. He thought, what am I doing this for? This is silly. I'm acting like a junior-high kid. Then he thought, what if I snore? Sometimes I wake myself up snoring. Marianne used to shove a pillow over my head to smother the sound. I hope I don't fall asleep. Then he got angry again.

The room was silent. He listened, hoping to hear the slow, even breath of sleep from the girl on the bed. He couldn't hear a thing.

His hip ached, jammed against the floor, and his right leg had a cramp. He eased onto his stomach. He thought of her laugh, her smile, her body. Stop thinking, he commanded. He tried to force himself to sleep. His arm, pinned by his head, had gone numb.

"Are you awake?" she asked.

"Yes." He buried his face in his pillow. She was awake. It was all a disaster.

"I can't sleep. I'm a little nervous about tonight."

"Sorry. Do you want a light on?" he suggested.

"Fuck no," she snorted. "A light on means someone outside looking in can see us." She raised up on one elbow. "Would you climb up here and hold me?"

"Okay."

"Just hold me," she warned. "That's all, okay?"

He pulled himself out of the sleeping bag. "I snore," he said, a warning of his own.

"I won't mind. It's too quiet in here." He pulled back the covers and climbed in. "I don't sleep very well anyway," she told him. "Maybe a few hours a night."

"Neither do I," he said. "Most nights, it takes me forever to doze off. Then I'm up again, and I can't get back to sleep. I'm always tired. It doesn't matter. I can't sleep."

"That's it. That's exactly right. That's what it's like for me."

He lay on his back, wrapping his arms around her. She pressed close to his side, planting her head on his chest.

"Is this okay?" she asked. "Am I crushing you?"

"No," he said. "It's nice."

She draped her top leg over his legs. He could feel her slender body pressed against him, an intimacy that had an immediate effect.

Then she shivered. She's afraid, he thought. He held her a little tighter and lay back. She was so tiny, so slight. He felt himself relax a little, and she seemed to do the same.

She murmured something. He eased into the mattress, like nestling in feathers, blanketed by the dark. The cramped muscles in his leg let go. A pleasant ache spread through him, and he sank deep into his pillow.

When he was still married, Daniel had liked the night. He loved spooning with Marianne. He loved listening to the house creak. He loved the drip of a soft rain, or the long, low moan of a windstorm. Night sounds. After Marianne, he'd grown to dread those little moments, but now, holding the girl, he found himself listening for a storm outside. A hint of wind tossed the curtain at the window he'd cracked open that morning. The air tasted stiff and clean.

It's the girl, he thought, half-asleep. I don't know her. I only know her pictures. But this is nice. This is peaceful. I deserve this, I deserve the rest. I've been very tired.

He closed his eyes. His thoughts usually irritated him. Bits of songs and fragments of sentences would bounce around in his head, keeping him awake. He was never still, never calm. Now, pressed close to her, he felt himself slip free of the noise. His mind was a lazy creek pushing through to the mud of dreams, the clutter of words swept away with the slow current.

He felt himself fall asleep. I must remember, he thought. I must try to remember what this was like.

Then, their breathing synchronized, as if one mouth could breath for two, and the rhythm of sleep took them.

XIV

http://www.truthzhammer.com

A man gave a dinner and invited
many guests, but at the appointed hour,
when the man sent his slave to fetch the guests,
they all began to make their excuses.
One said, "I must inspect my new-bought land."
One said, "I have bought five yolk of oxen,
and I must go verify their value."
Another said, "I am married today,
and ask that you consider me excused."
The slave returned and reported these things.
The man became angry and told his slave,
"Go out to the city streets and alleys
and gather the poor, blind, crippled and lame. Once,
when large crowds followed Jesus, he turned
and said to them, "If any follow me
who do not hate their father and mother,
who do not hate their own wife and children,
who do not hate their brothers and sisters,
and more still, who do not hate their own lives,
they cannot be one of my disciples.

XV

The sun angled up over the top of the window and woke them both. Rayleen sat up, sheet clutched to her chest. "What time is it?" she asked.

Daniel stared at his watch. "Eight o'clock."

"That can't be right. I never sleep past dawn. What time did we go to bed?"

"Midnight?" he guessed. "Maybe one o'clock?"

She shook her head in amazement, her brown hair tumbling over her face. "I never sleep like that."

Daniel slid out of bed, his knees and ankles stiff and rested. He stretched, his muscles groaning pleasantly. The room looked bright, sharp with color. His head was clear. Amazed, he thought, "This is what a night's sleep feels like."

Rayleen was out of bed, blanket around her shoulders, padding around the room. She checked the clock on the computer. "Oh my God," she said. "It is eight o'clock. You don't know how unusual it is for me to sleep like that. I must have been worn out."

"I was supposed to run with my jogging partner this morning," Daniel said. "I never miss. This is the first time."

"What time were you supposed to run?"

"Six," Daniel said. "I forgot to set the alarm. I usually wake up without it."

Rayleen sat down at the computer. "Do you have any food?" she asked. "I'm starving!"

"I can cook us something," Daniel said. He went into the kitchen and took a quick inventory of the refrigerator. He was a fair hand in the kitchen, thanks to lessons from his mother, who insisted that he know how to cook, clean, and do laundry. "When you get married," she told him, "you will marry a woman, not a housekeeper."

Within minutes he'd whipped up some scrambled eggs with salsa. He served them on platters topped with grated cheese and green onions, with warm tortillas, sliced cantaloupe and fresh blueberries. While he cooked, Rayleen poked at the computer, going into his history files, looking at the list of places he'd been on the net.

"Oh, I love you!" she said when he presented her with breakfast. "This looks so good!" She poked a fork at the fruit, staying away from the eggs.

He went back to the kitchen to clean up. He listened for sounds from the other room, wondering if she was eating or hiding the food in his desk drawers. When he returned, he found her plate stripped of fruit, and the eggs left intact, save a single bite. "I'm not big on eggs," she explained, "but I tried them, and they were very good. Thank you!"

Daniel called Thomas to apologize. "Hey, it's me," he said. "I missed the run. . .yes, I'm so sorry, I overslept. . .I know, I never do that. . .no, I'm fine. I feel great. . .no, I haven't had time to work on the case. I got sidetracked a little. . .no, nothing bad. . ."

Rayleen sat listening for a minute, and then bounded off into the bathroom. "I get the shower first," she called.

"Oh, that's a friend. . ." Daniel said. "No, just a friend. Someone I helped out of a jam." He was not interested in explaining Rayleen to his pastor, so he changed the subject back to running. "We run tomorrow, okay? Six o'clock? Great. . . tell your wife I said hello. Okay Thomas. . .goodby."

He hung up the phone. What now? He felt a tug in the pit of his stomach. The night before had been an adventure, but the adventure would end now. Perhaps she liked him enough to see him once in a while. He had been without a social life for the last year. Aside from Thomas, everyone he knew was on the Internet. It would be nice to have someone real to visit once in a while.

"Okay," she said, stepping from the bathroom, her hair slicked back from the shower. She was dressed in a white tee-shirt and blue jeans. The shirt was tight across the chest, very flattering. He decided that her breasts looked bigger than they did in the web-site pictures.

"Listen, I really have to thank you for everything. It was so nice of you to let me stay here last night. Can I ask another favor of you?"

"Of course," he said.

"I'm a little worried about my house and my computer. Could you drive me back to Boulder? Do you have other plans, or could we drive over?"

His heart sank. It was what he expected. He shrugged. "We can go now," he said. "Let me shower. We'll hit the road in five minutes."

"You don't have to rush," she insisted, but she began gathering her things right away.

In the bathroom, he allowed himself a glance at the mirror. His hair was pasted up in the air from the night's sleep. His shadow-beard made him look five years, no, ten years older. He scowled and turned away.

The initial silence on the drive back was broken by Rayleen. "When we get there, will you go in with me?"

"Absolutely," he answered, glad to be of some service. He'd dreaded every moment of the drive back because she would be out of his car soon, and probably out of his life as well. "What did you think? That I'd just drop you off and go?" He laughed and choked the steering wheel.

"No, but you were acting pissy, and I didn't know what to think."

He stole a glance and felt ashamed. "That wasn't pissy. That was contemplative."

"What are you contemplating?" she asked.

He paused to make something up. "I was thinking about your business."

"What about it?" She turned in her seat to face him, back against the passenger door, frowning.

"Just wondering how you got started. I mean, you have a nice computer set-up, and web sites cost money to maintain. Where'd you get the capital?"

She relaxed a little. "Waiting tables," she laughed. "I saved every penny I made for six months. I was living with a friends so I didn't have much rent. I put everything into the computer. My roommate helped me set up the site. At first, I made money by putting banners for other sites on my page. You know, advertising."

"Sites like yours?"

"Yeah. Hardcore sites, mostly. A lot of them were trap-sites, where you click on them and get captured. You can't get out without triple clicking the 'back' key, or just shutting down. They pay a little to post a banner."

"Then I set myself up with an age verification service. They pay by the click. If anyone visits me I get paid, and I don't have to worry about liability if some twelve-year old decides to cruise the Net."

"Who took the pictures?" Daniel asked.

"Lance. He's my roommate. He helped me set up the page, too. He's nice, you'd like him."

Not likely, Daniel thought. "So you made a lot of money from that?"

"Not really," she said. "You pay a lot to maintain a site. Bandwidth is expensive, and I wanted quality pictures. The next step was selling products. I tried selling still-shots, but they didn't sell. The pictures were the same as the ones I was posting on the net, so I wasn't offering anything different. That's when I started marketing tapes." She brushed her hair from her eyes and laughed. "We shot about five movies in two days. It was fucking crazy. Lance got a camera from a friend, and Michelle, that's my other roommate, she got some lights from somewhere, and we just shot film after film. I went through bottle after bottle of wine, because I just wanted to get the tapes done, you know?"

"I put the rest of my money into a tape duplicator and a DVD-burner, nice ones," she continued. "Lance loaned me some money, not much, but a little. And I had been applying for credit cards, lots of them. I maxed everything. Then I changed the web page, put some ads in for myself, and I waited for the orders to roll in."

Daniel turned off the highway, onto the Boulder Turnpike. The land was flat. Fenced cattle strolled over the patches of dirty snow that speckled the fields. Daniel passed a bicycler on the right shoulder of the road. "And you made a lot of money?" he guessed.

"Nothing. I was ready to panic. I'd get an order, here and there. Not enough to pay the interest on my cards. So I changed my strategy." She shifted in her seat, suddenly animated, her slender fingers stirring the air for punctuation. "I needed a client list. I began contacting everyone who e-mailed me at the web site, sending out "fliers." That's what I call them, anyway. You know how you get junk mail from places selling magazines? Well I sent letters with stories on them, and followed up with a sales pitch. It worked. I was out of money trouble in two weeks. In four months, I bought a car."

Daniel nodded, impressed.

"It was more than just sending out a letter with, 'Dear Friend' on the heading. I kept target phrases on file, so when I sent out a flier, it was tagged to the customer. If a guy complained about his wife, his flier would say, 'Hope things are better at home.' Or. . ."

"'How's the business going?' if he owns his own business?"

"Yes! That's it! It was as if the ad was theirs. But I didn't stop there. . ." She paused, her hands frozen, clear polish on her nails glistening like sunlight on ice. "Did I send something like that to you?"

"Sure," he said. "I thought it was good business."

"Thanks. You didn't think I was just writing to you, did you?"

He stopped at a light, checked his mirror, and then turned to her. "On one level, no, of course not. I mean, I knew you were selling. On another level though, the thing you're selling is fantasy, an illusion, a dream to believe in, so one is inclined to believe despite the evidence." He laughed. "That's what you had in mind, isn't it?"

"Of course," she beamed. "And I didn't stop there. If a guy told me his fantasies, I kept that on file. I had a code for each different video. If someone ordered certain video, I'd follow it up with a flier on a related video, and sell him a second one."

"I started altering the site based on my marketing needs. I put e-mail buttons on the page, and encouraged everyone to write me and make requests for pictures, poses, anything to get them to write. And I always answered back. Always."

"You answered me," Daniel said.

"I answered everyone. I set up a list of fliers, and tracked who got which flier. I put them in sequence, so I could run through the cycle, depending on the preferences of each client. I could punch up any customer on the computer, tell you what they did, what they liked, what I'd sent them, and what I was going to send them next."

"It's like you were orchestrating a hundred different relationships at once," he marveled. "Did they all fall in love with you?"

"Love?" she scoffed. "Sure, whatever." She stared him down. "Love is lust. The rest is just a pretty story to explain the drooling."

He pulled onto Rayleen's street. "You'll get no argument from me," he said. Up ahead, he could see that there were no cars in her driveway. "Your house looks okay."

She shifted around, and grabbed the door handle. "I just want to know if my computer is okay," she said. A glance back— "You're coming in, aren't you?"

He shut off the engine. "I'm leading the way," he said.

In the light of the sun, the walk to the front door wasn't threatening. "You unlock the door," Daniel said. "I'll go in first. Okay?"

She took out her key without answering, turned the lock, and stepped back.

The lights were off inside. It took a moment for Daniel's eyes to adjust. By then, she was inside, and there was no way to shield her.

The hanging plants were dumped and broken. Dirt and clay-pot shards littered the rug. The glass over the Monet print was shattered, and the print was slashed. The metal shelf holding Rayleen's videos had been tipped over, and many of the tapes were broken, stomped into pieces.

The computer monitor was smashed. The face of the processor had been kicked in. The Raggedy Ann doll from Rayleen's bedroom was tied spread-eagle to the legs of the computer desk, a pair of panties over its head, and a kitchen knife in its crotch, pinning the doll to the wood desktop.

On the wall above the computer, the intruder had drawn three crosses in red. The center one was larger than the other two. Beneath the crude pictures, he'd written in red letters, "I'm watching."

Rayleen stared at the wall, mesmerized. Daniel checked the processor first. The back end had been removed, and some of the insides were missing, torn out by hand. Pieces of the circuit board were scattered behind the desk.

Daniel untied the Raggedy Ann doll, removing the strings that bound the arms and legs. He pulled the panties off. The doll's eyes had been burned out, with matches, or a cigarette lighter. He covered the head back up, and set the doll aside. Then he checked the wall. The crosses had been done in paint, not blood. Blood would have dried brown.

Rayleen was still staring at the wall. "We need to call the police," he told her. "Now."

"I can't!" she groaned. "My roommate sells drugs, okay? I don't know what he's got hidden! I don't want to get him busted, and I don't want to get busted for his shit! He gets back tomorrow. I'll call then. Right now, I just want to get the fuck out of here!"

He took her by the hand and dragged her to the door. She stumbled along behind him, still staring at the wall. "Give me the key," he said. "I'll lock up."

She laughed, an ugly sound full of despair, and slapped the key in his hand. "Why are we bothering? It didn't keep him out last night. . ."

"We're calling the police tomorrow," he said after locking the door. "Whether your roommate comes home or not." He took her back to the car, glancing from side to side as he walked, the sidewalk and bushes suddenly not so benign. He stuffed her into the passenger's side of the Hyundai, and closed the door.

Up the street, a man was jogging toward the car. Daniel stared, trying to decide if it was the same man, the maniac who had broken into Rayleen's house. He felt his stomach twist into a taut, knotted bundle. He clenched his fists, and stepped closer to the sidewalk. He heard the car door lock. She was saying something. He couldn't hear it.

The jogger came closer. He was in his late twenties or early thirties, well-built. The right height, Daniel thought. Was it him? He braced himself, and even took a step, ready to launch himself at the man as he ran past. At the last moment, Daniel stopped himself, his nerves screaming— not him! not him! The jogger ran on, unaware, and Daniel returned to the car.

Rayleen grabbed his arm when he sat behind the wheel. "Oh my God," she said. "I saw that guy, and thought. . ."

"I thought so too," Daniel shrugged, trying to keep his voice casual, light. "Let's get out of here."

"Please," she said. She seemed to be okay. Her hair was a little disheveled, and her eyes had a hint of red, but her voice was calm and even. He started the car on the second try, and headed back to Fort Collins.

He waited until they were outside of Boulder city limits to speak again. "You can stay with me until your roommates are home." She didn't answer. "You'll be safe," he added. From the corner of his eye, he saw her scowl and turn away.

He nodded to himself. He was assuming he knew how she felt, and he didn't. Not really. "Do you know who did this to you?" he asked.

"No."

"I'll bet it's one of your customers. You probably have his information in your files. I can help you go through them and narrow the list, if you like."

"Maybe we'll do that," she said. The tone of her voice said no.

They had reached the highway. Traffic roared by. He shoved the gas pedal to the floor, begging the Hyundai to a higher speed. The sun was bright, and the inside of the car was heating up. He cracked the window. "Is this okay?" She didn't answer. He twisted in his seat and tried to stretch.

"When I was seventeen. . ." she started. She paused, and swallowed. Daniel kept quiet and listened.

"When I was seventeen, I left home." She stared out the passenger side window, not turning around to speak. "My father was a cold man, very. . .demanding. I grew up believing that he was perfect, perfect in every way. If he seemed distant, it was because I needed to try harder to be a good girl. I studied hard, because I needed to be smart. I didn't eat, because I needed to be pretty. I didn't argue, because I needed to be obedient. But nothing I did was ever quite enough."

"Mother was no help to me," she continued. "I think she was trying to please him herself. I saw that she was wasting her time, but it seemed like I was doomed to try the same things, looking for a smile or a little encouragement. And I succeeded– not often, but often enough to keep me trying."

"When I was sixteen, I published a poem. It was about my father. A love poem, I suppose. I waited to tell him until it came out in the magazine, a literary magazine, the kind nobody reads. I gave my only copy to him. He sat there reading it, and then he took out a pencil and started marking slashes over the lines, showing me where I should have put the line breaks. He told me later that criticism was the highest form of compliment. He said I was a professional, so he would treat me like one."

She paused, and took a deep breath. Her shoulders were shaking. "I met a boy, and fell in love. He had dark, curly hair, huge brown eyes, and a nice, tight ass." She gave a sad little laugh. "And he had a beautiful smile. Shy and sensual at the same time, you know? He was older, a college student, and he courted me. I was used to high school boys. Not very mature. Carlos was different. So polite and gallant. So romantic."

"One day I showed him my poetry. He read each poem very carefully, and when he got to the poem about my father, he cried. I did that, I made him cry. I saw the tears. It was. . ." She paused again.

"What did your father think of Carlos?" Daniel asked, guessing the answer before she said it.

"He told me I couldn't see him anymore. He thought I was too young." She shook her head. "I was thinking about marriage, and meanwhile, my father didn't want me to go to the movies with him. He had no idea."

"Carlos had a job with a photography studio, doing portraits. He wanted to be a freelance photographer, and sell pictures to magazines. I didn't know he was dealing on the side until later."

"Is Carlos your roommate?" Daniel asked.

"No," Rayleen sighed. "Lance is my roommate, remember? Lance and Michelle. Anyway, Carlos said he wanted to marry me. We'd travel the world, taking pictures, seeing the places I wanted to see, places I'd read about. I didn't believe it, not really, but I was so in love. When it came time to talk to my parents, Dad just freaked. He gave us one of his thirty-minute non-stop sermons, and we just sat there with our mouths open. Then he threw Carlos out of the house, and for the next two weeks, I didn't go to the bathroom without an escort."

"So you left," Daniel said.

"I left."

"It wasn't what you wanted?"

Rayleen shook her head. "It was a fucking disaster. As soon as I moved in, I was property. We had our first argument the day I left home. Carlos wanted to make love, and I was depressed and worried about Mom, and he threw a fit. I gave in that time. Other times I said no. It didn't matter."

"It was so strange. I found myself trying to please him. It was the same as my father, only. . .how do people make the same fucking mistakes over and over and over? I wanted to please him, that's all, and I couldn't do it. I didn't wash the shirts right. I wasn't dressed up nice enough for him when his friends came over. And I couldn't cook for shit." She laughed again.

"I hated cooking. He never cleaned his plate. He'd say, 'That was good,' and half the food would still be on the plate, and I'd think, if you like the fucking food, then eat the fucking food, you know? And when his friends came over, he'd shit on me in front of them. He'd say, 'Go buy some chips. Please don't cook anything, I like these guys.' And they'd laugh, and I'd laugh, and later, I'd study cook-books, looking for something he might like. Nothing. He didn't like food, the no-good, bony-ass, anorexic son-of-a-bitch. I hated cooking."

She took a breath, and stopped. Daniel started to speak, but bit his lip instead. Let her tell it. It's her story.

"So it ended. First, I found out about the drugs, and with my upbringing, dealing was like selling your soul, but even then I didn't say a thing, not yet. I didn't want to piss him off. He must have figured he could get away with anything, because he started doing everything. He cheated on me. He hit me. The first time it was a little slap, and I got pissed off and belted him. He got this look on his face like I'd insulted his manhood, and he pinned me down, and I thought, he's trying to scare me, and I didn't want to give him the satisfaction. But he wasn't bluffing. He pulled my pants down, and pushed me on to the bed. I couldn't stop him. He was too strong. And I kept thinking, he's just trying to scare me. Then he shoved my face into the pillow, and I couldn't breath. I tried to scream, but I was too frightened. Then he raped me. . ."

She stopped. She didn't speak again for several minutes.

The highway was flat, skirting the foothills through fields of stubble and dirty snow. Cars passed them as they drove. Daniel had slowed down to give her time to talk.

"I started working a few days after that. I saved most of the money. I gave some to Carlos and told him that the tips were bad at the restaurant, and he believed me. He was a shitty tipper himself."

"I couldn't go home. That was done. Jesus forgives, but not my Father. And I couldn't live alone. What was I supposed to do? I planned. I saved. I kept the money hidden, and when Carlos and I got into an fight, I'd sneak off and look at the cash, and tell my-self that it would be okay. Sometimes he was really nice. Once he brought me roses, two dozen, because he loved me twice as much as other men loved their 'women.' And I almost told him about the money. . ."

"Then I caught him with one of his girlfriends, fucking on the couch." She laughed. "That sounds ugly, doesn't it? Fucking. People look ridiculous when they're making love. They look like cans of spam slamming into each other." She shook her head, marveling. "But I stayed with him! I stayed with him for another two months. Can you believe it? I didn't have enough money to leave. I swore I'd never be caught in a situation like that again, that I'd always have enough money to do what was right for me. But my little envelope of cash wasn't enough, and anyway, I had it coming, right? I made my own problems."

"Then one day, we had an argument and he punched me, and I realized that it was only going to get worse. I went looking for my money, and most of it was gone. The fucker had found my hiding place. He took the money and put an IOU inside, for God's sake! He thought it was funny. I cried and cried, and I think I wanted to die then. He found me sitting there, tears running down my cheeks, and he tried to make up. He wanted to apologize."

Daniel took the exit from the highway. Fort Collins was minutes away.

"I waited until my next paycheck. Then I took his stereo and his television to the pawn shop, and got back about a third of what he took from me. I called it even. I moved to Boulder. I didn't leave a note. That first night, I went to a bar, and met Lance. I told him I had no place to stay, so I moved in with him and Michelle."

"I got two jobs, both waiting tables, and tried to put some money together. The whole time, I worried that Carlos would show up and do something. Then one day, Lance drags me into his room and sits me down at his computer. He tells me about the Internet, and says, 'I have bad news for you.' He went to a porn site, and there I was. Carlos had sold some pictures I posed for. They were supposed to be between us. And there I was with my tits showing for eighteen thousand visitors. He got even with me for the stereo, I guess."

"It bothered me, more than I can tell you. I thought, Oh my God, anyone with a computer can see me naked. I got so paranoid.

Wherever I went, out for a drink, even shopping for groceries, if some guy looked at me, I'd think, he knows, he recognizes me. He's seen me without my clothes on. I couldn't stand it."

"But I couldn't do anything about it. In the end, I decided that the pictures weren't me, they were my body. They could go ahead and have that, as long as my head and my heart were mine. The rest didn't matter, you know?"

"I thought about my future a lot. Sometimes I went to bars with Lance and Michelle, and did the meat-market thing. Guys would go through hoops for me. Buy me anything. Do anything for me. Anything except shut up and listen."

Point scored for me, Daniel thought.

"I watched people. I listened to them talk. And this is what I think: Love is a load of crap. It's chemicals and imagery. It's advertising. It's packaging. And if I wanted to make money, and be independent, I needed to get in the business."

"Lance knew the Net. When I had enough money saved, we set up a web-site." She turned in her seat, facing him. Her eyes were red and her mascara had streaked.

"I didn't like feeling helpless. I was broke. That was a year ago. Now I own a car, and I have ten thousand dollars in the bank. And until today, I thought I held the steering wheel. I thought I was driving. Then along comes some prick with a mental problem and I'm back to where I was before. I'm depending on others. I'm depending on you. And I could buy and sell you twice!"

Yikes, Daniel thought.

"I'm sorry," she said. Tears coursed down her cheeks, and she buried her face into her palms. "Shit! Shit!"

He touched her shoulder. She pulled away violently.

He let her cry. They were only seconds from his apartment. He pulled into the parking lot and shut the car down. It smelled of oil.

The engine is on its last legs, he thought. He turned to Rayleen and sighed.

"I know you're feeling helpless right now, but that's the fear talking. You're not helpless. It's a card game, and you have most of the cards. You have the guy's name and e-mail address in your files. And you're not alone. I'm here. You don't owe me anything. I don't like when nice girls are hounded by psychos. And if you have that much money in the bank, then the guy could smash five computers and you'd be back for more. Fuck him."

She stared at him. The tears made her dark brown eyes shine like onyx. She sniffed. "Okay, I'm done whining."

He smiled. "Good. You're messing with your makeup."

She turned the rearview mirror and moaned. "Oh, I look like crap!"

He shook his head. "Not possible." He opened the door. "Let's go inside."

She followed him to the apartment. He unlocked the door, and fumbled with the light. She moved past him, so when the light came on, she saw it first.

XVI

TO: Daniel Bain
FROM: Robert Wilkens
SUBJECT: RE: Multiple Graves
ATTACHMENT: Address/Immigrants/Ellis

Today at 10:38 A.M. you wrote:

>   Dear Bob,

>   Have a question for you. I'm looking into the back-
> ground of one Mordecai Ryan. A cemetery search yields up
> four graves, all children, all dead in 1905, all ten to twelve
> years of age, all named Mordecai Ryan. I'm thinking that my
> subject acquired the identity to cover a previous one, using a
> dead child's name, as the child would no longer be needing it.
> Good theory, but it doesn't explain the multiple-Mordecai's.

>   I know he entered the country through Ellis Island in
> 1904. After 1905, there's no record of him, until he reach-
> es his twenties. Profiles like a classic identity switch, but it
> smells wrong. Odd name, Mordecai— Help me out here.
> I can actually pay you on this one.

>   By the way, how's your brother? I owe him a hundred
> dollars from about two years ago, and I lost his address when
> I threw it away. Send me word so I can get him off my con-
> science.

>   Daniel

Dear Daniel,

This one is out of my league. Weird shit, brother. I'm attaching a list of addresses for historians who might be able to help you. I know the first two. Good guys. If there's an answer, they have it.Sorry I couldn't help you any more than that. No charge for the list. God bless search engines.

Bob

P.S.My brother doesn't expect the money. Send it to me instead. LOL.

XVII

The apartment had been ransacked. The desk drawers were open and their contents lay on the floor. Daniel's case of backup discs had been rifled, some of them left piled on the desk top. At the rear of the room, the dresser had been pulled out from the wall, and the drawers were open and emptied. Rayleen fell back against the apartment door, slamming it shut. "Oh shit," she said. "Look what I got you into."

"Don't touch anything," Daniel said. He walked to the phone and called the police. Rayleen slid down and sat cross-legged on the floor, her hands folded in her lap. Her eyes were locked on the monitor. "You can't tell them about my break-in," she said. "I don't want to explain why the police weren't called in Boulder."

Daniel put his hand over the receiver. "That's fine, but I need to get something on record here. This guy is a nut bag, and I want a paper trail on him, in case he hurts someone." Rayleen shuddered.

The police promised to send a patrol car. The next call went to his sister. Daniel spoke in a hushed voice, nodding as if Penny could see him through the phone.

When he was done with the call he turned his attention back to Rayleen. "I brought you here because I wanted you to be safe," he said. "I'm not really worried about this asshole coming here when I'm home. I think he's a coward. On the other hand, I'm not willing to bet your safety. I know a place where you'll be absolutely, perfectly safe. My sister does volunteer work at a hideaway for women in trouble. They have security guards, and this jerk couldn't get within a quarter-mile of that place without landing in jail. You'll be safe there until your roommates get home."

She looked up at him, her face blank. "Did I do this? Is this what I get for the business I'm in? Is this part of my 'cost of sales'?"

He thought about it for a moment and said, "No, I don't believe that. Neither do you. Nobody deserves to be stalked. This is random. Sick-tickets like this guy are out there, and who knows what triggers them? People are complex. It's never so simple as 'You sinned, so now you pay.' If it was that simple, we'd all pay."

He paused. She was near tears again, and he didn't seem to be helping. "Listen. I don't know what you're thinking, but I have a good feel for people. I don't get fooled, not often. You're a nice gal. You have a good heart. You wouldn't hurt anyone. This guy would. You don't deserve this."

She nodded, and started to cry. He sat down on the floor with her and put her head against his shoulder.

A police officer arrived within the hour. He was an older man in his late forties or early fifties. His uniform was crisp, but it smelled of cigarettes and strong cologne. He pulled at his mustache, making notes in a small spiral notebook. He asked what was missing. Daniel explained that a zip drive disc was gone, which meant his files had been stolen.

"Do you still have a back up copy?" he asked.

"Yes. The original files aren't damaged. They were copied. The guy who did this stole my business files."

"But you still have the files?"

"Yes," Daniel answered, suddenly very tired. His head ached. He pinched the top of his nose, and rubbed his eyes.

"And you don't know who the man is?" the officer asked again.

"No. We have his name on a disc. We suspect he's a customer of Rayleen's business."

"What business is that?"

"Self-help tapes," Daniel said with a straight face. "Mail order. I think he's a little taken with her, and he may view me as competition."

"Really?" The officer glanced up in disbelief. Daniel's face colored. He had spoken without thinking, and revealed too much.

"Well, I'll tell you folks," the officer said, putting away his pencil and book. "I don't think we're going to find an answer on this one. And I have to be honest. If nothing's missing, it will be hard to justify setting aside a lot of manpower on this case. Now if you get me a name, I'll be glad to look into it for you. I'm going to suggest that we save ourselves some time, and avoid filling out a report until we have something better to go on."

"Okay," Rayleen said.

"No," Daniel said. "Fill out the report." The officer scowled. "I want it on paper. This guy is a wacko, and I want a record of what he does, so that when he hurts someone, there will be documentation."

"I can fill out a report, but we're not going to be able to do much more than that. . ."

"Fill out the report, then."

"Fine," the officer snorted. "It's nice and warm in here. I was just trying to save you folks a little time." He spent the next forty minutes filling out fifteen minutes worth of papers, treating Rayleen like a child, and Daniel like a criminal.

When it came time to leave, the officer repeated, "I don't think we'll do too much with this one." His lip turned up on one side.

Daniel couldn't tell if the man was laughing or scowling. He felt his face flush hot as the frustration of dealing with the officer spilled out in a sudden rush. "I understand that you can't do much past take reports. And I understand you have a good reason for not taking reports. Less reports, less crime, right?"

The officer turned back, chest suddenly out. "I beg your pardon?"

"I want a paper trail," Daniel said, his own chest thrust out into the space between the two men. "If we don't fill out a report, the crime never happened. Nevertheless, I thank you for going through the steps. I want a copy of the report. Do you have a case number for me?"

"You can get a case number from the station," the officer said, still sizing Daniel up. "You won't be able to get a copy for three working days, and it will cost you five dollars."

"I'll put it in a picture frame," Daniel said.

The officer gave him a slow, fuck-you nod. Rayleen sat frowning at the desk. When the door closed, the officer gone, she asked, "What was that about a case number?"

"I wanted to make sure he filed the case," Daniel said. "I want a record of this. I'm probably being overly cautious."

"Oh, that's you all right. You're very cautious. What was that you said? 'Nevertheless?' I thought he was going to hit you."

"Nevertheless, he couldn't," Daniel joked. She was laughing again, a definite improvement.

But on the way to Penny's house, Rayleen became nervous. "What is this place again? Some kind of monastery?"

"It's a safe house," he laughed. "The people that run it are rabid, man-hating, post-modern Marxist-feminists, and they'd take a bullet before they let some guy get near you. You'll be bored. You'll be safe."

"Lovely," she said. She shifted around in her seat and faced him directly. "So tell me something. How come I can talk to you so easily? That stuff I told you about myself? I haven't told that to anyone. Not even my roommates, not the part about my father."

Daniel shrugged. "We speak the same language."

"What do you mean?"

"Ever been overseas?" he asked.

"Nope."

"Well, trust me, if you run into another American, you feel a connection. Everyone else is foreign, and you have this language bond. You both jabber away, drinking in the sound of English. You and I are like that. We share the same language."

"Language is a symbol," he continued. "Just like your apartment, for example. It's a little sparse. You made fun of my place too, remember? Now tell me, how come you don't make your place more like a real home?"

"Because it's just a place to live. Home? There's no such place as home."

He laughed, and she nodded. "Right," he said. "So we both understand that one. It's a symbol we share. And when you said, 'Love is a load of crap,' you were talking about Carlos. And you were talking about the fox-hunt that passes for dating. And you were talking about your relationship with your father. We share a similar perception about romantic love."

"Ah," she said. Her eyes narrowed, and a half-smile played out on her lips. "What happened? She must have dropped a bomb on you."

"I was married. I had a daughter. I lost them both, twice, within the space of sixty minutes." He turned onto his sister's street. "We're out of time," he said. "Some day I'll tell you the story." He pulled into the driveway, and parked. "This is it."

Rayleen grabbed her bag. "Let's see what you're getting me into."

Penny was at the door. Daniel could see Christine floating behind her, trying to get a glimpse without having to look at Daniel. "So nice to meet you Rayleen," Penny said, extending her hand.

Daniel's introduction died in his mouth, and he stood in awkward silence. Christine stepped from inside the house and grabbed Rayleen's hand as well. "You're safe now," she cooed, pulling her away from Daniel. She turned and fired a frown at him. "We'll take over from here. You can leave now."

"I'm not the bad guy, Christine," he protested.

"Maybe not. But if there weren't so many bad guys, there wouldn't be so many women in trouble."

"Christine." Penny stilled her partner with a word. Her eye was twitching, but she managed a smile for Daniel. "You did the right thing bringing Rayleen here," she said. "She's safe now." Her voice calmed him, and he nodded, backing away. He tried to catch Rayleen's eye with a smile, but Christine was already pulling her into the house. "I'll call you," Daniel shouted.

Penny walked him to the car. "She seems nice," she offered.

"She is nice."

"How did you meet her? She seems young."

"She is young. I met her on the Internet." He opened his car door. "We're friends." He wanted to say something else, but it sat on the tip of his tongue like a diver poised over cold water. Just say it, he thought.

"I'm glad I brought her here," he said at last. "I wouldn't trust anyone else. I don't ever say so, but I'm proud of you. Your life was a bomb crater, and you turned it around. I don't get along with Christine, but she treats you well, and you don't act like a doormat around her, so I figure you two are good for each other. And you're good at what you do. I know Rayleen will be safe."

Penny did a second take, caught off guard. "Thanks," she said, sounding tentative.

"If you're waiting for the punch line, there isn't one," he grinned. He climbed into the car. "Watch her. The guy who's after her is sick, and I think he'll hurt her if he gets the chance."

Penny waved as he backed out, her eyelid jumping. She had always been nervous, a thin bundle of raw energy. She was also athletic and clever, at the top of her class. The summer before eighth grade, she shot up three inches, taller than most of the boys in her class, and she developed the sloped-shoulders that would mark her posture from then on. Her grades were still good for the most part, though her math and science scores dropped off noticeably. Her figure developed slower than the other girls in her class. She took to wearing floppy, shapeless clothing, sweaters in the winter, baggy work-shirts in the summer.

Just after graduation, she married Dale Woods, her high school sweetheart. Dale worked at a local garage, doing repairs and running the pumps. He had plans of saving money and opening his own shop, a family-run service station, something that Penny endorsed, though her personal interests ran toward literature and modern art.

Dale turned out to be very good at planning and very poor at producing. He spent his spare time drinking and bowling. He placed occasional bets with a local bookie. Even without the expense of children, the couple found themselves deep in debt. Penny worked at two jobs, clerking at a dime store during the day and selling hamburgers at night. She managed to apply some of her checks to their debts, and after a year of hard work, they were nearly out of trouble. Then Dale lost his job.

Dale told Penny that the gas station owner had been "pushing him," and he left before the axe fell. A mutual friend told Penny that Dale got caught "working out of an open drawer," stealing cash by not ringing in the sales. Dale took a construction job, but it lasted just two weeks. "It was temporary, Babe," he explained. "Construction is on-again, off-again. Get used to it."

After six months, with the debts piling up and Dale at the bar five nights a week, Penny suggested that construction work was "off-again, off-again." That was the first time he beat her. It was then that she developed a twitch in her left eye.

Penny talked about leaving him. She made vows, set deadlines, and conferred with friends. In the end, he left her. He pinned the goodbye note to the refrigerator, the only appliance he left behind.

He took the television, the stereo, the air conditioner, and the remaining fifty-seven dollars in their checking account.

Devastated, Penny moved home. Louise held out hope that the marriage could be salvaged, but Dale sent divorce papers and that was that. Penny kept her jobs, working her way out of debt, spending nothing, never leaving the house except to work. Louise suggested that she try to relax, a suggestion she ignored until the evening she told Louise that she was "going out with friends." Within a week, she quit her night job and began going out twice a week. Louise was relieved, and told Daniel that Penny might even have a new boyfriend.

Then, one night at dinner, Penny announced that she was a lesbian. "I have always felt this way," she said. "I am only now beginning to understand my life in the context of being a lesbian. I am asking for your love and your support."

The announcement didn't matter much to Daniel. Then he met Christine. He had always had difficulty with a certain passive-aggressive personality, the kind of person who said, "Oh really?" instead of "You're full of shit," the kind of person who said, "Is that okay with you?" instead of "I don't care what you think." Daniel and Christine were at each other's throats from the first moment, and it was misunderstood by Penny as a judgement on her sexual preference. The truth was simpler. He thought Christine was a bitch.

Penny, though, was a saint. She had weathered the most brutal consequences love had to offer and responded with courage. She had a career and a life of love and friendship. She was still twitching, still confused, but she was not a quitter. He admired her, ached for her, and celebrated silently over her small victories.

As he drove away, he switched on the radio. Sometimes he listened to talk shows, soothed by the litany of easy opinions and unsupported claims, a form of "white noise" that blocked the strum and cackle of the world. Radio phrases mingled with Daniel's half-formed thoughts, like rocks in a tumbler, points grinding until they were smoothed-edged and harmless.

He turned up the volume. The newscast focused on the Pacific Rim flu. People were dying on the west coast. The hospitals were understaffed, probably the result of the low wages paid to nurses. Authorities were concerned by the short supply of antibiotics that seemed to have no effect on the virus. Daniel switched channels and found a car commercial. He didn't need a new car, he needed to repair the one he had. He shut the radio off.

Instead, he decided to sing himself out of a disturbing sense of loss. The car was empty, and with the windows rolled up, he could only hear the car's engine, his songs, and his uneven breathing. He felt lonely. He had enjoyed her company.

Back in the apartment, Daniel followed up on his Internet search for the new Messiah. Rayleen's idea that Jesus might be "hiding in plain sight" seemed worth pursuing. He compiled a list of twenty-two web sites and their locations, and was surprised to discover that one page originated in Boulder.

He laughed. Boulder had a nationwide reputation for being a home for radicals and assorted freaks. Palm readers and New-Age bookstores flecked the business district. If Jesus returned, where would he go if not Boulder?

The site was the very one that featured the "blank verse version" of the New Testament. The most recent posting featured a passage from Luke, Chapter Fourteen. It was clearly altered. Daniel wondered who would do such a thing. It would take a lot of nerve to rewrite the Bible.

He copied down the physical address of the web site, and tucked it in his pocket for future reference. Perhaps he could interview the owner of the site and then visit Rayleen. He might "drop in" and take her to lunch. "I'm in town on business," he would say, "and I thought I'd stop by." He would bring flowers, something fragrant with a splash of bright color, yellows and oranges. She would put them in a glass vase.

By late evening, Daniel had a severe case of cabin fever. He'd outlined his schedule for the following day. His preliminary searches had yielded some interesting possibilities. To go any further, though, he would need to know more about the old man's church in Wellington. Daniel sent e-mail inquiries to several places, including a Christian watch-dog group to see if they had any information. And he sent a follow-up letter to the F.B.I. If he kept after them, they might answer just to keep him out of their mail-box.

That done, he found himself anxious not to be alone. Veronica was closing Brian's Diner. He didn't want to see the big man again, not after breakfast the day before, but he had a desire to talk to a woman, to connect with someone from the opposite sex.

He wondered how Rayleen was doing in the Women's shelter.

Shut up, he thought. Go to Brian's.

He hadn't eaten since breakfast (how had that happened?) and a bowl of chili struck him as a good idea.

Veronica was there, but so was her boyfriend. He was thin, bones wrapped in Levis. Black hair and chin stubble made him look like a hard-lived thirty, older than he probably was. He stalked Veronica with flat brown eyes as she scurried from table to table. When he saw Daniel, he scowled. One more customer meant a longer wait.

Daniel sat down at the counter. He glanced over at the boyfriend again. He stared back at Daniel with needles in his eyes. Veronica stopped to pat his arm before serving Daniel.

"Bring me a beer and a bowl of chili," Daniel told her when she arrived with a menu. "And bring me the check. I'll close out right away so you can get out of here. It's late."

"Thanks," she gushed, clearly relieved. "You're the best."

Brian was in the back yelling at the dishwasher in Spanish. Every few minutes he poked his head out, checking on Veronica's boyfriend, never stopping to say hello. Daniel sipped his beer, and poked at the greasy chili, wishing he'd stayed home.

The front door slammed. Two college students came stumbling in, drunk and stupid, looking for a late meal, and maybe an off-duty waitress. Veronica steered them to a booth and dropped menus, warning them that the kitchen was closing. When one of them asked if she was getting off soon, the boyfriend's head snapped around.

"Yes I am, and my boyfriend and I are going out," she smiled.

"Boyfriend? Fuck him." The smaller of the two students had a voice that carried, and Veronica's boyfriend was out of his chair before she could warn them.

The larger of the two students, a blonde kid with a crew cut and a down vest, slapped his friend in the chest with the back of his hand. "Shut up," he said, but the boyfriend was already there, hands on the table top. "You boys got a problem?" he asked.

"Yeah," said the little one, his long brown hair tumbling over his forehead into his eyes. "We're hungry, and you're interrupting us."

The boyfriend's arm snaked out, grabbing the little one by the shirt collar. "What did you say?" The blonde sat back, hands in his lap, stunned. His eyes had a glazed, panicked look.

"Ricky, stop it!" Veronica pleaded. Ricky tightened his grip, twisting the little one's collar, shoving him back against the seat cushion. The crewcut blonde tried to stand up. Ricky let go of the little one, and raked his hands across the bigger one's face, tearing at his eyes. He followed with an open palm to his nose, driving the boy back into the booth.

"Ricky!" Veronica grabbed her boyfriend by the arm and shoulder. He stepped back and threw her to the side, bouncing her against the corner of another table. She yelped, clutching her hip.

Daniel vaulted off the counter stool and strode toward the booth. "Stop it!" he commanded. Veronica's boyfriend turned his way, squared up, and lashed out with a jab that caught Daniel on the side of the neck. As the attack came, Daniel launched a right round-kick, driving his foot above Ricky's knee on the outside of the thigh. Daniel could feel the leg buckle. Ricky tumbled forward. Daniel grabbed his hair with one hand and gripped his shoulder with the other, spinning him around, planting him face down on the table, bouncing the sugar caddy. He drew Ricky's arm up behind him, pulling until his feet kicked out.

Ricky tried to pull loose. Daniel cinched the arm up again. "If you move," he said, "I'll break your arm."

The blonde student stared open-mouthed, blood trickling from his nose. He leaned closer and drew back a fist. Daniel stopped him with a look. "Don't do it. . ."

"Let him go!" Veronica shrieked. She hit Daniel from behind with a tiny fist.

Brian came lumbering across the dining room, cursing. "This is a God-damned place of business, not a God-damned boxing ring." To Daniel's surprise, Brian grabbed him from behind and tossed him aside. "What's wrong with you?" the big man shouted. "This is my place of business!"

"Brian! It's me, Daniel!"

Brian's face was a stewed plum. "You're eighty-sixed! Get the hell out of here!"

Ricky sat down in the booth, rubbing his shoulder. Veronica stood behind him crying, her arms wrapped around him, hair spilled loose from her ribbon. The two students began to smirk.

Brian's eyes were wide with the rush of adrenaline. "Get the hell out of here," he repeated, but his had begun to tremble, and his eyes betrayed a wet, pleading fear behind the bluster. The big man was terrified.

Daniel nodded. "Let me pay my bill. . ."

"I don't want your God-damned money, I just want you to go."

The smaller of the students slid to the edge of the booth, talking to Brian. "Mister, if you need help throwing anybody out. . ."

Daniel backed away. "No need," he said, palms up. "I'm going." The smaller student stood, clenching his fists and shrugging, like a boxer trying to loosen up. Ricky stayed in the booth.

Daniel turned for the door. From behind, he heard, "Sorry about the misunderstanding, man." Daniel went to his car and drove away.

Going back to the apartment was out of the question. He went north down the center of Fort Collins until he reached the turnoff to Wellington, a small town to the northeast. He needed to think and the drive would do him good.

What had he done wrong? He traced the events in his mind, wincing when he recalled the way Veronica attacked him. "Stupid cowboy," he muttered, berating himself. "Who do I think I am, John Wayne?" He had enjoyed playing the role of Rayleen's protector. Perhaps he'd wanted another taste, spiced with a little physical contact.

He'd outweighed Veronica's boyfriend by at least sixty pounds, skinny little bastard. Daniel had acted like a bully, and he was ashamed of it. But there was something else gnawing at him. He needed to find out what it was.

Part of him wanted to ignore what had happened, to say to hell with it, and to hell with all of them. He wouldn't miss that crappy diner. (But that was a lie. He'd been a customer since Marianne passed.) If he talked to Brian in a day or so, the big man would let him return, but that wouldn't happen. He would never set foot in the diner again.

Brian's actions weren't any great mystery. He'd made it clear how little he thought of Veronica's boyfriend, but either the boyfriend scared him, or losing Veronica scared him. The fight made him feel angry and helpless, and he took control by ejecting the one person involved who treated him with respect. It was a safe move. Brian had nothing to lose but a customer, and the guarantor of his safety was Daniel himself. He could bet on Daniel's integrity.

Ricky was a scrawny little punk. And the students were stupid troublemakers who picked on the wrong thug. Daniel saved them from a beating, but he had no sympathy for them. They would behave the same way again, and eventually they would pay for it.

On the country road to Wellington, he realized that what still bothered him was Veronica. The memory of her fist on his back made him wince. Daniel had been trying to "save" her. Save her from what? Ricky? Whatever relationship those two had was based on a complementary set of needs and behaviors. Daniel had interfered with their pattern. It wasn't so much that she was ungrateful. She blamed him! Daniel was the bad guy, the one who threatened her partner, her balance, her world.

Daniel decided he'd been a fool. He thought of the woman in the gym, so angry at him for helping her. Some people just don't want to be saved. And creeps who insist on saving them get what they deserve. "No good deed goes unpunished," he whispered.

He pushed his car through the curves in the road, bald tires and tired engine squealing along the edge of the pavement. He rolled down a window, letting the winter wind blast in. No one else was on the road. There were no street lights. The moon scowled overhead.

A set of headlights popped up on the horizon. Daniel slowed down, but his car hit a sheet of ice and fish-tailed. He fought the slide, left, then right, whipping the wheel in his hands. For a moment, he thought he might spin, doing doughnuts across the pavement. Instead, the Hyundai righted itself just as the oncoming car drove past.

Shaken, he pulled over, finding himself near a field. The moon glared down on a building to the right. The black silhouette looked like a series of boxes stacked haphazardly in the dark, a cross perched on top. He turned off the engine, and listened to the wind. This is Ryan's church, he thought, and he knew it was true, the way a child knows the capital of a state, the way a zealot knows he is going to heaven. He believed. And the wind shrieked.

XVIII

TO: Daniel Bain

FROM: Dr. John Kitt, MD.

SUBJECT: Post-Operative State

Dear Mr. Bain,

I am certain you understand that doctor-patient confidentiality requires that I make no specific comment on Mr. Ryan's condition.

In general though, the conditions you described are not only possible, but probable, given multiple surgeries. It is sometimes advisable to leave easy access when a series of operations are required.

I hope this information has been of some service to you. I am not surprised that it seemed miraculous. I have been a practicing surgeon for more than twenty-five years, and I still have to remind myself that medicine is science, not magic. And given the rapid advances in the medical arts, it is not far-fetched to predict that what we will do five years from now would surely seem "miraculous" today.

Sincerely,

Dr. John Kitt

XIX

The e-mail from Mordecai Ryan's doctor confirmed what Daniel already believed. The mystery of the marked graves of children bearing Ryan's name had not been solved, but Mordecai Ryan was not an immortal centurion. He was a dockworker turned smuggler who had enough money to keep him alive long after he should have crumbled into dust.

There were still questions to ask, and Daniel was not inclined to wait until morning, not with a silent apartment urging him back out into the night. He called ahead this time, so Winthrop was at the door to greet him.

The old man was awake, having trouble sleeping himself. The pain was worse, he said, and the drugs were keeping him awake. He seemed glad for the company.

Winthrop drifted back to his quarters. Daniel waited until he was alone with the old man to tell him what he'd found.

"I heard from your doctor," he said. (That's not the way I meant to start, he thought. I sound like the doctor betrayed a confidence, and he didn't.)

"And what did you learn?" Ryan asked.

This time, Daniel thought before he spoke. "I learned that you're a courageous old man, battling death."

Ryan scowled. "Stop the bullshit."

"Good idea," Daniel said. "For example, you led me to believe that you were a Roman Centurion." Daniel's face flushed as he spoke. He'd almost believed, hadn't he? Ryan had played him for a fool.

Mordecai Ryan coughed out a laugh, driving mucous from his nose. He pawed at it with the bandages that held his I.V. in place. "People believe what they want to believe. You thought you'd discovered a great secret. I just nodded and let you talk."

"Why?" Daniel asked. "You've paid me a lot of money. Why would you waste your time and mine playing games?"

The old man closed his eyes for a moment. A faint smile crawled across his lips. "Your time is paid for. As for me, I'm an old man, and it's my dime. Or my hundred thousand, eh?" He opened his eyes. "Besides, sometimes a lie is more true than the facts. Sometimes a short, clever story cuts through the clutter of details, slicing down to the bone, to the heart of the marrow. Facts? Facts have no soul." The old man was slurring his words.

"Your centurion story amused me," he continued, "because there was so very much that was true about it. I am the walking dead. Do you see how I live? Can you imagine what it's like to lay here rotting?"

Spittle formed at the corners of his mouth. "The centurion in your story waits for the return of Jesus. And so do I. And the centurion's act, born of kindness, the hastening of Christ's death, was punished. Very fitting. Perhaps you've heard the saying? 'No good deed goes unpunished'." Daniel flinched.

Ryan's dark eyes locked onto Daniel's. "The men I've hired didn't believe me. You were willing to consider a supernatural explanation for my state. That, my young friend, showed an open mind. It was clever of you to find my connection to the Spear."

"What about the Spear? Do you think it had any special power?"

Ryan coughed again, and shook his head. "I handled dozens of artifacts before the war. Some were religious and some weren't. I believe what I see. They were pieces of art, or pieces of history. In the case of the Spear, they were simply pieces."

"Why did you hire me?" Daniel asked. "Why me?"

"The corporate world has a phrase for what I need. They call it, 'thinking outside of the box.' I've hired private investigators who log hours, putting themselves through the paces, never really looking. Why should they? I'm a crazy old man, an invalid. My money is good, very good, because they'll never have to come up with an answer. Jesus is a myth, and they'll never have to deliver him. Even the believers think Jesus will return 'some other time.' Never now, never this moment. So I hired you. And you surprised me right away. Too bad you're not working on the case this very moment."

"It's late," Daniel said. "I'm off the clock. What's the matter? You don't want any company?"

The old man shrugged, shaking his tubes. "No, I don't mind talking to you. Winthrop has been my ears, but he has heard all of my stories."

"Tell me your stories," Daniel said.

The old man's eyes darted away. "My personal story is unimportant. But since you are in the mood for a tale, let me tell you a good one. It's a familiar story, one you were taught in school at an early age, early enough so that you didn't question it. You took it at face value. As I tell it to you now, try hard not to hear it with a child's ears. Listen with an adult's sense of irony and outrage."

Ryan stopped to rest, wetting his lips with his tongue. "A young woman is visited by an angel," he continued. "She is told that God has chosen her, 'cast his shadow' on her, and that she is pregnant. She is engaged to a man, but she has been chaste. She questions the angel: How can this be?"

"You're talking about Mary, the mother of Christ," Daniel said.

"The girl is told to visit her relative," Ryan continued, "a barren woman who, at an advanced age, is suddenly pregnant, a sign of

God's potency. Mary goes to the relative, Elizabeth, and finds that the angel has been truthful. Mary is indeed pregnant."

"At the same time, an angel visits Mary's fiancé in a dream. The fiancé knows that his beloved is with child. He does not wish to embarrass her, so he plans to break the engagement quietly, so as not to humiliate her. The dream-angel convinces him to marry the girl anyway, since the Holy Spirit was responsible for the pregnancy."

"And so he marries her. Immediately, according to Matthew. After the child was born, according to Luke. Matthew adds that Joseph did not consummate the marriage until after the birth. There. Wasn't that lovely?"

Daniel waited.

"I said, 'wasn't that lovely?'"

"Not the way you told it," Daniel said.

The old man grunted. "The Biblical accounts differ in fact, but also in intent. Matthew notes the possible stigma for Joseph, giving him a sign, freeing him from the concerns a man might have in such a situation. Luke focuses on Mary instead, looking at how she is convinced, how she comes to accept her role. Joseph's role is not mentioned." He paused. "And what do you think Joseph's role was?"

Daniel shrugged. "To shut up and raise the kid?" he guessed.

Ryan laughed, a sound that came from deep inside his open chest. Then the mirth descended into a fit of coughing, and finally, silence.

"Yes," he said finally. "Raise the child. Joseph the father. But what of Joseph the husband? How would you feel, Mr. Bain? Cuckolded by God, forbidden social redress, forbidden even the catharsis of anger. How did you put it? 'Shut up, and raise the kid.' Well spoken, my friend."

Daniel thought of Marianne. He thought, I've been cheated on. He kept it to himself. Instead, he said, "I never thought of Joseph as a cuckold."

"He thought of it, I assure you. Sexual matters were a matter of public speculation, then as now. Elizabeth, for example, had a sense of 'public disgrace' for her previous infertility. To be barren was to be useless. She was patient. The late baby was a reward, and a redemption."

"You seem to know a lot about the Bible," Daniel said.

"I'm a pastor," he said. "I'm also a scholar. I had to be knowledgeable. There was a time when my business demanded that I know the difference between an icon and a fetish, between art and Duchamp's urinal. I studied theology, archaeology, history, as well as painting and sculpture. You would be surprised at the things I know. I'm an old man. I've had years to learn. And I've forgotten nothing." He leaned forward a little as he spoke, biting off the last word like a chunk of bitterroot.

He lay back and rested for a few moments. Daniel waited, wondering how to change the subject, but as the machines clicked away the time, he realized that the old man was finished. Daniel cleared his throat. "Are you tired? Do you want me to leave?"

Ryan shook his head.

"Can you talk?"

"I'm not dead, I'm ill," he growled.

"Tell me about your partner. According to the records, he died in 1945. Was he in combat?"

"Oh no! Of course not!" The old man smirked. "Robert was ill-suited for combat."

"Did his death have anything to do with. . ."

"Robert Wilkins was an investor. That's all. I used his money, and he used Ryan-Wilkins to pretend that he had some use in life, which he didn't. He was dead for almost two decades before. . ." he stopped, and waved his hand at Daniel.

"You met Hitler. What was he like?" Daniel wanted the old man to keep talking, to tell something about himself. He was tired of parables, riddles he couldn't solve. He needed to know Mordecai Ryan. He had facts, pages of facts, but no sense of how they fit together. How did Ryan see himself? What were his beliefs? His values? He needed the old man to talk.

"Hitler was a little man," Ryan said.

"Short?"

"No, I suppose not," Ryan said. "Average. Not really noticeable. Not very imposing. I expected a Viking, a robust vision of Aryan strength, the eater of nations, the boot and the fist. He looked more like a clerk."

"Did you get a chance to speak to him?"

"We shook hands. That's all, really. I was there for the photo. Bring in an expert, make the whole thing look academic. He was stealing Austrian treasures, and having me in the picture let them pretend, as if they were a college or a museum arranging a new exhibition instead of a gang of butchers confiscating great works of art."

"I did my part to stop them, you know. I cooperated fully with the United States Government. I gave them my list of contacts, I gave them reports on anyone they wanted. I knew some of the people on Hitler's staff. But it was too late. By the time the United States got around to acting, Hitler had all of Europe and half of Russia." He stopped and stared at the ceiling.

"Is that all you remember? About Hitler, I mean."

"He had a cold," Ryan said. "He kept patting his nose with a tissue, and he told the story about how he caught the cold a half-dozen times. Whenever someone noticed the tissue they would ask, 'Do you have a cold, Fuhrer?' he would repeat how it had rained the night before, and how he had insisted on reviewing the troops, despite advise to the contrary."

"Himmler followed him like a dog, just like a little puppy dog, always there to agree. 'I told him to stay out of the rain,' he said, 'but where the men are concerned, he will not listen.' And Hitler would beam and pat his nose with the tissue, and wait to be congratulated again for his dedication to 'the men.'"

"He liked attention, huh?"

The old man snorted. "I saw him for all of five minutes, and he couldn't get enough of it. As I said, he was a little man. I have seen his type before. Sad, angry people who need constant attention, to be confirmed, to be validated."

"Why did you build the church?" Daniel asked.

Ryan's face went blank. "Not interested in Hitler anymore?"

Daniel sat forward and put his hand on Ryan's bed. He looked directly into the old man's eyes. "I drove past your church this evening. On the road to Wellington. That is your church, isn't it?"

The old man shrugged.

"I'm wondering how an old dockworker turned smuggler. . ."

"Importer," Ryan corrected.

"Importer. Whatever. How did you end up a pastor?"

"I'm not the story here," the old man said, spitting as he talked.

"You want me to find Jesus for you," Daniel said. "I'm guessing the church is part of the story."

The old man shut his eyes, and tugged at the covers, trying to pull them up. His fingers slipped over the material, unable to grip the fabric. "Let me get that for you," Daniel whispered, pulling the sheet and blanket up under the old man's chin.

Ryan sank back into his pillow, eyes closed. Daniel waited for a few moments more, but it was clear that the old man wanted to rest. "I'll let you sleep now," he said.

"I already answered your question," Ryan said. "Were you listening? Did you pay attention?" His voice was a shallow breath, nothing more.

Daniel thought back over the conversation. "You told me that you only 'believe what you see.' Is that it?" No answer. "You saw something. Something that changed you."

The old man gave him the slightest nod.

Daniel remembered the Biblical story. "This thing you saw. Did you see it in a dream?"

The old man pursed his lips and frowned. "I believe my eyes, Mr. Bain. The rest of the world is asleep. I'm wide awake."

TO: Daniel Bain

FROM: Rayleen

SUBJECT: PARTEEEEE !!!

Dear Daniel,

I'm home again! My roommates got back this morning. We picked up a new computer, and as you see, I'm back on line. Lance was plenty pissed about the damage. I called the house to see if they were back, and he yells, "Who is this?" like he was ready to kick some ass. I told him what happened, and he thinks it was pretty cool of you to help me.

That place you put me in last night was very interesting. Thanks.

Anyway, Michelle and I decided to throw a back-in-business party. It starts at nine, but no one will show up until eleven. Don't bring anything, everything you need will be here. I invited half of Boulder, and you'll have a chance to meet a lot of cool people. Hope you can make it— Ray

XXI

When the alarm went off, Daniel slapped at it and rolled over on his back. Time to get up and run. He turned his head to the side. Her smell was still in his bed, in the sheets and on his pillow. He had noticed the hint of her presence when he went to sleep just hours earlier, tired, aggravated and eye-sore from another fruitless night at the computer. At first he wasn't able to sleep. The fight at the diner still bothered him. Brian's sweat-soaked face leered at him from under his eyelids, and Veronica's voice jerked him awake as he dozed. Then Daniel noticed the smell, her smell, and he relaxed, sleeping until the alarm went off.

He could not miss another morning run. Thomas was there waiting for him. "I'm glad you made it," he smiled.

Daniel shucked his coat and started off at a jog. "Let's go, I'm ready now. I'll warm up along the way."

Thomas followed, his strides smooth and easy. "I was worried about you yesterday," he said. "You never miss a run. I figured you were either hurt or with a girl. I'm glad you weren't hurt."

Daniel snorted.

"How are you today? Is everything all right?"

"I'm fine," Daniel said, speeding up a little. For some reason, he didn't want to talk. He wanted to run, to stretch himself, to race until his heart punched a hole through his chest. And he wanted to beat Thomas, to finish first for once.

"I've been thinking about what you told me on Sunday," Thomas said. "I don't think I gave you a very good answer to your questions.

151

I was paying more attention to my own problems. At any rate, I've been thinking about Jesus' return. If he did come again, that is, now, if he was here now, I don't think he would hide. I think he'd be shouting his message to a world cluttered with messages." Daniel stepped up the pace, and Thomas kept with him, his fluid strides seeming effortless. "I'm going to suggest something a little far out. If Jesus has returned, he might be found on the Internet."

Daniel snorted again.

"It's not such a weird idea," Thomas protested.

"Not at all," Daniel said. "It's a very smart idea."

"You've already thought of it," Thomas guessed.

"No, a friend," Daniel huffed. His chest was beginning to ache pleasantly.

"You know, computers could have been invented long before they actually were," Thomas said. "The problem was vacuum tubes. They knew how to build computers, but the failure rate on the tubes just about guaranteed that some part of the machine would be broken down at any given time."

They were running now. Thomas flew along the pavement while Daniel slammed through the slush puddles. "Resisters were invented, and then integrated circuits, and the failure-rate problem was solved," Thomas continued. "We are very clever animals, we human beings. We can build things, but we don't solve the problem of communication, because the problem is us. If you get onto the Internet, you find a hundred-thousand opinions shouted in capital letters. No one agrees, no one listens. We have built the Tower of Babel all over again, and we are drowning in the cacophony."

He paused to breathe. "You're pushing it today, aren't you?" Daniel answered with a grim nod. "Good. Keep it up." Then, "You know the story of the Tower of Babel, don't you?" Daniel didn't answer.

"Men decided to build a tower so great and so high that it would mark them and symbolize their achievements," he continued. "God looked down and said, 'They are united. They speak the same language, and look what they've accomplished.' His solution was to "confuse the language of the world," that is, to make different languages and dialects, so that man would be foiled in his attempt to become God. It's a neat story. The verb "babble" comes from the tale. Also, interestingly enough, the word barbarian, which is derived from the same root. People who speak differently from us are assumed to be barbarians, get it?"

"So what's your point?" Daniel gasped. "Jesus is having trouble getting the word out because God stirred the language pot? Jesus is suffering from God's anger at the Babylonians?"

Thomas laughed. "It's a story, Daniel, a parable. Man spends his energy being clever, and building things, instead of listening."

"But God split the languages as a punishment. For what? It sounds like Eden again. Men won't obey, so here's the punishment. . ."

Thomas shrugged, and drew in deep breaths. He was working to keep up. Daniel went faster still. The morning air was like ice in his throat. He ignored it.

"I think," Thomas said, drawing air between phrases, "that mankind was meant to be together, that we weren't meant to be alone, and the convolutions of language are both the barrier and the punishment for misspent efforts."

Daniel considered this, and then shook his head. "I disagree. I think that people understand each other perfectly well." He wiped sweat from his eyes. "I think they understand each other too well. . .I think language is our way of hiding who we are. . .from ourselves and from others." His chest was screaming now, and his calves were knotting up. He pushed harder. "I think we're all screwed-up units. . .we don't want anyone else to know. . .I think we all believe we're the only ones. . .that everyone else has it 'together'. . .and language is how we hide our faults. . ." He could feel a second wind rip through him like a surge of adrenaline, and he started to pull away. Thomas was running flat out now, his long legs eating up the pavement. His mouth dropped open and he sucked in huge mouthfuls of air.

For a moment, Daniel thought he could keep it up, that he could outrace his friend. Then, just as suddenly as it had come, the kick went out of him. His stomach went up into his throat, and for a horrible moment he thought he might vomit. He slowed, and Thomas slowed with him, clutching at his chest. "You did good," he said, "You really pushed me," but as they finished, Daniel was struggling to maintain a slow jog, and Thomas was clearly holding back.

They walked the Oval one last lap before leaving. The morning sun hid behind a bank of thick black clouds. "Snow?" Thomas said, pointing at the coming storm.

Daniel nodded. "Hey?" he said at last. "What if the Babel story is backwards? What if I'm right, and man uses language to block communication, not facilitate it? What if God said, 'I sent Jesus down, and no one got it.' What if the message was garbled?"

"Jesus lived in a simple world," Daniel continued. "Communication was oral. Maybe getting out a message back then was like trying to build a computer with tubes. People are unreliable, and the message gets changed during the transmission. Did you ever play telephone? You know, whisper a message from person to person? The message always gets screwed up."

"That's why Jesus spoke in Parables. So his message could be remembered."

"But now we have television, radio, and the Internet. Everyone could get the Word, straight from the horse's mouth. No more breakdowns. Only no one's listening. Maybe we're like a vacuum tube computer. Maybe God's plan won't work as long as it needs humans to carry it out. . ."

Thomas stared at him. "You're very pessimistic today."

"Well, what if Christ has returned? What do you think we'll do to him?"

Thomas's face clouded, the light in his eyes swallowed by a black expression. "Man crucified him the first time. They will try that much or worse. Most men serve evil, and cannot stand to hear the truth."

"Who's the pessimist?" Daniel asked.

When he could breathe again, Daniel headed for the gym, lifting until every muscle in his body ached. He couldn't lift as much as usual, which confused him at first. Then he remembered that he hadn't eaten. That was beginning to happen a lot.

When he climbed on the scale, he got a shock. He had dropped six pounds in a single week. He checked his weight three times, not trusting the machine. Was he forgetting to eat that often? He hadn't finished dinner at the diner the night before. In fact, he hadn't finished a meal in days. He decided that it was a good thing.

At home, he checked his e-mail and was elated to find a letter from Rayleen, inviting him to a party. The letter was full of double meanings, he was certain, and he read and reread, searching for hidden revelations. The line about the women's shelter being "interesting" made him wince every time. He wondered what they had said to her, and if she thought less of him because of it.

He wrote a short note back, thanking her for the invitation, promising to be there. She had only lasted a single night at the shelter. Party guests would deter a stalker, but what about later? He hoped that her roommate Lance was big enough to protect her, and he felt the sting of jealousy at the thought that someone else would be looking after her safety. Then he berated himself for the thought. He had no business worrying over her. He had already done the white-knight thing, the cowboy thing, and everyone at Brian's Diner hated him. It wasn't his place to protect her. He hardly knew the girl.

Then he wondered what he would wear, and just as quickly wondered what the hell it mattered. He was middle-aged as far as the girl was concerned, and he was certain that he looked like a giant pear with legs anyway. And to hell with anyone who didn't like the way he looked, they could face the wall when he walked by if he didn't suit them. . .

He stopped. He had been through this before, back in junior high, and again when he gained weight in his mid-twenties. He was older now. Why did he insist on replaying emotional responses he should have grown out of? He wasn't in school anymore, damn it.

He went to the mirror, and took a hard look. He was fairly trim, really. The weight loss was flattering. He shrugged. For what it was worth, he looked okay. Besides, what mattered was the person inside. Inside. He grinned, and the grin turned maniacal. His eyes widened, his teeth bared. He laughed and shook his head. What was inside should stay locked inside.

He pushed the party from his mind. He had work to do. He had nine thousand dollars worth of retainer to work off. He would focus himself on business.

Checking the computer, he confirmed that the church he'd seen the previous night was indeed owned by Mordecai Ryan. Daniel resolved to drive out and look around while the sun was still up.

It would do him good to get out of the apartment. He had been checking his e-mail every few minutes in case Rayleen wrote him again. (She signed her letter "Ray." Was he supposed to call her that now?) He needed to go outside and breathe the November air until his head cleared.

He drove slowly this time, taking care with the sharp curves on the road to Wellington. The storm that had threatened the morning seemed to have dissipated, leaving a cold, overcast sky behind. The late afternoon sun was a yellow glow over the mountains. By the time he reached the church, a pink sunset painted the bottoms of the clouds.

He parked the car and got out, circling the building on foot. The church was a wood-frame building with a single steeple topped with a wrought-iron cross. Long vertical stained-glass windows marked the side of the main structure. Rooms, perhaps offices, were stacked on the left side like tiny boxes. The architecture was an odd amalgamation of gothic, modern, and western. He imagined that Ryan had a hand in the design, because no reputable architect would have proposed the aesthetic catastrophe in front of him.

Worse, time and neglect had done damage to the place. Paint had peeled. Tumbleweeds nestled in the entryway, protecting the door like an abatis of wire and stakes. One office window was shattered, with shards of glass pointed in at wind-blown curtains.

Daniel peered inside. The room was dark, but he could make out a desk, a pile of papers, and shelves stripped of their books. He poked at the broken glass. It was loose. He pulled at a shard, pinching it between his thumb and index finger. It came out of the frame easily enough. He dropped the fragment inside and pulled at another. The sun was going down. He could feel the chill of evening creep along his back as he pulled at the glass, stripping the window piece by piece. A few shards were tough, like dagger blades, and he had to use two hands, working the glass from side to side until they pulled free. He looked around. The highway was empty, the fields around the church bare, corn stubble and snow in flat sheets as far as he could see. He hoisted himself into the window and dropped inside.

He crept through the office into the hallway, listening as he walked. A rustling at one end of the hall. Rats? He wished for a flashlight. He felt along the hallway, kicking something as he walked. A cardboard box. He stepped around, feeling for a door. Light from the stained glass panels showed him the entryway to the church itself. The colored windows were unbroken, an eerie exemption from the general decay of the building. Daniel walked slowly, his hands in front of him so he wouldn't run into the pews. When he found his way into a row, he crossed over to the windows and sat down, curling up on the bench, knees tucked under his chin.

He studied the glass. A twilight sun lit the red and blue scenes, throwing colored shadows into the gray room. The crucifixion scene was crude, but in the dim light, more terrible and sad than he had ever seen it depicted. He felt a sudden yearning to believe, to embrace something bigger than himself, something worth dedicating his life to.

The Christ on the glass panels was separated from his mourners. His mother, Mary Magdalene, and the other apostles were clustered at the bottom of the panel, comforting each other, while the Christ suffered alone at the top of the glass. The clean-shaven Christ looked toward heaven, straining against the nails that pinned his palms to the cross.

Was there a more poignant story ever told? A hero wronged, betrayed, suffering, finally succumbing, only to return triumphant? Conflict, the blood and bones of a well-told tale, infused the narrative— conflict between Christ and the God who demanded his pain and sacrifice, conflict between Christ and the disciples who failed him, disciples who must live on with the memory of their failure— conflict between Mary and her duty, to conceive and nurture a child so that he could be delivered to the pain of the cross— conflict between the crowds of onlookers and a Christ who would save anyone who would acknowledge him. It was a good story.

The sense of longing was overwhelming. He thought of the people he loved, and how he had failed each one. He had not been supportive enough of his sister. His mother just wanted him to be happy, and in return, Daniel wore his misery like a uniform when he was around her. He'd let Marianne down somehow, and his daughter died in the wreckage of their marriage.

Then he thought of Rayleen, surprised to find her mingling with his most wretched blunders.

Daniel stood. It was almost dark now, and he needed to leave. As he headed down the row, back to the open door, he heard a sound, a plop, a soft thump that might have been a footstep, or something else. He stopped, anchoring himself with a hand to the wall, and listened. Something scuttled closer from the end of the hall. Daniel forced himself to swallow, and then to move.

At every step he waited for a blow to the head, or a bite at the calves, or a dozen other possible attacks. He could imagine each so vividly that he cringed in pain. He searched for the door to the office and the shattered window, his way out. He moved on, step by sliding step. Something flew past him, brushing his ear, and he yelped. "Shit!" He rubbed at his ear, disgusted. Bats? He sniffed the hall, searching the air for the smell of guano. He found none, though the air was stale, dying, trapped in an old church that no one wanted.

Then the hallway ended.

He tapped the wall that blocked his path and turned around with his back to it. At the other end of the black hallway he could see a hint of red and blue from the stained glass. He had gone too far and missed the office. He steeled himself, and headed back.

A fluttering sound warned him, and he ducked as something flew by again. He tried not to panic but blood pounded in his ears. When his hand found the office entry, he tumbled inside, grateful and anxious to leave.

Near the window, he spotted the pile of papers. It was nearly dark in the room and he was badly frightened, but there were a few picture frames poking out of a stack of papers. He had come to find something he could use, and perhaps there it was, conveniently piled, waiting for his inspection. He checked the doorway to see if some creature had followed him into the office. Then he turned his attention to the pile.

He found Sunday service fliers with the songs and agenda marked. He pocketed them. He found a notice announcing a family picnic and barbecue. It was too dark to read the date. He found discarded copies of an evangelical magazine from an affiliated church. When he got to the pictures he tried to make sense of the images, but it was just too dark.

There were three frames. He took them to the window. Then he heard the snap of a step on brittle wood just outside the window.

Police. The word popped into his head, bringing with it a tangible fear. What if a patrol car had spotted his Hyundai outside the church and stopped to investigate? He was technically breaking and entering. He could be arrested.

I am the world's worst detective, he thought. He crept to the window, and tried to spot the source of the sound. He had a hunch that when he stuck his head out the window, someone would be there to hit him, or put a gun to his head. He could stay in the office, forcing a move, he supposed, but if a policeman had stopped, he would not leave until the empty car outside was explained. "I'm coming out," he announced. He set the pictures on the window sill, and climbed out.

He was alone. The Hyundai sat out front, unattended. He walked to the trunk, put the pictures inside, and then sat on the hood of the car, contemplating the church from the outside.

Clouds blotted out the sky. The jagged edge of the mountains were backlit by the indigo sunset. The church was a silhouette, looking much as it had the night before, a stack of boxes topped by a cross.

Back in his apartment, Daniel stacked the photographs at the computer table. He still had a few hours before the party, and he was determined to take something of value from his trip to the Wellington church.

The first photo was a construction shot, showing Mordecai Ryan pointing to a section of the newly erected frame of the church. A foreman was listening, patiently, while workers waited in the background for instructions. The photo had the stiff, orchestrated look of a posed shot.

The second photo showed the finished church, shot from the side. Viewed from that angle, the box-shaped rooms that had appeared to be attached to the building in random fashion actually served as huge steps leading up to the steeple and cross. The design of the church had a certain logic, even beauty. Daniel wondered why the stairway to the steeple didn't face the highway so everyone could see it. He remembered the way the dying sun had illuminated the stained glass. Perhaps the sun's angle had been more important to the old man than the stairway.

The third photo showed Mordecai Ryan shaking the hand of a younger man. It was a posed shot. Both men wore sport coats. Mordecai looked old, as always, his face like a chunk of lava rock, pitted and lined with crevices. The younger man was willow-thin, with shoulder-length hair. His dark eyes were piercing, intense, and Daniel frowned at the sight of them. There was no inscription on the picture. Mordecai had been the pastor of the church. Who was the young man? The youth pastor? An assistant?

Daniel turned the picture over. It had a cardboard back. He worked at the small tacks that pinned the cardboard, prying them back until he could remove the photo itself. There, on the back, was an inscription in pencil. "Mordecai and Derek."

Derek Becker. He had been a pastor in the church. Daniel flipped the picture over, and stared at it. The pose was odd. The two men faced the camera. Derek's face was guarded, reserved. Mordecai looked happy, even a little silly, grinning as he shook the younger man's hand. Daniel studied the pose, trying to extract a meaning. He mimicked the pose, taking Mordecai's place. What was the man thinking? Daniel stood in the middle of his apartment, a silly grin on his face, holding out his hand, and an idea came to him.

"No," he whispered. He flipped through his notes. The name was Hagan, he was sure of it. He flipped through pages of notes on his legal pad, and found the name he was looking for. He'd remembered correctly. Hagan.

He signed on to the Internet, and went back to a site he had previously researched. Mordecai Ryan had married in 1963, to a divorcee named Margaret Hagan. Daniel did a quick search on the bride, and found what he expected. Hagan was her name after the divorce. Her maiden name was Becker.

"Gotcha," he whispered. He did a search on birth records, and again found what he expected. The couple had a child in 1964. Margaret Hagan Ryan died from complications in child birth. The boy's name was Derek.

XXII

TO: Daniel Bain
FROM: Wendell Lindsay
SUBJECT: Multiple Graves

Dear Daniel,

Yes, Bob Wilkins mentioned that you'd be contacting me. I'm sorry I can't be more help to you. The conundrum of the multiple graves is a curious one, and I would have loved to provide you with an answer. Alas, I must disappoint you.

As you might imagine, record keeping was less effective at the turn of the century, and though there may be some way of discovering the answer you seek, I can't imagine what it is.

You also asked me to speculate as to scenarios that might explain the graves. As a historian, I am painfully aware of the temporal, narrative nature of history itself. Speculation is, in the end, the "nature of the beast." What I think you meant was, "Make a guess," and that is something a disciplined historian struggles to avoid (a losing struggle, I might add).

That said, let me answer your question.

Entry into this country at the turn of the century through Ellis Island was, to state it plainly, an unpleasant experience. Immigrants were herded off ships into fenced lanes, like cattle in chutes, and left to stand for hours in lines maintained by government clerks. These clerks were all-powerful, the "keepers of the gateway to America."

And they were poorly paid, a dangerous combination. People who feel powerless and find themselves in a position of power can be callous, even brutal. The potential for abuse, from bribes to arbitrary cruelty, was always present and often realized.

The procedure for processing an immigrant involved the drawing of official papers, with a legal name. Some immigrants, sensitive to their status as a "greenhorn," chose names that were "Americanized."

Imagine a clerk who processed papers day after day, staring into the tired, frightened faces of foreigners. And imagine that he had a sense of humor that crossed the boundary of what was appropriate. Since his pen-stroke carried the authority of his country, he could play out his pranks with impunity. Perhaps he happened upon a name that amused him, or perhaps he selected a name that he thought comical. And perhaps he attached that name (Mordecai Ryan?) to every young man who came through his line, entertaining himself by sending them off with the same name. The New Americans would not protest, how could they?

As for the graves, the flu epidemic of that year claimed many children (an unhappy circumstance that is presently repeating itself on the West Coast).

There you have it. I have imagined such a scenario, and found it to be possible, even plausible. I cannot claim to have "solved" your conundrum, however. But if a theory supplants a mystery, we all feel better, do we not?

Best wishes. W.

XXIII

The Derek Becker that Daniel was looking for was the old man's son. Daniel found him in the Boulder phone book under the name Derek Hagan. The address matched the physical location of the web site that featured rewritten Biblical passages. He was— what had Rayleen called it? — "hiding in plain sight," using his mother's divorced name.

Why hadn't Mordecai Ryan simply asked Daniel to find his son? Daniel couldn't understand what the old man expected to gain from the misdirection, and it bothered him. Why had he chosen Daniel? What was Daniel supposed to do now? Go tell Derek Ryan that his Dad wanted to speak to him?

And what about Derek Ryan? Daniel did a furious search, filling in the holes in the story. Derek had graduated from a theology school and was installed as pastor in the newly reopened Wellington church. The change coincided with a change in affiliation by the church to Derek's denomination. Prior to the change, the church had been unaffiliated. Mordecai Ryan had acted on his own, a loose-cannon who advertised himself as a "Christian Shepherd."

Derek was apparently a bit of a prodigy, graduating first in his class, bypassing protocol in acquiring his first position as pastor. Daniel suspected that Mordecai's money might have had something to do with Derek's ability to circumvent the usual church placement as assistant pastor or youth pastor. Either way, young Derek Ryan was a wunderkind, publishing essays in both theological and philosophical journals. Daniel clicked his way to the papers he could find, printing them off. One was titled, Obscuring the Message: Authorial Intrusion in the Four Gospels.

Daniel glanced at the clock. It was nearly eleven, and he hadn't even showered. He threw himself from the chair and stripped off his clothes, pitching them onto the bed, and then headed for the bathroom. The man in the mirror was thinner than he remembered, muscular, a good-looking man. There was a touch of grey at the temples that gave his face character. He stopped and stared. "I'll be damned."

He drove to Boulder, pushing his car, cursing at the stumbling engine that threatened to quit before he reached Rayleen's. He relaxed a little when he neared her house, only to find a new excuse for anxiety. The street was lined with cars on either side. No parking spots. Music blared from closed windows. People wandered the street and sidewalks ahead. How many friends had she invited?

He parked two blocks away and walked. Head down, hands in his pants pockets, it hadn't occurred to him to wonder who else would be at the party. He passed a young man in his early twenties with spiked blonde hair, a ruby nose ring, baggy jeans with pockets down to his thighs, and a yellow basketball jersey draped over his coat-hanger body. He mumbled a hello at Daniel, and Daniel mumbled back, his mouth suddenly dry.

Daniel had put on a nice sweater. Sweaters were always appropriate. He looked good in sweaters. He crossed over into Rayleen's yard and walked up to her door. The front step was blocked by a dozen young men, beers in hand, shuffling in place, breaking their sentences with the same verbal filler— "Dude, it was, like. . .fuck, Dude. . ." They stopped talking when he reached the bottom step. I am the only one, Daniel thought, wearing a sweater.

"Excuse me, gentlemen," he said, and the group parted as if the police had arrived. Daniel pulled open the door and Reggae music rolled out, tumbling over him, knocking him back, a musical closet stuffed full and opened suddenly. He took a deep breath and walked in.

"Can I help you?" a young woman shouted into his ear. The room was dark, lit from behind by the kitchen. Thirty people were jammed into the living room, bouncing off one another, clumping into twos and threes, swirling and breaking off, forming other clusters. The music pounded the windows and shook the joists in the walls.

"I'm here to see Rayleen," he shouted. The girl was already spinning away, chasing a young man with sunglasses and a goatee.

Daniel stood still. He searched the bobbing faces for Rayleen. No one spoke to him. An unpleasant memory came. He had been swimming laps at the health club when an attendant stopped him and asked him to leave the pool. "A child had an accident," he explained. A three-inch piece of fecal matter floated between the ropes in the next lane, a health hazard. Now, floating in a sea of young people, he was the malapropism, out of place, and unwanted.

He turned to his left, and at that moment, Rayleen turned to her right, and they found themselves face-to-face. She grinned, and in a burst of spontaneous joy, hugged him. "You made it!" she shouted. "I didn't think you were coming!"

"I said I'd be here," he said.

"What?" The music bounced between the floor and ceiling.

"I missed you!" he shouted. She pulled back a little and squinted, searching his face.

"There's a keg in the kitchen," she answered.

A tall man in his early twenties grabbed her from behind, wrapping his arms around her, locking his hands just under her breasts. He said something into her ear, and she twisted around, hugging him. Another man, shorter, darker, with a slender build and huge brown eyes, tapped her shoulder. She disengaged from the tall one and fell into the other's arms, leaning into him with a deep kiss that took Daniel by the heart and twisted it. Of course she had friends. Of course she was close to other men, even intimate. She was a porn model. Surely he hadn't pictured her as a waif? He backed away.

Beer, he thought. He headed for the kitchen, weaving through thatches of boys in bagged-trousers and girls in jeans and white tee-shirts.

A girl with a Denver Broncos ball-cap spun around as he passed, bumping into him. Her cap dropped to the floor. "I'm so sorry, sir!" she moaned, covering her mouth with her hands. Daniel bent to retrieve the cap from the floor, but she was much quicker, snatching it up without effort. "I've got it sir, no problem." By the time he reached the keg, Daniel was ready to drink.

The music was still loud in the kitchen. The back door was open, and the keg stood just outside the door. Daniel pawed past half-full and quarter-full cups of beer discarded on the table, finding an empty one that looked as if it might not yet have been used.

As he stood, cup in hand, a girl came drifting through the kitchen, a ghost in a diaphanous blouse, like white gauze clinging to her body. She moved as if in a trance, taking slow, careful, deliberate steps. Around her neck was a length of twine, fashioned into a noose. An angry red welt circumscribed her neck. She floated into the back yard, and Daniel, curious, followed her.

A group of four young men stood around the keg. They stopped talking as the girl with the noose approached. She pulled back her blonde hair, revealing a pretty face caked in ruined makeup. "I just tried to kill myself," she announced.

A cold wind pulled at her blouse. She stood in bare feet on a patch of ice. One young man with red hair rising off the top of his head like a mott of trees, turned to the girl. "Jesus, Kirsten. How fucked-up are you?"

"The rope broke," she said dully.

"It's twine," he told her. "Where are your shoes?"

"I can't find them," the girl moaned, bursting into tears.

"Go find your shoes, and then go home," he said. She waited for a few moments, sobbing. The young man with the red hair began to speak again. "Every culture on the planet has a storytelling tradition.

168

Stories are how we make sense of what we see. But it's more complicated than that. Stories are how we help construct reality." (He cupped his hands together as he said this last, as if he were fashioning an invisible snowball.) "The stories we tell shape the way we see things in each of our individual realities. . ." The girl with the noose dried her eyes with her sleeve and drifted back into the house, her face a smeared mask, hair draped down to cover her eyes.

"What was she thinking?" one boy muttered.

Red Hair shook his head. "We can never know what another person thinks. For that matter, we can't know anything at all. The universe is in a constant state of flux. Reality is different for everyone." He paused. "And Kirsten's reality is really, really different."

"There's only one reality," a chubby young man interrupted. He had a glass pitcher half-full of beer clutched in his fist, and he was very drunk, shifting side-to-side, trying to maintain his balance.

"You personally can only perceive one reality," Red Hair said, adding, "that is, if you can still perceive one." Everyone chuckled, except the young man with the pitcher.

"You seem to know a lot about what we can't know," Daniel said. The group stopped talking and stared at the intrusion. Well jump right in, Daniel thought. That's the way to make friends.

Red Hair glared straight ahead, as if he hadn't heard. "Anyone who thinks they know something can be proven wrong in short order," he said.

"Philosophy major?" Daniel guessed.

"Pre-law," the boy sneered. "But take your best shot."

Daniel nodded at the others, and held up his beer. "I know this is a beer," he said. "Let that be your test case."

"Too easy," Red Hair said. "You haven't taken a sip, have you? What if you do, and discover it's gasoline? Do you know for sure until you taste it? And if you think it's beer, why do you? Because it came from a keg, and you've been conditioned to expect it. People get what they expect, don't they?"

"Let me help your argument," Daniel said. "When I say 'beer,' do I mean the type or the token? Beer in general, or this specific beverage? There's an ambiguity. Plus, the definition is 'soft.' Does hard cider count? Porter or ale? Beyond that is the problem of naming things in general. If the item were here, we'd point, and say 'this here.' Calling something by its name usually means it's not there, and using the name has as much to do with the name, the symbol itself, as it does with the thing it's meant to signify."

"Philosophy major," the boy accused.

"No," Daniel laughed. "Literature. Now the skeptic, and you sir are a sceptic, asks, 'Is this really beer?' meaning, 'are appearances deceiving?' Then he asks, 'Is it a real beer?' meaning authentic, genuine beer, and finally, 'Is beer real?' as if everything might be phony. And if you can't know a beer, then you can't know anything. Right?"

Red Hair waved him on.

"The problem comes from the question itself," he continued. While you're debating the nature of reality and the symbols that inhabit it. . ." He paused and took a sip. "I'm drinking the beer." He made a sour face. "And this isn't real beer, by the way. It's Coors." The chubby one howled and took a long draw from his pitcher. The others shuffled around, losing interest.

"But you can't know things for sure or be certain that others encounter them the same way you do," Red Hair scowled.

"No, you can't. Not in the sense you mean. We have limits. We're not Gods. We'll never really know what others are thinking. Too bad. Get over it."

"Then you admit I'm right?"

"No, I think you have unreasonable expectations. You can't know what others think, but you can get a good sense of it from experiences and interests you share. If two people are close, really close, it almost works like ESP. . ."

"Name one time where you have that kind of connection with someone else," the boy demanded.

"Love," Daniel said. He stopped suddenly, trying to suck the word back in and leave it unspoken.

Red Hair laughed. "I rest my case," he said.

"So Dude, how about them Broncos?" another said, his nasal delivery meant to mock, to move the conversation out of the theoretical and back to a topic someone might actually care about. Daniel felt simultaneously ashamed for having imposed himself on the others and angry at the rejection. He refilled his cup and slid away. The others allowed him to leave without so much as a glance.

Find Rayleen, he thought. He drank half of the beer in a single gulp, and ditched the cup on the kitchen table. Commercial beer, he thought. Water.

Techno blared from the stereo, and the people in the living room were dancing. A boy in the corner had a flashlight, and he was annoying girls by spotlighting their faces. The stairway was lined with people watching, drinking, all clearly having a good time. Everyone was enjoying themselves, everyone not wearing a sweater.

A pair of girls came in the front door as Daniel passed by. The thinner, prettier of the two bolted into the crowd, arms waving, dancing to the music, leaving the other girl behind. The heavy-set friend backed up against the door frame, looking miserable. She pulled at her blouse, trying to smooth the wrinkles. Then she patted her hair into place, and waited, sucking her stomach in. Rayleen came walking by, holding onto another man's arm. When she saw the girl, Rayleen disengaged, and stopped to say hello. The heavy girl took Rayleen's offered hand with a surprised look. Rayleen bent forward, speaking directly into the girl's ear, and then led her into the living room, where she introduced her to the boy with the flashlight.

Daniel watched as yet another man tugged at Rayleen, calling for her attention. She bowed away from the two in the corner, and turned to the new demand, gracious and attentive.

171

Daniel went upstairs to find a bathroom. There was a line.

Waiting, he heard a commotion. Through a bedroom door, he saw a boy in his early twenties rocking himself at the end of a bed, laughing and crying at the top of his lungs. "Let's all die! Let's all do it now!" Suddenly, the boy locked up, his back rigid, a look of horror on his face. He pitched himself to the floor. Two girls dropped down to huddle over him, trying to comfort and quiet him. He lay babbling. Strings of words spewed out in a rush of incoherence.

Others went to his side, reaching out, offering their help, kneeling, touching his tee-shirt, his hands, his hair. It's okay, it's over now, we're here, we're with you. You're not alone.

The bathroom line was growing in front of Daniel as friends joined friends already in line. Two boys ahead of him were talking about the celebration after the Bronco's most recent playoff victory. "They were firing tear gas into the street, and we were climbing up lamp posts, screaming, trying to get above the gas. A row of cops came rolling across the street, swinging clubs at everyone who didn't run. My roommate got maced with pepper-spray because they caught him starting a fire in a trash can. I couldn't breathe, and I was swinging my arms around, hitting anyone who tried to fuck with me." He took a breath. "It was fucking great."

I'm out of here, Daniel thought. There were bathrooms on the road home.

The police walked in the front door as Daniel reached the bottom of the steps. In the corner, the heavy-set girl sat next to her new friend, pointing the boy's flashlight at the officers. Rayleen was nowhere in sight. Someone cut the music and there was a noisy outcry. Some of the kids pushed their way to the back door, trying to get out before the cops started carding people.

One officer spotted Daniel and asked, "Is this your home?"

"No," Daniel frowned. "But I know the people who are throwing the party. Is there a problem?"

"Noise," the officer shouted. "It's out of control. We're shutting this down now. If you know the people who live here, you need to tell them to clear the house. They've broken a dozen ordinances, including underage drinking, and they're going to spend the rest of the night in jail if they don't clear everyone out."

A boy with jeans down around his thighs and a Colorado University tee-shirt pushed in front of Daniel. "I can handle this, officer. What seems to be the problem?" He spoke with exaggerated precision, trying to hide the slur in his voice.

"Do you live here?" the officer said.

"No sir, I do not, but if. . ."

"Shut up and go home son," the officer said. "And get someone to drive you. Your breath is ninety-proof."

Daniel tried the kitchen. Rayleen stood by the sink, her hand on her hips. Someone was ranting at her, his voice rising above the general chaos. "It's that Christian family down the street. I know it. Those God-damned, right-wing, in-your-face, hypocritical bastards called the police because someone's having fun that they don't dare have themselves. Don't let anyone bend a law, for God's sake, unless it's blowing up a fucking abortion clinic, or pistol-whipping a gay man. That's okay, God doesn't like abortions or fags, so have at 'em, right? Am I right? Fuck them. We ought to march over there, and burn a cross on their front lawn, and sing hymns while we roast marshmallows."

"The KKK does that too," Rayleen said, weary of the tirade.

The boy waved his hand, moving past her point. "Yeah, yeah, but someone ought to cry bullshit when bullshit is out there, and this is bullshit, you know? It's bullshit."

"The police are here," Daniel said. "They want the place cleared. Do you want some help?"

Rayleen wouldn't meet his eyes. She nodded, angry.

Daniel went back to the officers. "I talked to the gal that lives here. I'm going to help clear the place," he said. Without waiting for a response, he headed up the stairs to the furthest corner of the house and began herding people to the door.

Most were cooperative, sensing that the fun was elsewhere now. A knot of four boys ignored him, and left him hovering in Rayleen's bedroom doorway, waiting while they talked. Finally, one glanced to the side and said, "Fuck the police. And fuck you." Daniel shrugged and moved on. When the house was clear, the cops could have those four.

Moving down the stairs, he found the lower level nearly empty. Rayleen had moved everyone out on to the lawn, and she was holding her own with the police. Four more officers had joined the first two. One of the new arrivals pointed at Daniel and asked, "Do you live here?"

"No."

"Then go home."

Daniel started to protest, but there was no reason. He'd wanted to leave twenty minutes earlier. Rayleen was butting heads with the oldest cop. Daniel gave up trying to catch her eye. "I'm leaving now, Officer," he said, pointing a finger up the stairs. "Check the bedroom at the top of the stairs. Four guys up there said to tell the cops to fuck off." Then he headed out the door to his car.

The lawn was filled with people milling around, blowing trails of vapor into the night air. A giant in a football jersey was peeing into a bush that lined the walkway. A young girl knelt nearby to vomit. As he walked, Daniel noticed a man standing still, facing the front steps. Daniel guessed that the man was in his early thirties, older than the rest of the crowd. He found himself staring as he drifted toward the street, and when he reached the sidewalk, he turned right instead of left, away from his car. He slowed, passing a tree that blocked his view of the house. On the other side, he saw that the man had turned and was facing him, hands in his pockets, no expression on his face.

A chill raced along Daniel's back, drilling into the base of his neck. It was the jogger, the man who threatened Rayleen. He knew it in his bones.

He took a step toward the house. The man whirled and ran. Daniel followed, racing into the shadows that cloaked the side of the house. Night-blind, Daniel slowed as he rounded the corner of the house. When his eyes adjusted, he saw the jogger slipping over the back fence, down into the alley.

Walking back, Daniel recalled the way the jogger had turned to face him. The bastard definitely knew who he was. He hurried to his car, suddenly worried about his apartment. Then he thought of the doll with the burned out eyes, and he was frightened for Rayleen. This bastard wasn't going to give up. He was going to hurt her.

But how to help her? She had her own friends, people she relied on. And he didn't have to convince her of the danger, she was already afraid. He chewed on the problem as he drove home, windows open to wash the smell of cigarettes from his clothes. He had already made an idiot of himself at Brian's Diner. The world didn't appreciate heroics, perhaps with good reason. It was too easy to mistake the motives or the methods of others. You couldn't always tell the good guys from the bad. In this case, the bad guy was obvious enough. But what was Daniel's interest? And what good could he do?

He decided that he couldn't do anything at all. When he got home, he sent Rayleen an e-mail, thanking her for a wonderful time, reminding her that he was at her service. He added that he'd seen a person that looked like the stalker at her party, and though he couldn't be sure, she ought to pass the information on to her roommates. He finished, restating his willingness to help.

That finished, he checked his mail. He had two letters commissioning his services. The first job involved a simple trace. He did most of the work right away, happy to have something to take his mind off the empty room. He opened a beer, but only took a sip. He thought about making himself a sandwich, but decided against it.

The second job was more complicated. A finance company wanted to locate and contact someone who had left Denver. The company suspected that the man had relocated in southern Wyoming. Daniel would have to find him and pay him a visit. With luck, the debtor would be intimidated into making a payment, even a post-dated one. A bounced check was as useful as a good check. If the check cleared, the company collected. If the check was hot, the company had more leverage in the courts. Daniel had most of the following day planned, so he penciled in the day after for the trip north. The finance company was a good customer, and Daniel would enjoy the drive.

Both letters answered, Daniel felt the silence. He sat at the computer and listened to the wind blow against the window. He looked around the room. What am I doing here? he thought. This isn't a home. It's a cell. I need to find a real apartment. My credit is still good. I could buy a condo or something. The money from Ryan would make a good down payment.

He thought briefly about the hundred-thousand that Ryan promised. There was no way the old man would pay it. You can't get something for nothing, Daniel decided.

Still, he had the makings of a good business. He needed to wake up and go to work. He could buy a place of his own and write off some of the mortgage as office space. It would be cheaper than paying rent. "And I need to get some plants," he whispered.

A knock at the door made him jump. No one ever visited him. Ever. He glanced at his watch. It was three in the morning. He stood and clenched his fist. Someone had rifled his files. Maybe someone wanted a confrontation.

He didn't ask who was there. Instead, he unlocked the deadbolt and yanked open the door, ready to swing.

Rayleen. Startled, she stepped back. He squinted into the dark. "Are you okay?" he asked with an incredulous voice.

She moved into the light. Her eyes were red, and she spoke with a slow mumble. "I couldn't sleep. I was kind of hoping I could crash here."

XXIV

C:\MyFiles\Truth\Nov

That I am to act soon is a certainty. What action I must take, however, is uncertain. How will I know my course? I have received a sign, but it does not tell me what I am to do. I must empty myself, cast out my wishes, my needs, and make myself open to Him. Then whatever action I take will be His will, a piece in His puzzle, a lever in His machine.

I will fast. I will not sleep. I will pray. When I am empty, I will go to her, and I will do what the Lord would have me do. I know that the choice will be a hard one. Perhaps she has seemed sweet to me so that I will learn the wisdom of sour. She may be a test, or she may be poisoned fruit. Whatever God commands, I will obey.

The man that shadows her is a nuisance, a thug, a familiar. I will give him what he deserves. I know how he will end up.

She ignored my warning, of course. As I watched her celebrate, I was reminded of the etymology of the word, "carnival." The word comes from the Latin root, "carne"— meat. A carnival is a "meat festival." How perfect! Could any other word describe the sight of so many lost souls, celebrating the flesh? Animals! They grope each other, dressed to confuse and confound the separation of the sexes. They drink until they stagger, and then they urinate in the bushes like dogs. Meat. I wonder at the INFINITE MERCY OF GOD,

179

that He doesn't light the crust of the planet and
burn it to cinders. And we, in His image, defiling
that image with every foul action, we deserve to
burn.

I long for a chance to strike a blow for His
word. I long to serve the world notice that the
celebration is over, and the bill is due. The plan
is in motion. His plan. I am a part, a small but
significant part, because any part, no matter how
small, is significant in His eyes if it serves His
purpose.

What will I say to her if it is His will that
she suffer the consequences of her behavior? I
will express my sorrow. I know that much. I have
watched her for too long not to acknowledge the
profound spiritual feeling that I hold for her in my
heart. While others coveted the flesh, I saw past
that, to the small kernel of truth at the center of
her being. I would have loved that tiny heart of
goodness. I would have nourished it, and it would
have grown until it bloomed, full-flower. That love
is stillborn. She holds it, dead in her vile hands.
In its honor, I will weep when I do what must be
done, but I will not regret serving Him.

As for the thug, the familiar, I know who he is
now. I know who he is and who he works for. The
thread that connects us all is the ONE SIGN I have
received, the proof that ALL THINGS ARE CONNECTED in
HIS WORLD. I am not surprised.

XXV

After Rayleen showered, she asked him for the fourth time if it was really all right if she spent the night. "I feel really stupid right now. I shouldn't have bothered you." She was draped in one of his tee-shirts, her legs tucked under as she sat on the bed.

"It's not a big deal," he lied.

"My roommates crashed after the police left. I was too wound up and I thought I couldn't sleep, so I decided to clean the house. I started in the kitchen. I had my rubber gloves on, a sink full of soapy water, and all of a sudden. . . ." She turned away. "I thought I heard something outside the window. It scared me."

"What did you hear?"

"Wind," she growled. "That stupid old house has a lot of noises. I was tired, and I scared myself."

"Did you get my e-mail?"

"No," she said. "What did you say?"

"Just to be careful. I thought I saw someone who looked like the guy who's been bothering you. He was out on the lawn when I left the party." Her eyes widened. He tried to change the subject. "So anyway, you came here. . ."

"I know, I should have gone somewhere else— "

"No!" he blurted. They both stopped, and then they both started giggling. "No," he repeated, in a reasoned voice this time. "It's nice that you feel comfortable here. I like the company." He took a breath. "You should go to sleep. Do you want me to get the sleeping bag?"

"If you want to," she said. He stood helpless. "What do you want?"

"I want you to get some sleep."

"Then get in here," she said, sliding under the covers.

He shut off the lights, and climbed under the sheets, rolling onto his back. She waited until he was still and then put her head on his chest, holding him the way she had two nights before.

Daniel tried to relax, but a disturbing thought came. What if she couldn't sleep tonight? The two things he offered her were safe conversation and a chance to rest. He didn't want to lose that. Suddenly he was tense. An itch worked at the small of his back.

"I don't know what's wrong with me," she said at last. "I was so tired, and now all I feel like is talking."

"I've been waiting for you to say something," he said, relieved.

"I don't really have anything to say. I just want to talk." She paused. "How come you left the party without saying goodby?"

"The cops told me to leave, and you had enough trouble without me adding to it." He considered telling her about trying to force a confrontation with the jogger, but decided against it. He didn't want her worrying in his bed.

"I got off with a noise-ordinance ticket," she explained. "It's a bunch of bullshit, but I guess they could have hit me with 'disturbing the peace' and put me in jail for a month." She sighed. "Tell me about your wife. You said you lost her twice in one hour."

He closed his eyes. He had changed into sweats when she arrived, selecting a tight-fitting tee shirt, hoping that she might notice his weight loss. He could feel her body through the shirt. She was a slender and tight with muscle. He felt old and soft laying next to her. "My wife left me," he started. "We had a daughter, just eighteen months old. Her name was Courtney. My daughter, that is. My wife's name was Marianne."

Rayleen nestled in closer, draping a leg over his. He felt her relax. "I thought things were going well," he continued. "I was happy. She must not have been. One day, I came home and found everybody gone. There was a note in the baby's crib, explaining that she had to leave, that there was someone she needed to be with, and that she was leaving the state. I couldn't believe it, really, and I ran around the house looking in drawers, seeing if she'd taken enough clothes to actually leave me. I remember thinking that if she took just two or three outfits, then she was at a motel somewhere close, just trying to teach me a lesson. If she took everything, then she was gone for good. I tried to picture all of her outfits. I counted them off in my head."

"Why would she want to teach you a lesson?"

He shrugged. "Maybe I ignored her, I don't know. I don't think I did. If she felt that way, she certainly never mentioned it. If she was unhappy, you'd think she'd say so."

He thought for a few moments. Why was he telling her so much? The next part was the most painful. He wondered if he could say it out loud. She didn't interrupt his silence, wrapping her arms around him instead.

"Anyway," he said at last, "I heard a knock at the door. It was the police. On her way out of town, Marianne hit an ice patch. She'd been going about fifty. She slid sideways into a cement embankment, and flipped the car over the rail and down into a creek. The car landed on the roof. They were both dead, pretty much instantly."

"Oh God, I'm so sorry," she said. Her voice was hollow, trembling.

"So I lost them twice. She left me, and then she died. I couldn't even grieve for her. Any feelings I had were a lie after that goodby note. She didn't want me in her life. I wasn't the one she'd want to mourn her."

"I had to arrange the funeral. All of her relatives knew she was leaving me. She'd told everyone, everyone except me. They weren't comfortable with me running the funeral, but what could I do? I was her husband, and I was expected to make the arrangements." He thought that she was trembling, and he lifted her chin. "Are you crying?" he asked.

"It's very damned sad," she said.

He put her head back down and held her, waiting to continue until he had control of his voice. "I assumed that someone told her boyfriend that she'd died. I never heard from him, and he stayed away from the service. That was the thing that saved me, not having to be polite to that bastard."

"There was great dramatic irony at that funeral. The people who didn't know what was going on, my side of the family, were so sympathetic. 'You have to go on for them, be strong for them. They'd want it that way.' Right. And I'd nod, and thank them for coming, feeling ashamed for them and for me."

"Marianne's mother said that she knew 'it was hard for me.' That's what passed for condolences from Marianne's family. Her father was a little more blunt. He told me, 'If you were worth a damn as a husband, she'd have never been on the road that night.' I didn't argue with him. I tried to say kind things about her and remind him what a special soul Courtney was. He was too angry to listen."

"I sat through the memorial service and the little reception after. My mother arranged that. She set everything up, and then wondered why no one from Marianne's family showed up. I couldn't tell her. The words wouldn't come out. What could I say? 'She left me, Mom, and the whole family blames me for her death.' Mom wouldn't let anyone eat. She wanted us to wait for Marianne's family. I just sat there with my mouth shut. She took it personally, and. . ."

He was quiet. "What?" Rayleen asked.

"I should have let my mother know that it wasn't her fault," he said. "She thought she did something wrong. The subject never came up again— imagine that! She probably still blames herself. I ought to call her." Looking back, it was hard to see why hiding his marital troubles had ever been important. Certainly not as important as his mother's feelings.

"I've never told the whole story to anyone," he said, wonder in his voice. "Partly because it's all 'woe is me,' and I hate that. But also because I don't know how to grasp the whole story. It isn't about her leaving me, because she died. It isn't about her death either, because I was being cut out of her life. As for Courtney, she'd have been raised by someone else. She wouldn't have had a thing to do with me, beyond the accident of biology. How are you supposed to make sense of a story like that?"

Rayleen was quiet for a while, pressed close. When she spoke, her voice was drowsy, soft and low. "The story explains a lot, though."

"Explains what?" he yawned.

"Your job, this little room," she whispered. She was asleep moments later. He lay still, his arms wrapped around her. He could feel her chest rise and fall with each breath. After a time, he fell asleep as well.

When she woke up, he was nearly done making breakfast. The late morning sun was starting to warm the room. He'd crept to the kitchen to prepare the meal, trying not to bang cabinet doors or drop utensils. He was only partly successful. When he brought her breakfast out, she was awake, sitting up in bed, her back against the wall, the covers pulled up around her waist.

"I know you're not big on eggs," he explained. He gave her a desert dish with layers of fruit, granola, and yogurt, garnished with an orange slice. It was the dish she'd ordered at the all-night restaurant.

"This is perfect!" she gushed. "This is so nice!"

He shrugged, and sat at the edge of the bed as she dove into the fruit. He had stopped at the store the previous day, searching for lighter foods, and had purchased two of the parfait glasses from the housewares aisle, thinking of such a breakfast.

"I love this," she told him. "The fruit is fresh, not canned. This is so healthy for you." She brushed a strand of hair from her eyes, and caught him staring at her. She smiled, and he realized that she didn't mind.

"What time is it?" she asked between bites.

"Ten," he said.

She stopped, and stared at him, a spoon of yogurt floating in the air. Her brown eyes locked onto his, and he nodded. "I know," he said.

"But I don't sleep," she said. "Only when. . ."

"And I don't. . ."

"Then how?" She remembered the yogurt, and put the spoon in her mouth. "It's really, like. . ."

"Yes," he finished. He stood up. "By the way, I found Jesus. He lives in Boulder." She laughed. "I'm going to pay him a visit today. Want to come along?"

She nodded, suddenly serious. "I'd like that. I'm wondering how this will all come out." Her eyes drifted off. She appeared to be considering something. "You don't think he's the real Jesus, do you?

"It doesn't matter," Daniel said. "I'm going to get my fee." He patted the bedspread where her leg was. "I'm glad you're here." Then he went to shower, leaving her to her thoughts.

By the time she finished her turn in the shower, her mood had turned icy. Her eyes seemed darker. The corners of her mouth had hardened, and she wasn't talking.

Rayleen's car was in the parking lot. When he asked if she wanted to go back to Boulder in one car, she declined, saying it would be wiser to take both vehicles to "save time." Disappointed, he asked if she still wanted to go with him to visit Jesus.

"Sure. It'll be interesting," she said.

On the way to the car, he asked, "Are you all right? You seem upset about something."

"No," she said, shaking her head as if he was imagining something. She had a scowl in her voice, so he didn't believe her.

"Let's meet at your place," he said. "Then I can drop you off after we take care of business."

"That will be great," she said, turning away. He went to his car, talking to himself. As he drove, he traced the morning in his mind, wondering what he'd said that had been taken wrong. He started to punch the steering wheel, another outburst of smothered rage like the dented door panel. "I'm so fucking angry," he thought, and it out loud, the anger lessened enough to let in another realization.

It's not me. She has her own things to deal with. It's not me.

He thought of how she made him feel when they sat on the bed talking, and then how he felt when she went cold. He was deeply affected by her behavior. Her mood changes were lethal.

If she was going to go silent on him after he had opened himself up to her, then he ought to be cautious. He didn't have to end the relationship, but he needed to protect himself.

In Boulder, he pulled the Hyundai over and parked, not wanting to drive the last block and a half.

"What relationship?" he said out loud. "I don't have a relationship with this girl. This is crazy. I'm in my thirties!" His breathing was shallow and rapid. He thought of the last year, locked in his apartment, playing detective. "What the hell have I been doing? Was I crazy, and didn't know it?" He considered that. The loss of his wife and daughter was devastating. He'd recognized that he was wounded, but had never considered that he might be seriously damaged. "Wow," he whispered. "Maybe I'm losing it."

Even as the thought reached his lips, he dismissed it. More likely, he was waking up after a long, painful sleep. He sat for a few minutes more, listening to the engine flutter. Finally, he put the car in gear. He had work to do.

She was waiting for him in the front yard when he arrived, her hands on her hips. She yanked the door open and climbed in. "Where did you go?"

He didn't answer. He handed her a slip of paper with an address. "Do you know where this is?" he asked.

She nodded. "It's about four blocks away. Is this where Jesus lives?"

He nodded.

"Well that figures. Drive to the stop sign, and turn left." She sat in silence while he drove. "What are you so pissed off about?" she said at last.

Daniel ignored the question. "I have to convince this guy, Jesus, to come to Fort Collins and see the old man. That's the only way I can collect the rest of the fee." He paused. "It's a pretty significant sum of money, so I'm thinking of how to get the guy to go."

"Why wouldn't he?" she asked.

"I'm guessing he doesn't want to see Mordecai Ryan," Daniel said. "The old man is his father."

"What?" Rayleen said. "You're joking."

Daniel shook his head. "He didn't hire me to find his son, he hired me to find Jesus. I don't know what's going on here, but I'll play along. The old man's first check cleared. If he wants to pay me a hundred grand to bring the guy in for a question or two, that's fine with me."

"A hundred grand!" Rayleen gasped. "No fucking way!"

"Yes fucking way," he frowned. "I don't know what sort of falling out they had. I think it had something to do with a church in Windsor. The old man built it, and his son was the Pastor. Then something happened. Now the old man wants to reconcile, and I have to convince the boy to talk to his Daddy."

"If he doesn't want to see his father, he won't," she said. She folded her arms and leaned against the car door. "Maybe his father is a prick, and he doesn't want him in his life. You can't make him go."

"I can't make them shake hands," he said. "But if the old man gets a face-to-face, I get paid. Job done. I'd like to ask his son about the web page anyway." He explained that Derek Ryan was the author of the page that featured gospel rewritten in blank verse. "Actually, it was your suggestion to look for Jesus on the Internet, remember? We found the page that first night you stayed over."

"I still say the son shouldn't have to make up with his father if his father's a jerk," she said.

Daniel twisted the steering wheel in his hands. "You're missing the point. I don't care. It would be nice if they got together again, but I want the money."

"C'mon, Daniel," she said. "The truth is, you think everyone ought to make up and hold hands because it would be swell. You can act all pissed off, but you're hoping the old man gets his way. If the old man's a jerk then I hope he gets what's coming to him. That's the difference between you and me."

"That's just a difference of age," Daniel said. "The young want justice. The old want mercy."

"Screw mercy," she said. "That isn't the way the world runs. Big fish eat little fish. When the big fish get sick and old, the little fish nibble them to death. Turnabout's fair play."

"We're here," Daniel said, pleased to change the subject. He pulled the car over. The apartment house was just ahead. "I think this might be tricky. Let me do the talking."

"Sure, I'll just shut up and look pretty."

He turned, his face blank. "I meant no offense." As he left the car, he told himself that he would not call her again. Whatever he'd done to become the focus for her irritation had been inadvertent. He did not deserve her hostility and would not subject himself to it again. (A lie. If she called him, he would gladly pretend this day had never happened, because he was being every bit as difficult as she was.)

The apartment house was an old brick building. He looked up and spotted a second floor apartment without curtains, nothing visible on the walls. "That would be the one," he thought. It would not surprise him to find that he had guessed correctly. He was not clairvoyant. He had some solid assumptions about the man who wrote the web site. "Jesus" was a scholar and a hermit. He would have books, if not on shelves, then stacked. Beyond the books, he would have few personal belongings. He would be withdrawn, sullen, perhaps angry at the intrusion. He would avoid eye-contact, and be uncooperative, even frightened. He might even be paranoid.

Daniel knocked on the door. The man who answered was clearly the Derek Ryan in the church photo, but his face had aged a decade in just a few years. His short hair was silver at the temples. The skin around his eyes was laced with crows feet. When he extended a hand to shake, his brown sweater pulled back, revealing a wrist the size of a small wooden dowel. He smiled. "Hi! How can I help you folks?"

Daniel handed him a card. "My name's Daniel, and this is my associate, Rayleen." He rushed on. "I've been hired to find someone, and I have good reason to believe you're the someone I'm supposed to find."

His eyes widened, but the smile stayed on. "Really? I didn't know I was lost! Oh well, it would be just like me to misplace myself!" He laughed, and opened the door. "Come on in. Let's see if we can sort through this."

He closed the door behind them. "The young lady is welcome to sit at my desk," he said. "I don't have much furniture. I don't do a lot of entertaining." The room was nearly empty. Off-white walls and tan carpet did nothing to hide the stark, vacant look of the room. A few piles of books were stacked near the computer desk, and a single potted plant sat on the floor near the window. The room was cold, despite a small fire in the fireplace. A couple of bundles of wood were stacked on the tile floor nearby, and a framed picture sat on top of the mantle. Otherwise, the room was empty.

"I will put some tea on," he said. "It will only take a moment.

"Don't bother. . ."

"Oh, it's no bother!" he said, and he was gone, whistling.

"I thought your place was bare," Rayleen whispered.

"Look who's talking," Daniel said. Derek Ryan was still chirping a tune at the other end of the apartment. Okay, Daniel thought, he's not sullen and he's definitely not paranoid. Paranoids don't let strangers into their house and fix them tea. Derek Ryan seemed simple and friendly. His voice had a pleasant southern tang to it. What was it about the man, the apartment, that put Daniel on his guard?

He stooped to check the books stacked on the floor. As he'd anticipated, there was a selection of Biblical criticism, some philosophy, and a surprise, a book of love poems. Rayleen stood at the fire, her arms outstretched, trying to warm up. The window by the plant was open a few inches. He could feel the draft. "This place is an icebox," he said as he walked over to her. "You could store meat in here." He stood behind her, and glanced up.

And stopped breathing.

His stomach convulsed and his legs turned to gelatin. He closed his eyes, trying not to vomit. The floor began to sway, and he dropped down, catching himself in a squat. He heard Rayleen ask him if he was okay. He didn't answer. Blood pounded in his ears, drowning her voice. He took a deep, ragged breath, nearly choking on the cold air.

He sat down flat on the carpet, eyes closed. He felt her hands on his shoulders, helpless hands. He could do nothing to comfort her. He took another breath, and then shut down. The only sound he could hear was the thunder of blood.

The smell of ammonia jolted him, and he opened his eyes. Smelling salts. He was flat on his back. Derek Ryan knelt over him, holding fingers up. "How many do you see?"

"Move your hand, or I'll break your fingers," Daniel said.

Derek did a double-take, and sat back.

Daniel forced himself up on one elbow. The back of his head was sore. He had done a head-plant when he'd passed out. Daniel was glad the floor was carpeted. "Don't move," Rayleen ordered.

He sat up, fighting off the nausea. "I'm sorry. I'm ill," he said. "I will have to postpone this meeting."

Derek reached out, but Daniel brushed him away. "I have to go now." He stood and stumbled for the door, walking into the hall without waiting for Rayleen. She caught up with him halfway to the stairs.

"Daniel, wait!"

"I passed out," he mumbled.

"I know that. Are you all right?"

Daniel shrugged, starting down the steps. He had a firm grip on the handrail, squeezing as if to tear the rail out of the wall.

"Don't even think you're going to drive," she said, following him. "You don't pass out and then get behind the wheel."

"I have to go now," he said, reaching the bottom step.

"Daniel!" The sound of his name stopped him, but only for a moment. "What is this? What the hell is going on?"

He turned and headed for the car. Fatigue was draining him like a sink with the stopper pulled. He thought of Derek Becker and anger cleared his head for a moment. The whole thing was a game, a sick game. He wanted to know why. He would go to Mordecai Ryan and grab the old man by the throat and demand an answer. "Why me?" he would ask. "Why are you fucking with me?" He would get an answer. He would know the truth.

He started the car and put it in gear. Rayleen grabbed the door and flung herself into the front seat. "What, are you going to leave me here? What's wrong with you?"

"Sorry," he said. "I'll drop you at home."

She made a sound, part growl and part moan. He realized she was crying. His anger didn't disappear, but it slipped into the background, like a fire in the distance. He had scared her. It wasn't his intention. She was a bystander at an accident. She'd been caught in the wreckage. "Sorry," he said. "I have to get away and think this through."

"Think what through?"

He started to tell her, then stopped. How could he say it without sounding crazy? There had to be a reason for what he'd seen, but he couldn't put the pieces together in a way that made sense. He drove on, biting his lip.

"You aren't going to tell me?" she said. "Fine. Keep it to yourself." She sounded like a child then, and he felt ashamed. If he reached her house before explaining, she would fling herself from the car, and he would never hear from her again.

"It was the picture," he said. "The picture on the mantle."

She waited. When he didn't finish, she said, "Okay, I saw it. A woman and a little girl."

Daniel nodded. "My wife and daughter."

XXVI

TO: Thomas Rodgers

FROM: Daniel Bain

SUBJECT: No reason. . .

Dear Thomas,

I just realized that I missed our morning run. Again. I am so sorry. It might appear from my actions that I don't take our workouts seriously. Not so. I have enjoyed the running, and there is simply no way I could push myself the way I have without the benefit of your support, and your competitive drive.

I am going through a crisis of sorts. I realize that since the death of my wife and daughter, I have been in hiding. I am thinking back over the conversations we have had, and I know that you've tried to tell me as much. There have been other indications– I lose my temper at odd times, as if everything that's been covered over or bottled up is breaking loose. Last week I put a hole in my apartment wall. I put dents in my car.

Something is happening now to change me. I feel as if I'm waking from a dream, and the process is painful. I think I liked being asleep. (That sounds dramatic and pitiful, hahaha) But I know that I need to wake up. I need to get back to the real world.

In the course of trying to find the old man's Jesus, I found the guy that Marianne left me for. I haven't confronted him yet. When I do, it will be a sort of closure for me. I think I want to move on.

I want to let the past be the past, so I can start paying attention to the future.

I'll tell you all about it in a few days. In the meantime, I want to pass on running for a day, maybe two. I think I can close this case today. I'll call when it's all over.

Your Friend,

Daniel

XXVII

After he dropped Rayleen off, Daniel raced back to Ft. Collins, jamming the gas pedal of the Hyundai into the floorboard. By the time he was half-way there, he had a plan. He stopped at his apartment, checked his e-mail (no letters) and sent a note to Thomas apologizing for missing another morning run. On the way out, he put a strip of tape at the top of the door to help spot intruders. Then he threw himself back into the car. Time to pay Mordecai Ryan a visit.

The office door to Ryan Enterprises was locked. Daniel rapped on the glass. No one came. He pounded on the metal door-frame and paused, waiting for an answer. Then he hammered again, rattling the door. Open up you bastards, he thought. If he had to call, he would let the phone ring until they were sick of the sound.

Winthrop arrived. Ryan's secretary stood staring through the glass door, hands limp at his side, no expression on his face.

"Open the door," Daniel said.

"What do you want, Mr. Bain?"

"I want you to open the door."

"Mr. Ryan is asleep. He is not to be disturbed."

"Mr. Ryan is disturbed, asleep or awake," Daniel said. Winthrop didn't smile. No sense of humor. "I have what Mr. Ryan hired me for. Wake him up."

Winthrop's face betrayed him at last. His mouth dropped open and his eyes widened. That's it, Daniel thought, as Winthrop pulled the keys from his pocket. Unlock the fucking door. The latch popped, and Daniel yanked on the handle. Winthrop flinched, stumbling back from the door as Daniel swept inside with the wind.

On the way to the elevator, Daniel glanced back at Winthrop. The man scurried to keep up, his arms pinned to his side. Winthrop, he thought. Is that a first or a last name?

Winthrop pushed the elevator button.

"Where does someone get a name like Winthrop?" Daniel asked. "Did your mother say, 'Here is a boy born to service. Let us call him Winthrop'?"

Winthrop stepped into the elevator without answering and pushed the button.

"Second floor, Winthrop."

Winthrop's gaze remained fixed on elevator controls.

Daniel stared at the back of the man's head. I ought to ram your funny little head through the elevator wall, he thought.

When the door opened, Winthrop said, "You will wait here while I wake Mr. Ryan."

Daniel walked down the hall, brushing past him. "And you will kiss my ass."

"Mr. Bain!" Winthrop called. "Have you been robbed of your senses as well as your manners?"

Daniel froze, and then turned around. "My apologies," he said. The tendons on his neck betrayed his effort to appear calm. "I can't help but feel I've been played for a fool here, and since you are privy to Mr. Ryan's plans, you are bearing the brunt of my anger. Please wake the old man up, so I can direct my anger where it belongs."

Winthrop crept past him, his hand to the wall, and scuttled off to the penthouse. Ten minutes later, Daniel had another audience with Mordecai Ryan.

"I have what you want," Daniel started. "I can bring him here tonight."

Ryan huddled under his blankets. He made a show of trying to wake up. He rubbed his eyes, yawned, stretched his spindle arms under the blankets, groaned, and felt at his face with his fingers. "Winthrop tells me you have good news."

"I found your Jesus."

"Where was he?" the old man asked. "What state?"

"Here in Colorado. He has an apartment in Boulder."

The old man barked a laugh, and then sat up. "I'm confused, Mr. Bain," he said. "If he's here in the state, why didn't you bring him?"

"You want to ask him a question, right?"

"Yes. . ."

"Well I have a question for you. Several, actually. Why did you hire me?"

The old man seemed fully awake now. He stared, a slight grin on his face. "I like your work," he said.

"I trace people who skip out on their bills," Daniel said. "I don't do surveillance. I don't use high-tech bugs. I slog through files on my computer. I am to private investigating what a rubber raft is to sailing. Why me?"

"You belittle yourself. . ."

"Listen old man," Daniel hissed. "I know what the game is. I know who Jesus is. He's your son."

Ryan shrugged his frail shoulders. "I am his guardian."

"Why me?"

"Why not?"

"I don't want to fence with you," Daniel said. "I know who your son is. I know what he's done. And I know what his connection is to me. I want to know what you gain out of this. Are you trying to buy me off? Is this supposed to be restitution for my wife and daughter?"

Ryan's coy demeanor disappeared, and Daniel got a glimpse of the businessman, the old blackheart at work. His eyes narrowed to little black points and his wet lips pressed flat. "You're babbling, Mr. Bain. I'll be glad to chat with you, but you need to make some sense. Otherwise, this interview is over."

Daniel stood, a rush of fury burning in the back of his throat. He started to spit the hot words out, but he needed to think. What did he want to gain? He took a deep breath. I want the truth, he decided.

"I've got what you want, so I guess I'll tell you when the interview is over. What happened in 1980? A robber baron turns into a preacher. How did that happen?"

Mordecai Ryan stopped moving. He coughed once. "All right, Mr. Bain. I have no idea what has triggered your anger, but I'll humor you for a few moments. I'm not going anywhere."

He sat up a little, wiggling to the top of his pillow. "I came to Colorado on business. I was trying to diversify, to branch into new investments. I looked at all sorts of schemes. My accountant and I went to Wellington to look at a cattle feed-lot. It was a nice, honest business, a steady business, the sort of thing we looked for. The weather was hot. Not quite a hundred degrees. The smell of manure was oppressive. I felt weak."

"I remember looking up, and the sun swallowed everything. An angel came, and told me that my son was the Christ, come again, and that I was to prepare him for his ministry. That was all. I woke up with the owner of the feed lot kneeling over me, fanning me with his stupid hat." He snorted at the memory. "And I followed the angel's instructions. What else do you wish to know, Mr. Bain?"

"You passed out in a feed lot and dreamed you saw an angel," Daniel repeated.

"A creative rewording of the details," Ryan said. "Have you dismissed my story out of hand?"

Daniel waved him off. "Angelic visitation? Okay. Let's say I believe you. Aside from all of that, you want to talk to your son, and he doesn't want to talk to you. Why didn't you just tell the truth?"

"Your truth has no hook. A hundred thousand dollars, now that's a hook. And I wanted you hooked, Mr. Bain. Were you hooked?"

"This fish wants to know why."

Mordecai Ryan gave another snort. "Bring me the one I sent you for. I'll have a check ready."

Daniel went home and checked his e-mail again. Still nothing. He filled the Hyundai at the gas station and headed back to Boulder.

The case was solved, as far as he was concerned. He thought about the old man's story and decided that Mordecai might have had his vision after all. Perhaps a lifetime of illicit business had eaten at his conscience. Perhaps the years of Biblical scholarship left its residue in a fever dream. Or perhaps Ryan really was visited by an angel.

It was a convenient vision. Derek Ryan would be the Second Coming and a lifetime of scams would be redeemed. The old man built a church, sent his son to theology school, and waited for the end-time. Derek, though, did not cooperate. The son, the key to the old man's vision, had his own agenda, and there was a rift, a schism. The son stopped talking to the father. How could Mordecai convince the boy to accept his proper destiny? The old man had all the money in the world, but the boy was apparently unimpressed by money. So Mordecai Ryan offered the money to a go-between, trusting Daniel to be properly impressed by the cash.

And Daniel was impressed. The kicker was the added incentive of meeting the man who took away his wife and child.

What would the old man say to make things different between his son and himself? Daniel couldn't imagine. Perhaps the meeting would go badly, and the old man would welch on the balance of the fee. It wouldn't matter. The most important thing was to close off the past, to jettison this case. After, he could decide what to do with the rest of his life.

All he needed to do was get Derek Ryan-Becker-Hagan to Ft. Collins. And that would not be a problem.

By the time Daniel reached Derek Ryan's apartment, he was wound up inside, twisted to the point of nausea. He forced himself to walk slowly, and go over once again what he would say. "I'm back," he would explain. "I have a confession to make. You and I have a connection, and it concerns a request I have." He repeated the opening three times on the way, stopped only by the door.

When Derek opened up, the plan disappeared. Daniel threw out an arm, slamming the door open. "Get a coat, freak-show," he ordered. Derek tumbled back into the apartment. "Get a coat and come with me."

"Who are you, and what do you want?" Derek demanded. He straightened up, his eyes meeting Daniel's without flinching. If he was frightened, he was doing a good job of hiding it.

"I'm going to take you to meet your father," Daniel said. "He wants to talk to you. He lives in Fort Collins, and I will drive you there. When you're done with your little reunion, I'll drive you back. Then you'll be finished with me, and you'll be relieved, because you'll have gotten off easy."

Derek shook his head, clearly confused. "My father?"

"Mordecai Ryan. He wants to ask you a question. He's paying me a lot of money to produce you. You will oblige me."

"Friend," he said. "I don't even know who you are. And I'm certainly not going to drive somewhere with you. As for my father, we no longer speak."

"You will speak to him for me."

Derek's mouth narrowed into a pucker. His gaze shot from side to side and then locked on the floor. "I can't stop you from hurting me. That is in your control. But I won't go with you. I have left that part of my life behind, and I will not waste time looking back." He folded his arms, his shoulders hunched, his lower lip extended.

Daniel pointed at the picture over the mantle. "That's my wife Marianne and my daughter Courtney."

Derek Ryan's eyes went white. He started to speak, an angry scowl, but Daniel took him by the arm and dragged him to the door. "You're coming with me," Daniel said, his face just inches away. "You owe me."

The drive back was silent at first. Daniel had no intention of speaking. Ryan twisted in his seat, fingers to his temple, nodding, with an occasional grunt. Then for minutes at a stretch, he would sit absolutely still, staring off in the distance.

Finally, he said, "There's nothing I can do to ease my father's heart."

Daniel shrugged. "I don't care." The highway was a snake. He'd taken this route too often in the last few days. The sun set to the left, burrowing into the mountain tops. Daniel missed the mountains. He loved to hike and camp, and he hadn't gone in a very long time. Too many memories of his wife and daughter to battle. A sudden yearning almost overwhelmed him, and he found himself making a vow.

Derek Ryan hummed to himself.

Well, Daniel thought, I have a captive audience with Jesus. Perhaps I ought to chat. "Can I ask you something?"

"Given our situation, I find it odd that you would ask for permission."

"Why are you rewriting the gospels?"

Derek Ryan blinked. "Well. I suppose I don't think of it as rewriting. I think of it as returning to the original Word, cutting away the editorial intrusions of the gospel-writers, the translators, the editors, and the publishers. Somewhere, the message got lost. I am trying to restate the message, within a familiar framework, so that it cannot be ignored." He steepled his fingers and nodded.

"Is it working?" Daniel asked.

Derek's lips flattened into a frown. "I get e-mail every day. Most of it begins, 'I understand you to mean. . .' or, 'I think what you're trying to say is. . .' And they're never right! Not even close. I have stated my position so that it can't possibly be misunderstood, yet people argue with me about what I meant."

"I have ongoing dialogues with self-styled critics, interpreting what I've written. Marxists and Freudians tell me what I've left out, and how my suppression reveals an agenda. New Historians tell me how twentieth-century culture has infused itself in the rhythms of my lines. Feminists write me hate mail, telling me that Gaea is angry." Derek scowled, and then took a breath. When he resumed, his voice was even, perhaps a little sad. "The truth is, people don't want the truth."

I want the truth, Daniel thought.

Derek continued, his soft, southern drawl stitched with a hint of anger. "But the letters that frustrate me the most come from people who read the scriptures and derive exactly the opposite meaning from what was intended. I write that you must sever the past now, follow the Lord's path now, and I get letters thanking me for helping them to weave the spirit of Jesus into their daily lives, their jobs, their homes. They are all like the man on the road to Jerusalem who said, 'I will follow you, but first, let me say goodby.' They simply will not listen!" He was louder now. His hands jumped in his lap, angry fingers pointing for emphasis.

"I think you're assuming that people use words to communicate. I think they use words to avoid it." Daniel glanced over and smiled. "In fact, you're avoiding communicating now with that little speech of yours. There's a dead woman and a dead child sitting here with us, and you seem to think that if you don't name them, I won't notice it." Derek Ryan stopped, his hands cupped in mid-air.

"I won't help you pretend," Daniel continued. "You don't gain anything by faking reality. You lose. You lose your judgement. You lose your perspective. And if you let others help you fake it, you lose your freedom. You end up needing them to plug the holes in your lie."

Derek leaned closer, putting a hand on his shoulder. "I loved her," he whispered. "But not in the way that you think, friend."

"Get your hand off me."

Derek sat back, a tiny smile at the corners of his mouth. "Tell me, why are you angry with her?"

"She broke her promise to me. And she did it for you."

"She could make her own choices. You didn't own her."

Daniel shifted in his seat. "Fine. She was an adult. What about my baby girl?"

"She was a gift from God. You soil her memory with your anger..."

Daniel swerved to the right, slamming on the breaks. His hand shot out, catching Derek Ryan in the head with the flat of his palm, slamming him against the passenger-side window. Stunned, Derek wavered, and then turned in his seat, offering his other cheek.

"Don't mind if I do," Daniel said, backhanding him.

Derek raised his gaze, sullen and flushed. "Did that do it?" he asked. "Is she back now? Perhaps you can take her somewhere against her will, and interrogate her, and she will love you again."

Daniel willed himself to be still. When he had his breath again, he put the car in drive and pulled back onto the highway.

For the rest of the ride, they were silent. When they reached the parking lot of Mordecai Ryan's building, Derek reached out again, a finger brushing his shoulder. "You're not alone, you know. If you follow in God's path, he is with you, always. . ."

"Well that's the bait, isn't it?" Daniel interrupted. "We're all lonely."

"We were together once," Derek insisted. "The Eden story is about being together with God. We were one. Now we're separated, and we long to reestablish the link. It's the thing we all yearn for. Some people try to fill the hole by buying things. Others. . ."

". . .turn to religion," Daniel interrupted. (And some to politics, he thought, remembering Christine.)

"Don't let yourself be alone because of what has happened."

"But we are alone, aren't we? People have friends, and lovers, and support groups, but the one thing they know, the one thing they can count on is that they're alone. Maybe they have the memory of belonging, of being in the womb, or a memory of nursing. But the moment that they become a "self," the moment they look in a mirror and say, 'That's me!' they stop belonging. Because to be a person means to be a person alone."

Derek sat staring. His father's office building loomed through the windshield. He seemed in no hurry to go inside.

"From the moment we become a person, we fear others, wondering what makes everyone else seem to belong, when we know, we know that we don't belong. So we hide from one another, trying to keep that dirty little secret from getting out. That's why you can't get anyone to listen to you. They're busy hiding, just like you, using words as a shield."

"You're wrong," he said. "You could belong."

"Not and still be me," Daniel said. "There's. . ." He laughed, remembering an old saying. He would repeat it now, because it had been finally revealed as truth. "There's no 'I' in team."

"I'm sorry," Derek said, returning to the soothing voice of a counselor. "You have misunderstood the decisions your wife made, and it has made you turn away." He brushed his bruised cheek with the back of his hand.

"Go inside and talk to your father," Daniel offered. "I'll call it even."

Winthrop answered at the first knock. The three men went straight upstairs. Daniel's heart hammered against his ribs. He had never expected to see the balance of the fee. Now he wondered. Ninety-thousand dollars more. For the first time, he allowed himself to spend some of the money in his mind.

The little corner light was on in Mordecai Ryan's room. He sat huddled under the sheets, strung with his tubes and wires. He recognized Derek immediately.

Daniel started to sit in the corner of the room, but Mordecai pointed a hooked finger at him. "We won't be needing you any more this evening, Mr. Bain. This is a family matter. I'm sure you understand." He turned to Winthrop. "Mr. Winthrop. The check?" Winthrop handed Daniel an envelope, and escorted him back downstairs.

"Goodby Mr. Bain," the secretary said. He locked the door behind him, leaving Daniel alone in the parking lot. Daniel took two steps toward the car before remembering his promise to give Derek a ride back to Boulder. "Fuck him," he whispered. "Let him sprout wings and fly home."

The check was for ninety thousand, five hundred dollars. Daniel took it straight to the ATM, and deposited it in his checking account. Then he headed home. As he approached the parking lot, he found himself looking for Rayleen. Her car wasn't in the lot. He was disappointed, but it was still early. He hadn't checked his e-mail. He might have a letter.

Or he might have scared her off with his feinting spell at Derek Ryan's apartment. The thought chilled him. Maybe she enjoyed his company because he was strong, mature, someone she could depend on. The incident with the picture made him look confused, vulnerable, weak. Maybe she'd discovered that he wasn't what she was looking for.

He stopped, remembering what he had told Derek Ryan just an hour earlier about faking reality. If showing that he was human had ruined everything, then it was for the best. Let it all crumble and be swallowed with weeds. I am who I am, he thought.

He checked his e-mail. No letter. He considered sending her one, but he couldn't think of anything to say. "Thinking of you" was too trite to mean anything. "Come over tonight" was a demand he had no right to make. "Write me please, I'm feeling lonely" was pathetic. And he wasn't feeling pathetic. In the end, he grabbed a beer and planted himself on the bed, back against the corner of the walls.

"I need a television," he thought. "And I need to move out of this dungeon and get a real place." The nine thousand dollars was a windfall. Paradoxically, ninety-thousand seemed less an end in itself, than a stake in something bigger. He could put money down on a house, or go back to school, or expand his business. The money was a beginning, not an end.

Something nagged at him. He sorted through his thoughts, trying to identify the source of his uneasiness. Though he'd struck him, the confrontation with Derek Becker-Ryan was nothing like the violent fantasies that had been the center of his daydreams since the death of his wife. He had beaten his wife's lover senseless a thousand times in his imagination, mixing literary dialogue with one-liners, punches with kicks. Now, his anger was diffused. He took another sip of beer. "Ahhh," he said, imitating Thomas. "I'm attaining closure."

Derek wasn't what was bothering him. Money? The check might not clear. That was a worry, since he was beginning to enjoy the idea of having resources. Mordecai might stop payment if he didn't get satisfaction from his meeting with Derek. But that wasn't the source of his uneasiness either. Daniel had some cash in the bank, and his tastes were simple. He had gotten along well enough without a big bank account.

His stomach growled. "That's it!" he thought. "I'm hungry!" He hadn't eaten since morning, when he'd had the granola, yogurt and fruit with Rayleen. He slid off the bed and headed for the kitchen, glancing at the window curtains as he passed. A chill raced along his back and shoulders.

Eyes. Someone was staring through the window. He stepped up, pulled the curtain, and jumped back in shock. The man behind the glass bared his teeth, slapping at the window pane with his hands.

XXVIII

TO: Daniel Bain

FROM: H. Gerlach

SUBJECT: Associates/Derek Ryan

Dear Mr. Bain,

Enclosed is a list of roommates, study-group members, and possible friends for Derek Ryan. It's a short list. Ryan spent most of his time studying. Everyone I spoke to remembered him as a loner.

Roommates:

Barry Walker

Jeremy Booth

Friends/Study Group Members

James Worthy

Sean Purnell

Seth Jenkins

Aaron Leverington

Hope this was of some help to you. The usual fee?

Harold Gerlach

XXIX

Daniel stumbled away from the window, pulling the curtain shut. He stood paralyzed for a moment. Then fear was replaced with a sudden surge of anger. The day had been, in turns, frustrating, humiliating, and finally, frightening, emotions that came to a head in a single, focused moment of indignation. His home, his little cell, was under assault.

He raced for the front door, undid the bolt, and sprinted outside, rounding the shrubs, arms pin-wheeling with the effort to stay balanced. As the outside of his window came into view, he saw a figure duck behind the far corner of the apartment building, a hundred feet away. Daniel nearly shrieked with frustration. The bastard was running again! He started to give chase, but remembered his open apartment door, left behind in a rush. If he played circle the building, the man might find the open door, and go inside to damage the computer.

Daniel turned back, still sprinting. He would lock the door, and run around to the other side, hoping to catch the intruder. If he was headed off to a parked car somewhere, then he was already gone, and Daniel would never catch him. But if he was circling, he would get what he deserved.

Daniel's keys were in his pocket. He rounded the shrubs, and stopped. A figure blocked his path. He drew back his fist.

"Hey!" Rayleen stood in the open door.

Daniel stopped and let out a deep breath.

"What are you doing?" Her eyes were wide with surprise and dismay. "What's going on?"

"Someone was outside my window, looking in," he explained. "He scared the crap out of me. When I went out, I left the door open."

She glanced around, shivering. "You're weird. No other guy I know would admit he was scared."

Daniel frowned. "Fear is a legitimate motivator."

"I know," she said. "Let's go inside."

"You go in," he said. "I'm going to check the parking lot. Lock up. I have a key."

"Please don't." Her face betrayed her fear. "He got in here once and if something happens to you. . ."

"Nothing's going to happen to me."

"There! Now you sound like every other guy."

Daniel hung his head. "Okay, let's just go inside."

She went straight to the bed and sat on the corner. "You haven't asked me what I'm doing here again."

"I'm glad to see you, so who cares?" he said. "But if you're in the mood for a question, here's one. You were pretty angry with me today, and I still don't know why."

"That's not a question," she mumbled.

He waited. He had been verbally fencing all day, and he did not intend to do it again. Not with her. Anyone but her.

She pointed at the computer, and said, "I brought some programs with me. I thought I'd download some things to help your business."

He nodded, and waited.

"Look, I don't want to talk about today, okay?" Her mouth hardened, and she wouldn't meet his gaze.

"Okay, that's fair," he said.

"And it isn't about you, although you're involved. You got caught in some old business," she said. "Just like I did. It's this whole 'stalker thing.' It pisses me off that I have to change my life because some guy wants to scare me. I jump at noises in my house, and it's my house! Mine! I live there, not him, but he's in my head so much, it's like he moved in with me."

Daniel started to joke, to try to lighten things, but something in her eyes told him she wouldn't appreciate the humor.

"And I'm not mad at you, not really," she said.

"Sounds like you're not sure."

She sighed. "No, I'm not. I don't like having to depend on anyone. And I'm not used to people treating me like you do."

"How is that?" he asked. Had she gone her life without encountering any gallantry?

She looked into his eyes, her voice dropping. "You treat me like a business woman."

He held his face in check, and waited. Then he thought, no, she's not joking. He did think highly of her marketing skills. After all, he'd been taken in by a web site, a marketing scheme. Her marketing scheme. He was forced to admire the person behind the product. Her eyes told him that she was not used to being recognized. The recognition was important to her. He nodded to show that he was listening.

She looked away. He thought she might cry. "Anyway," she continued after a few moments, "the thing is, I hate changing anything for this guy. I didn't even tell my roommates about him."

"What?" Daniel was surprised and a little dismayed.

"I didn't tell them," she repeated. "The guy is fucking with me, not them. I told them we had a break-in, and that some of my stuff was stolen. I told them I worried that they might walk in on somebody robbing the place and get hurt. Lance was worried that it might be somebody after his drugs, so he moved out some of his shit, which is just fine with me. I don't want it in the house anyway. . ."

"But your computer," Daniel said. "What did you tell them about that?"

"I told them I was upgrading," she said. "I got out of that women's shelter early, and went home to clean up. I hauled everything to the dump and bought a new set-up before they got home. Lance helped me put it together when they got back from the mountains."

"You should have told them," Daniel said.

"No! I'm changing everything because of this guy. I hate it. I won't let him win."

"We need to find him. My other case is over. I got the money. I can concentrate on you."

"See?" she said. "That's what I mean. Everything's changed. I don't want your help. I don't want to need your help." Now she was crying, and it enraged her. She buried her face in her hands.

He sat down next to her on the bed and put an arm on her shoulder. He thought of things to say, but words wouldn't change anything. He let her cry.

"Sorry," she said.

"For what? Sometimes all you can do is cry."

She nodded and leaned into him. He put his arms around her. Then she pushed him away, lightly, but with some resentment. "That's what I don't want," she said.

He put his hands in his lap. "Okay."

"See? That's what I mean. You're a nice guy, and you don't try to take over or tell me what to do."

"Well damn me for that," Daniel joked.

"No, you don't understand."

He stood up. "I understand plenty. This guy is in your head, and it's not about you or me. It's about him. He's a sick ticket. We

216

need to get him off the streets. I can help you find him. If it makes you feel less used, you can pay me my standard fee. Like I said, I have the time to concentrate on this jerk." He told her about his second encounter with Derek, how he had taken the son to see his father, and how he'd already deposited the check.

"I hate to tell you this, but the check might not clear."

"I know. But the fact that he wrote it gives me a little leverage. I might be able to collect something from him. In the meantime, I have enough cash in the bank to last a while. And a little extra to splurge. We should go somewhere. This place is too easy for him."

She thought about it for a moment. "Where do you want to go?"

"If it wasn't the middle of November, I'd drag you off into the mountains." Rayleen's roommates, Lance and Michelle, had just come back from a ski resort. "We wouldn't go to a resort. We'd go camping."

"I love camping," she said.

"I'm not sure you'd like it the way I do it. I like to pack in, and camp off-site."

"That's what I do!" she said. "Most of the people who camp stick to park sites. If you go off-site, you can be alone, really alone. No noise, no Winnebagos with televisions, no kids on skateboards. Just the mountains."

"No restrooms."

"Oh whatever, I knew how to dig a hole and squat when I was three. My family went camping all the time."

"You never mention them. Your family."

"Don't start," she warned. "You've pried enough out of me for one night."

"Okay," he laughed. "I do love camping, though. I like to camp near water."

"I love the sound of a river," she said. "It's so peaceful. I went with Lance and Michelle last summer. We packed up behind Chambers Lake. There are a bunch of creeks up there, feeding the lake with runoff. We went halfway up a ridge, and camped right next to one of the creeks. There was a little drop, a tiny little three-foot waterfall that splashed all night. Lance hated it. He said the sound made him want to go to the bathroom." They both laughed.

"Anyway, I just lay there in my sleeping bag that night, listening to the water, looking at the stars. There were so many stars. You don't know how many stars there are until you see them. . ."

". . .without city lights," he agreed.

"Yes! And it was a new moon. . ."

"In August, you can see. . ."

". . .shooting stars! Meteors! They leave tracers in the sky. . ."

"And the Milky Way. . ."

"Yes! Yes! It's so bright, like someone reached up. . ."

". . .and painted it with a brush."

"It was so peaceful," she sighed. "Not to sound psychotic, but the noise in my head stopped, and I could rest. It was like, it was like. . ."

Daniel stood, rigid. He knew what she meant, and he knew what she would have compared it to if she hadn't bit her lip to shut herself up. It was like sleeping here. It was like being with you.

"I love camping," she finished.

"Too bad it's not June. Or even April."

"April? Too cold."

"Let's go someplace warm," he said. "Have you eaten?"

"I had a salad."

"Have you eaten real food?"

She shook her head. He stood up. "Come on, I'll take you to dinner. Then we can decide what to do next."

"I'll drive," she said. "Believe me, if he's out there, he won't be able to follow me."

Daniel left the apartment first, stopping to let his eyes adjust to the night. Though they were alone, Daniel couldn't dismiss the feeling of being watched. He tried to keep an eye in all directions without being obvious. He didn't want to worry Rayleen. He thought he was being discreet, turning his head as if he was stretching, or enjoying the night, but when they reached the car, Rayleen said, "I don't think he's out here."

Behind the wheel, Rayleen was true to her word. They drove west, hitting a stretch of asphalt paved directly over the historic Overland Trail, a covered-wagon route from the days of the early settlers. The road sat at the western edge of town, skirting the foothills, running parallel to Horsetooth Dam. At night, the road was flat and deserted, and a driver could spot the headlights from another car two miles away. Rayleen's car roared over the swells in the road, topping out at sixty, until the empty fields gave way to houses. Turning east, she cut across to the opposite side of town. "Where am I going?" she asked.

He directed her to Bissetti's, a small Italian restaurant in downtown Fort Collins. They had to park a few blocks away and walk in. On the way, he took her arm, and she leaned in, tucking her head in his chest when the wind kicked up.

Inside the restaurant, she stopped and pulled free. Small, intimate tables were topped with candles in wicker-covered wine bottles. Burgundy tablecloths and dark wood gave the room an elegant look. Men in suits and women in evening clothes whispered over crystal wine glasses. "We can't eat here," she said. "I'm a mess!"

She was wearing a knit top that flattered her figure, and a skirt short enough to do justice to her legs. Her wind-tousled hair tumbled over her shoulders, not at all like the hair-sprayed heads that turned to look at them as they stood in the door. "You're lovely," he told her.

She stared at him as if he'd revealed a brain defect. "I look inappropriate," she said.

The restaurant was crowded. The only open spot was a small table for two in the center of the dining room. Daniel noticed that men on either side of them turned to admire Rayleen. She sat quietly, eyes on her menu, arms pressed to her sides. The candlelight caressed her skin. Loving shadows flickered across her face.

". . .something to drink?" A waitress was trying to take an order. Rayleen shook her head. Daniel was relieved. She was underage, after all. He ordered a glass of Chianti and an appetizer. "The calamari are excellent here. Do you know what they are?"

"Squid," she sighed, her eyes locked on the menu.

When the wine came, Daniel took a tiny sip, the flavor playing on the tip of his tongue. He let himself stare at Rayleen, drinking in the sight of her. Her dark eyes were black gemstones, glistening in the candle's flame. She felt his gaze, and slowly lifted her eyes, meeting his. He felt helpless for a moment, unable to express what he was feeling. He took another sip of wine. "Do you know how beautiful you are?" he said at last.

"I'll let my parents know you approve of the gene pool," she frowned. She had caught him staring at her before, and it hadn't seemed to matter. She didn't appear to be comfortable with it now.

The waitress dropped off a plate of calamari, topped with marinara sauce and sprinkles of cheese. Rayleen stared at it, baring her teeth.

"You're not going to try this, are you?" he asked.

"Nope. I will live and die without eating squid. Ever."

"I should have asked first."

"Yes, you should have," she said. She leaned closer, trying to speak without being heard by tables that were paying close attention to her. "Tell me, Daniel. What do you like most about me? Physically, I mean."

He didn't hesitate. "Your eyes."

She nodded, and sat back. "Yes, that's the usual answer. Guys just love my eyes." Her voice was getting louder. "Except that when they tell me how great my eyes are, they're looking at my tits."

Daniel put his fork down. "Fair enough," he said. "But if you had empty sockets, no one would be looking at your breasts. They'd be wondering what the hell happened to your eyes."

She stifled a laugh and tried to frown. "That's so stupid. It's not logical."

A man alone in a booth along the wall watched Rayleen as he ate. He was older, in his fifties. He ducked his chin to shovel in another fork of linguine, chewing slowly, noisily, his lips coated with sauce and his eyes never leaving Rayleen.

Daniel glared, but the man didn't seem to notice. "Did you find something you like on the menu?" he asked, turning back to Rayleen.

She closed the leather menu cover and set it aside. "Actually, I've never been very big on Italian food."

Daniel slumped down in his chair. "I should have taken you to Brian's Diner," he whispered. "Except I've been eighty-sixed there."

"Why? What happened?"

"Just another one of my adventures in chivalry," he laughed. He flagged the waitress, and pulled his wallet out. "I'm sorry," he explained. "It turns out I'm just not feeling terribly well, and I would like to close out my tab."

"Is everything all right?" the waitress asked, frowning.

"Wonderful," he lied, setting a twenty dollar bill on the table top. "Please keep the change. I'm sorry we couldn't stay."

221

The waitress eyed the untouched calamari, Rayleen, and then the money. She smiled. "So sorry you're not feeling well," she said. "Do come back and visit us."

"We didn't have to leave," Rayleen whispered when the waitress was gone. "I could have picked something."

"I wanted you to enjoy yourself and relax," he said. "This is my kind of place, not yours. You're not comfortable here."

She nodded her agreement. "It's so quiet, and everyone's so old. They ought to turn up the music and do shots." She laughed, and he did his best to laugh with her.

On the way out, Rayleen jammed her hands in her coat pockets and raced back to the car. "I'm not really hungry," she said. "Let's just go get a room at a motel somewhere. I don't want to stay at my place, and your place is feeling a little spooky too, with that guy showing up and all. Do you mind? Are you worried about your computer?"

He was worried, but he didn't say so. Rayleen drove east, to the highway that ran south to Denver. The chain motels all had locations at the highway junction. She chose the nicest of them and pulled up to the front door. Daniel started to get out, but Rayleen stopped him. "You stay here," she ordered. "This one's on me." She left the car running.

In the room, Rayleen was quiet, not angry as she had been earlier in the day, but withdrawn. "I'm really tired," she said. "I think I'm going to go to sleep. I hope you don't mind." The room was a double. She pointed at the bed against the wall. "I'll take that one, okay?"

He shrugged.

Daniel wasn't sure what he'd expected, but this wasn't it. He felt terribly uneasy. He started to take his shoes off, and stopped. He sat on the edge of a concrete slab the motel provided as a bed. The bedspread had a yellow floral print splattered with purples. The room smelled of disinfectant.

"Are you going to go to sleep?" she asked. She was already under the covers, her back to him. Her voice came out of the pillow she had buried her head in.

"I don't know," he said. It was ten o'clock. He wouldn't normally try to sleep for another four or five hours. His computer, his diversion, was back in the apartment. He wouldn't have slept well there, not with the memory of the jogger growling at him through the window. Nor would he sleep well here, in a strange room, stretched out on starched sheets with nylon blankets and a bedspread. He poked his finger at a pillow. It was like poking a sandbag.

He stood up. "Will you turn out the lights?" she asked. Her voice was distant, fading. She would be able to sleep, and he would lay on his back in the dark. The room was hot. He checked the thermostat. The air conditioning was on medium. He gave thought to opening a window. When he checked behind the blinds, the window was jammed closed. He tugged at it a few times, but he was making noise, so he left it alone.

Lights off, he stripped off his pants and shirt and climbed into bed. He replayed the events of the day, changing them to suit his mood. This time he caught the jogger trying to run away, and he pummeled him, hammering his head with his fists.

Then he revisited Mordecai Ryan's office building. He was upstairs with Winthrop, walking the hall outside of Ryan's bedroom, grabbing the personal secretary from behind, shoving him into a wall. "I'm tired of you both," his daydream screamed. Daniel opened his eyes. The room was black. He could hear a drunk couple walking down the corridor, past the door, laughing at something.

I'm beating up people in my imagination, he thought. Bad sign. I think I'm feeling helpless. On the face of it, this would be the finest day of my life. I collected ninety-thousand dollars in fees, confronted my wife's lover, and ended up in a hotel room with the most beautiful girl I've ever known. Except that the check might bounce, I'm feeling guilty about hitting Ryan, and the beautiful girl is sleeping in another bed.

He rolled over on his stomach. Rayleen was silent. Good. Let her sleep. He thought about going down to the restaurant lounge and having a beer or two, but he hadn't been drinking as much, and he didn't want to break the new trend simply out of boredom. His stomach growled. He should have had dinner.

He heard her stir. He had been shifting around on the bed. Was he keeping her awake? She shuffled the blankets once, then twice, and finally tossed them aside. He heard her pad over to his bed, felt her pull back the covers, and climb under with him. Thank God, he thought. Maybe now I can get some sleep. She slid next to him, and his eyes jolted open. He could feel her skin, her naked body pressed close, satin and steel wrapping around him. Her breasts trailed across his chest as she reached down, finding the waistband of his shorts, slipping her fingers underneath. She stroked him, sending a shock of pleasure through his body. She lay her head on his chest, flicking her tongue at his nipple.

He reached for her, hungry. She sat up, laughing softly, pulling at him. Then she hovered over him, her breasts close to his face, her nipple trailing over his lips.

He lay back and gasped. He stared at the ceiling as she pressed close, soft, warm, sliding against him. She arched her back, and he cupped her breast, his palm burning at the touch. Then she cooed, and there was something in the sound that stopped him.

He knew. The revelation came in a single instant, complete and irrefutable. He sat up, gently easing her away. "No," he said. "We're not going to do this."

"What's wrong?" she asked, a little out of breath.

"Nothing's wrong. We just aren't going to do this."

"You don't want me?"

The question was a lie. She knew damn well he wanted her. "Don't be ridiculous," he said. "Of course I do. But this isn't what you want, and you're not going to dismiss me like this."

She sat up, and snapped on the desk light. Her hair had fallen in front of her face, and her cheeks were flushed. He couldn't help staring. Her breasts were lovely, perfect. She was angry, and her eyes were molten glass, searing him. "God, you're beautiful," he whispered.

She rolled her eyes and smirked.

"There," he said. "That's just what you want. You want me to say the same things that everyone's always said. Then you can file me away with every other guy you've known. You can tell yourself that I'm just one more man, that all I want is to get laid, and all I see is your body."

He lay back on the pillow, looking away. "You and I are so much alike. We get hurt, and we decide that it's easier to deny love than to go looking for it." He thought briefly of Penny and Christine, and how courageous his sister was.

"I'm a romantic," he said. "I believe love exists, but I figure it's for anyone but me. I tell myself that my one chance at love died, and there will never be another chance."

"You? You're so cynical. Love is a crock. Love doesn't exist. All the while, you're afraid, aren't you? You're afraid love really doesn't exist, and that scares you. Because if it doesn't exist, then there's nothing to live for."

"That's bullshit. . ."

"But it's not enough just to be a cynic, is it?" he continued. She was talking now, arguing, but he talked over her. "You've got to go after happiness with an axe to prove it doesn't exist." She stopped trying to interrupt him, and pulled a sheet up over her breasts. "Every time we share a nice moment, you turn on it. It pisses you off, as if any moment of happiness was a shackle."

"I ruin the theory, don't I Rayleen? I'm a nice guy, and if you got to know me, I might be dangerous. If you could fuck me, you could dismiss me, couldn't you?"

She sat, flushed and angry. He lay still, his body aching for her. Don't look at her, he told himself.

"Do you think that if you say 'no' now, I'll suddenly trust you, and you can have me later?"

He flinched. He had to answer her honestly. "It sounds terrible, doesn't it?" he admitted. "And part of that is true, I guess. But there's something else. . ."

"There's nothing else," she said, standing up. He stared. Her body was a sculpture. Or maybe a weapon. "Don't spend a lot of time thinking about it. I thought you were a lonely old guy who could use a fuck." She climbed under her covers, and turned her back to him.

He shut off the light. His insides were contracting, crumbling. This is pain, he thought. Welcome back to the world of the living.

"There is something else," he said to the dark. "You and I made a connection somewhere along the line. You can say we didn't, but you're lying. I know what you're thinking a lot of the time, and you've got a pretty good idea what I'm thinking. We finish each other's sentences. We share things, our thoughts, our pasts, and the rest of the world is not invited. And when we're uneasy, we look to hide with each other. So don't tell yourself that there's no such thing as intimacy. We were intimate the day we met. Whether we make love or not has nothing to do with it."

Then he was silent, but his last words echoed in his head, and he realized that he believed them. A wave of shock passed through him, and he reeled in the dark with the force of the epiphany.

After Marianne, he thought he would never open up to anyone again. He had been wrong.

XXX

TO: Daniel Bain

FROM: Dee Taylor

SUBJECT: Frozen Account

Dear Mr. Bain,

It is our bank's policy to send form notification when an account irregularity occurs, and you will be receiving such a form. Given the large size of the deposit you made, I thought it prudent to notify you by e-mail. I tried to call as well, but have been unable to reach you by phone.

The check you deposited from Mr. Mordecai Ryan will not clear his bank. His account has been frozen, and his bank is refusing payment. Perhaps you can reach Mr. Ryan, and come to other accommodations.

I hope this additional information is useful. If there is anything else I can do to service your account, please feel free to call.

Dee Taylor, Account Executive

XXXI

Daniel came out of the grocery store with a carton of yogurt in one hand and a house plant in the other. The brown and white ceramic pot was nice, but he'd chosen the Boston Fern because he'd seen one in Rayleen's apartment. When he climbed into the car, she glared at the plant without comment.

Daniel sat on the passenger side, wondering what to say. Rayleen drove in silence. They hadn't exchanged two sentences since the sun came up. He felt their friendship was damaged. He wanted to tell her that it made him sad to think so. He tried different phrases, sorting through them as the car raced closer to his apartment. The morning sun was sharp and bright. Leftover snow from the last batch of flurries would be gone by the afternoon.

The parking lot came too soon. He gave up on clever words in despair. "Hey?"

She glanced his way.

"I'm afraid that our friendship might have been damaged by last night. It makes me sad to think that."

She parked her car and closed her eyes. "Me too. I owe you an apology for what I said. It was rude."

"We're friends. You get to be rude," he said. She had parked near enough to his apartment to see the front door from the car. "Hey," he said again.

"What?" There was still a touch of irritation in her voice.

"My apartment door is open." He hopped out of the car. "Stay here," he ordered.

She opened her door and followed him. "Like I ever listen to you. . ."

Had the intruder at the window returned? Was the intruder the jogger? Daniel raced to the door and stepped inside. The bright sun was blinding, and he needed a moment to adjust. Two men stood over his computer. They wore suits, one charcoal grey, the other navy blue. They had short haircuts, trim figures, and ears that lifted away from the sides of their heads like wings on an airplane. "Daniel Bain?" they asked.

"Who are you?" He walked past the computer desk and turned.

A wallet opened, giving him a glimpse of an I.D. "We're with the Internal Revenue Service."

"Let me see your warrant," Daniel said. Rayleen stood in the kitchen, watching.

"Do you know a Mr. Mordecai Ryan?" the one in the blue suit asked.

"Yes, I did a job for him," Daniel said. "Let me see your warrant."

"Do you know what money-laundering is, Mr. Bain?" the one in the gray suit asked.

Daniel shrugged. "Lots of money and a box of Tide. Show me your warrant."

The two men looked at each other and then back at Daniel. "Do you know how many years you're looking at? You can say goodby to your daughter there. She'll be a grandmother by the time you get out."

Grey Suit waved a piece of paper. "Here's all the warrant you deserve. You've been doing high-volume transactions with that old bastard. Nine-thousand, something. Amateur move, by the way.

The government tracks anything over five thousand dollars. Then you deposit ninety-thousand more. What did you do for the cash?"

"Payment for services rendered. I found Jesus for him."

"What a smart-ass," Grey Suit said. "You're shooting yourself in the foot, cowboy. You want to tell us anything that could help you?" They began to advance around the table, Grey Suit first.

"I want to tell you that you need a warrant," Daniel said.

Grey Suit kept talking, poking Daniel's in the chest. Daniel moved suddenly, shoving two fingers into the man's trachea. Grey Suit fell back against the wall. The man in blue tried to step in, but Daniel pushed harder into Grey Suit's throat, gagging him. "Back up!"

Blue Suit backed up a step, sliding his hand into his jacket.

He's bluffing, Daniel thought. If he had a gun, it would already be out. "Go ahead. If I see a gun, I'll crush his windpipe."

Blue Suit stood still, his hand in his jacket, his face like a white fence. Grey Suit slid down the wall, thrashing. Daniel followed him with his fingers, pinning his throat.

Blue Suit opened his coat. No gun. "You're hurting my partner," he said, anguish suddenly animating his face. "Let him go." He turned to Rayleen. "Stop him. . ."

"Daniel?"

Grey Suit sat flat on the floor, back to the wall. He tried to roll out of Daniel's hold, but Daniel grabbed him by the ear with his free hand. "Don't move around, Van Gogh," Daniel threatened, giving the ear a tug.

"You can be prosecuted for this, you know," Blue Suit said. "You're making a terrible mistake."

"Really? I don't think so," Daniel said. "You boys don't have a warrant. You're 'off-sides.' I'm like a quarterback with a free shot at the end-zone." He tugged on the man's ear again. "How about you?" he asked cheerfully. "Are you going to file a complaint on me?"

231

Blue Suit turned to Rayleen again. "He's hurting Bob. . ."

"Daniel, these guys are Feds. . ."

"I don't think so. I think they're free-lance. I think the people that hired them will be angry when they find what fuck-ups they are." Bob tried to pull loose again, so Daniel pushed his fingers deeper into his throat.

"Please. . ."

"Let him go, Daniel."

Daniel stopped pushing. He could let the man go without much risk. The partner was more of a threat, but he didn't seem to want a confrontation. Daniel took a deep breath and stood up, releasing his hold.

"Are you all right Bob?" The man in the blue suit knelt by his partner's side and grabbed his shoulder.

Bob coughed, clutched his windpipe, then rubbed his sore ear. Finally he nodded, patting his partner's arm. "I'm okay," he whispered.

Rayleen brought Bob a glass of water. He sipped it gratefully, pausing to cough again.

"You two need to get out of here," Daniel said.

"We're leaving. Just give us a moment, will you? My partner is trying to breath."

"Breaking and entering is against the law."

"The door was open, for Christ's sake. We knocked, and came in because no one answered. We were here for all of fifteen seconds before you came busting in. . ."

"It's my apartment."

Bob struggled to his feet with his partner's help. "We're leaving now. But this isn't over." The two men walked out without another word, Bob leaning heavily on his partner for support. After a few moments, Daniel went to the door and shut it.

"What was that?" Rayleen asked.

"They were breaking and entering. . ."

"I mean, why is the IRS after you?"

Daniel did some quick calculating. The IRS had Mordecai Ryan under observation. They thought he was helping the old man hide cash. Or, the two men weren't agents at all, and they were shaking Ryan down for cash. They had been fairly inept, after all. Then he remembered that while researching the case, he'd found a lien on Ryan's property. Maybe the old man was in serious trouble with the government. Maybe Ryan's past was catching up with him. Or maybe the government was after him because he had money. And a church.

"I don't know." He grunted. "That break-in I had? Somebody was in my files, right?" She nodded. "I'm wondering if these guys have been here before."

"What about your night visitor?" she asked.

He shrugged. "I don't know." He couldn't be certain that the man at his window had been the jogger.

She sighed. "We didn't even need to go to the motel, did we?"

"Maybe not," he said.

"It didn't have to. . ."

"Nope, it could have been. . ."

". . .different," she finished.

"Are you going to get in trouble?" she asked. "For hurting that man?"

"They didn't have a warrant," he said. "Then again, they say they're the IRS. So who knows?" He sat down at the desk, his legs weak with the flush of adrenaline. "What now?"

"I don't know," she said. "I guess I should go home."

"You don't have to."

"I have to eventually. I can't stay out of my own house because some asshole wants to bully me."

Daniel considered telling her to stay. He wanted her to stay. He didn't think she was safe, not yet. But what could he tell her? He had nothing but a hunch to argue with. Besides, she'd had enough of his chivalry, and she never listened to him anyway.

"It's not like I'm alone," she said. "I can tell my roommates. Lance is a pretty tough guy."

Daniel chuckled. She stood still, and he realized that she was ready to leave. "You're going right now?"

"Yes." She brushed the hair from her eyes. "I probably won't be over for a while."

"Don't lose touch," he said, suddenly feeling as if he was saying goodby.

"I won't," she said, sounding like goodby.

She gave him a quick kiss on the cheek and left. He watched her walk to her car. Then he sat at the computer, staring at the sun beams through the window. His heart was aching, he decided.

The new plant waited on the kitchen counter. He ought to find a place for it. The computer desk was too full, and that was a workspace anyway. The window ledge was too narrow. There were no end tables, no night stand next to the bed. There was no point in an end table without a couch, but a night stand would be a good idea. He really ought to get one of those.

Walking the apartment, plant in hand, he decided that there were too many strikes against them. Age didn't seem to matter when they were alone, but he didn't fit in her social circles. He'd been miserable at her party. And she didn't fit in his world. Was she any less miserable on their dinner date?

He replayed the conversation from the night before. If he had it to do over, he'd have told her that she couldn't have it both ways. She couldn't separate sex and her soul for marketing purposes without getting confused when it came to personal relationships.

He placed the plant in an open corner behind the desk, but the file cabinet blocked it from view, and no sunshine would ever find it there. It wouldn't survive. There just wasn't any place for the plant in the apartment. He put it back on the kitchen sink and left it.

He couldn't ignore her career, could he? The events of the past days left him little time to consider what she did for money. He wanted to believe that he was not a judgmental man, but how could he have a serious relationship with someone who posed nude for tens of thousands of Internet watchers?

He was an Internet watcher, of course.

He slumped down in the chair. "Oh my God," he whispered.

She was just a girl, a mixed-up girl. He was older. He was supposed to be wiser.

Everything tumbled in the rush of a single moment. Marianne's death. Courtney's death. Two years of hiding. His lost career. The idiocy of playing detective, chasing after Jesus, chasing a girl a decade too young for him. Gospel. Pornography. A single cry burst from his lips, raw and confused. He covered his eyes, hiding for just a moment. Then he sat up, nodding.

The sun had moved across the sky by the time he had it straight in his mind. A little distance between them was a good idea. How could he do the right thing for her if he was so twisted up in his own problems? He'd been a zombie for two years. Now he was awake.

He didn't regret meeting her. He'd been convinced that there was no more trust left in him, and he'd found himself opening up to her in curious ways. It said a lot about the possibility for love.

In the meantime, he had real problems. He would probably be arrested for assault. The man in the suit had been jabbing him in the chest. Both men had advanced on him, in his house, without presenting a warrant. No matter. Government employees did whatever they were not prevented from doing. And to anyone investigating

Mordecai Ryan, Daniel Bain was a peripheral player. They would hurt him if they could.

He missed Rayleen, but that was fallout from two years of solitary confinement. He needed to do what was right for her. He could still help her, though. He could do something tangible.

He turned on his computer and went to work. He would find out who was terrorizing her. He slipped her backup file into the drive and began looking. She kept profiles, personal notes on anyone who'd written her. Perhaps the jogger had corresponded with her over the net, and she'd made notes, something for her marketing plan, something he could recognize and use.

The customer file was extensive. He began with the "A's," checking the personal information. There were notes culled from e-mails, followed by "strings," automatically accessed phrases that would be added to a bulk mailer, tailored specifically to each customer. One man had written that he loved the scenes in the videos that depicted fellatio. The first string said, "I know what you like, Brent, and this video is for you!" The second string said, "I remember your letter, and thought of you when I filmed this one, Brent!"

Daniel flipped ahead to the "B's," and clicked onto his own data. The personal information stated, "Owns his own business." The first string said, "By the way, how's your business going?" The second string said, "Hope your business is keeping you busy!" Daniel stared. "Wow," he muttered. "I was pretty fucking exciting."

There had to be a way to limit the number of files he went through. The obvious one was location. The jogger was likely a Colorado resident. He did a search, eliminating out of state customers, and found himself down to two hundred files. He had all day. He would slog his way through the list. He stayed in the "B's," crossing off names from a master list as he searched.

The file on Ronald Baird had the notation, "Loves to watch. Creep." Daniel wrote the name on the pad. Baird lived in Littleton, a suburb of Denver. Certainly within driving distance of Boulder.

Jeremy Booth was a "Theology student. Tried to save me." The strings said, "Hope you find your church, Jeremy, but I hope you don't stop writing," and the more provocative, "This video will RE-ALLY make you see God!" Daniel wrote that name down too. Then he thought of Derek Ryan.

He jumped to the "R's," looking to see if Derek Ryan had purchased any videos. He hadn't. Nor had Derek Becker, or Derek Hagan. Daniel hadn't really expected to find those names on the list, but he was playing a hunch, and sometimes his hunches paid off. Checking further, Daniel found no listing for Mordecai Ryan.

He turned back to the notepad. Jeremy Booth. The name seemed familiar. He ran a check, looking for information. He had the man's social security number, courtesy of Rayleen's records, so the check was easy. He had been, as her notes stated, a theology student. Booth had attended a college several years earlier, though he had not graduated. Daniel started to take notes, places and dates, but his pencil froze on the pad. He did a quick check, first in Derek Ryan's file, and then in an e-mail he had saved.

The connection was there. He didn't know what it meant, but the connection screamed at him from the page. Derek Ryan and Jeremy Booth were roommates at college. He put the pencil down, and stared at the screen. There was no mistaking it. The solitary Mr. Derek Ryan-Becker-Hagan, the Second Coming of Christ, with two roommates and a handful of friends, knew Jeremy Booth and lived with him. Was Jeremy Booth the jogger? Daniel believed so, with nothing more than coincidence and a hunch to go on.

He found Booth's address. Then he went to an on-line street atlas, one of the new programs that Rayleen brought him, and plotted the location. No surprise. He lived a few blocks from Rayleen in one direction, and a few blocks from Derek in the other direction. The shape of the three locations was an imperfect triangle, but as Daniel printed off the map, the triangle became a perfect form in his mind, three equal sides, the geometric symbol he would use to uncover and expose the truth.

Daniel had seen the jogger on several occasions, and the jogger had definitely seen him. Daniel could drive to Boulder and confront the man. A simple face-to-face at his door should confirm or deny the theory. If Jeremy Booth was the jogger, Daniel would leave and report the matter to the police. And if they were a little slow to react, he would retain a lawyer to push the issue.

Unless, of course, the jogger attacked him, in which case he would hurt the man.

It was still early afternoon. The jogger was likely working. Daniel didn't want to make the drive and then wait for hours with nowhere in town to go except her house.

If Booth was the culprit, Daniel did have a question for him. What was Booth's connection to Derek Ryan? Was he doing bidding for Mordecai?

The thought of the old man soured Daniel's stomach. Mordecai had never answered the question, "Why did you hire me?" Daniel had a link to Derek's past, and perhaps a link to his present. It was a puzzle that fit together nicely, but gave no real picture. It revealed nothing.

"I need to know the truth," he whispered. He would pursue the mystery until he had an answer.

He took a short break to check his e-mail. There was a letter from his bank, telling him that Ryan's check was not going to clear. The ninety-thousand dollars was gone.

Daniel threw on a coat, jabbing his arms into the sleeves, cursing. He would make one more trip to Ryan's office building. There would be a reckoning. He was out of the apartment in a moment, slamming the door behind him.

He tried to start the car, but the engine wouldn't fire. He slammed both palms into the dashboard, raging. A sound to the left warned him. A young girl from the apartment complex, no more than six, was standing in the parking lot holding a Barbie and a small bag full of doll clothes. She stared at Daniel, frightened.

He rolled down the window, and smiled. "Sorry I scared you," he croaked. "I was mad. Not at you, though. Sorry."

The girl turned and ran away. Daniel put his head on the steering wheel. He was angry at Mordecai Ryan, not for the money, but because the old man had made a fool of him, pulling him in as a pawn in an elaborate, inexplicable game. And Daniel had a right to be angry.

But by the time he reached the office building and found the doors chained and padlocked, by order of the Internal Revenue Service, the anger was gone. Mordecai Ryan had his own problems.

Daniel stood in the parking lot, hands jammed into his pockets. A cloud cut across the sun, and the wind crept into his collar, chilling him. He saw Winthrop out of the corner of his eye, sitting in his car, staring at the office doors. Daniel walked over to the car, a gray late-model Ford, and tapped.

Winthrop cracked the window and said, "I can't help you with your check, Mr. Bain."

"I know that," Daniel said. His voice was calm, even melancholy.

Winthrop rolled the window down a little more. "I'm out of a job myself," he said.

Daniel nodded, staring at the office building. "Winthrop, I'm going to ask you a question. You might know the answer, and you might not. You might choose not to tell me. But if you know, and if you can tell me, it would give me a great deal of satisfaction. Why did Ryan choose me for this job?"

Winthrop shook his head. "I won't be able to give you any satisfaction."

Daniel sighed. "You see, two years ago, my wife and daughter left me to go be with Derek Ryan."

"I know," Winthrop said. "That little dalliance was the reason for the animosity between Mr. Ryan and his son."

"Really?" Daniel was surprised. "I had thought that maybe Derek didn't want the burden of his father's plans."

"No," Winthrop laughed. He rolled the window down a few more inches. "Derek was perfectly fine with his father's vision. They conversed about it all the time. Two self-important fools, if you ask me. The trouble came when Derek decided he to save the world with someone else's wife and child at his side. Mordecai wouldn't allow it, said that it was a sin. Derek blathered on about female disciples and other such nonsense." Winthrop rolled his eyes for emphasis.

"Derek finally left the church," he continued, "and moved down to his father's old office in Texas. When the word came that the woman and child had died, Mordecai was inconsolable. He felt that Derek had committed an inexpiable sin, something unforgivable, and the wrath of God would surely come next. It nearly killed him." He shook his head.

"He's dying now, isn't he?"

"They gutted him like a fish. Pardon the indelicate phrase, but it's most accurate, isn't it? He mutters about being the 'living dead,' and by God's Blood, he is a corpse, isn't he? It's horrible what medical science can do in the name of healing." His lips curled back in a sneer. Daniel wasn't sure if his words were directed at Ryan, or at doctors, or at the world in general.

"Why the game? Why was I looking for Christ, instead of the old man's son?"

"Why indeed?" Winthrop shrugged. "He believes the boy is Christ. And he's a manipulator. And he's as crazy as a loon. Pick an answer."

"Why did he hire me?" Daniel repeated.

Winthrop rolled the window down all the way and leaned his head out. "After your wife's death, the two never spoke. Guilt? Anger? I never understood it. Derek moved out of his father's apartment and we lost track of him. He stopped using his father's name. He didn't need to work. When he went to Texas, he cleaned out his bank accounts. He had some cash, enough to be comfortable and lay low."

"We tried investigation services. They are notorious for taking monthly checks and feeding bits of false hope in return. Mr. Ryan wanted to hedge his bet. He tried several approaches at once, a 'shot-gun' strategy,' if you will. He even tried psychics, if you can imagine that. And he wanted to hire someone small, someone hungry, a skip-tracer."

"When we hired you, we went to the phone book and started combing through the process-servers and skip-tracers, the Double-A agency and the Triple-A agency and so on. Mr. Ryan became impatient and told me to flip ahead, and get someone from the 'B's.' You were there first, Mr. Bain."

Daniel shook his head. "You hired me because my name started with the letter 'B'. . ."

"I told you the answer wouldn't be satisfactory."

"But surely you checked on me. . ."

"No, not at all," Winthrop laughed. "The whole thing is a coincidence. Mr. Ryan had no idea who you were. The night you came barging in, demanding to know everything, Mordecai had me look into your background. We had one of your competitors check you out. When Mr. Ryan found out who you were, he was flabbergasted. He told me, 'It's a sign!'" Winthrop laughed again, a cackle this time. "Who's to say? Maybe it is. It's quite a stunning coincidence, really."

"So you got fired?" Daniel asked.

"Oh no!" Winthrop said, smirking. "Mr. Ryan can't pay me what he was paying me, not with his funds tied up. So I've quit. I have secured another position in advance. . ."

Daniel turned and walked away, not bothering to say goodby. Winthrop was a mean-spirited little man. Life was too short to squander any more of his attention on smirks and cackles.

It was time to drive to Boulder and meet Jeremy Booth, but he'd been in such a hurry to see Ryan that he'd left the map and the address behind. He had to return to his apartment.

When Daniel pulled into the parking lot, he saw a squad car. Two uniformed officers stood at his apartment door. The IRS agents had complained.

Daniel left the car and approached the officers. They seemed startled by him, so he slowed down, not wanting to alarm them. "You gentlemen are here to see me," he declared. "I'm Daniel Bain."

The officer in front, a thin, blond-haired man in his twenties, pulled his weapon from his holster, extending the gun with both hands. "Put your hands in the air," he said. Daniel was calm, and despite the barrel pointed his way, he didn't flinch. At least he was dealing with pros. The other officer drew his weapon as well. Daniel put his hands on top of his head and turned slowly to face the wall at the entrance to his apartment.

"Put your hands behind your back, please," the smaller officer said. Daniel complied, and the officer cuffed him.

The second officer, a tall, muscular black man in his late thirties or early forties, pulled a radio speaker from his sleeve. "We've got him," he said.

Daniel shook his head. He shouldn't have hit the agent. He should have known better. The court wasn't going to take his word against the word of two Federal employees. Perhaps Rayleen would back him up. If he was lucky, he could make bail and no lasting harm would be done. He certainly didn't want a felony assault on his record.

The smaller officer chanted the Miranda litany. Daniel nodded his way through the questions, declining a lawyer. "I don't need one," he said. "I don't have anything to hide." He glanced out at the parking lot and then back at the arresting officers. Several things registered in his mind simultaneously. More police cars had pulled in behind him. Another three officers raced up the walk from the far side of the apartment building. Meanwhile, the thin, blond officer was crowding him. Daniel felt a sudden jolt of fear.

The black officer was talking, but Daniel didn't understand the question. Too much was happening at once. "What the hell?" he muttered. "It was self-defense."

The blond officer grabbed him by the back of the neck and shoved his face into the wall, pinning him. "Really? Well at what point did self-defense become torture? Was it when you burned her fucking eyes out?" He shoved Daniel's teeth into the wood slats.

Daniel turned his head, and spit blood. "What am I being charged with?" he demanded. The answer occurred to him a moment before the officer responded.

"You're being charged with the murder of Rayleen Rogers."

XXXII

Http://www.truthzhammer.com

Heaven's Kingdom is like the field of wheat,
visited by an enemy at night,
who sowed weeds into the good seed and left.
When the wheat sprouted and bore heads of grain
the tares, the enemy's weeds, sprouted too.
The slaves asked their master, "Didn't you sow
good seed in your wheat field? Why then the tares?"
The master said, "An enemy did this."
The slaves asked, "Shall we pull the weeds up?"

"No," he replied, "Lest you damage the wheat.
For now, allow them to grow together.
Come the harvest, I will tell the reapers
to gather the weeds in bundles for pyres,
then gather the wheat to my granary."

"Harvest will mark the end of the seasons,
and ledgers will mark the fate of the wheat,
the Enemy's sabotage made useless.
As for the tares, we will char the bundles,
a conspiracy of weeds set ablaze."

XXXIII

The police stuffed Daniel into the back seat of the patrol car. "I want a lawyer," he said, and then he was silent. He remembered the disfigured rag doll in Rayleen's apartment and he could hear the officer's words, "burned her fucking eyes out." He knew what had happened. There was nothing to be done.

He stumbled through the next three hours, a jagged assortment of moments to be survived. They took his picture and repeated his rights. He sat alone in a holding cell while a dozen officers talked past him. "Give this son-of-a-bitch the same," one said, peering into the cell, his face a flesh balloon squeezing between the bars, disfigured, ready to pop.

From the holding cell, he could see a television. Two men and three women moved through a plot involving a dog and a dresser, played to the frantic beat of a laugh track. Daniel tried to watch, to make sense of the story, anything to divert his attention, but the scenes he watched refused comprehension. He could not string the fragments of action into anything resembling a continuous narrative.

A court-appointed lawyer in a puckered brown suit appeared, chain-smoking Camels. He sat close to Daniel, his face hovering inches away, whispering in confidence. He seemed intent on finding what information Daniel could trade for a plea bargain. The ash at the end of the cigarette grew, a full inch of curved, filthy gray, poised to fall.

The room had a wooden table and a two-way mirror on the back wall. A guard stood in the corner while two cops interrogated him. "Listen to me," Daniel explained. "Jeremy Booth! He lives in Boulder. I think that's who killed her. He was stalking us both."

"So you like young girls?" The lead cop sat in his chair, studying his nails. He had dark, curly hair, and a battered nose. His eyes were small black pellets that darted to his older partner, a fat, graying cop in his sixties.

"There are two ways to verify what I'm telling you," Daniel said. "I checked Rayleen into a women's shelter two, no, three days ago. My sister can verify that. Her name is Penny Bain. She's in the book. And check your own field records. You took a report on a breaking and entering Monday afternoon. The cop didn't want to take a report, but I made him do it."

"Did you fuck her?" the younger cop asked. "Or did she tell you to kiss off? Is that what this was about?"

"The guy ransacked her apartment! He smashed her computer, and he burned the eyes out of her rag doll. . ." Daniel's voice broke. The lawyer put a hand on his shoulder.

"The neighbor who reported the murder called it in as a noise complaint," the detective said. "She told the dispatcher that the screaming had gone on for ten minutes, and she wasn't going to stand for it any more. Ten minutes." The lawyer took his hand back.

Daniel focused on the detective's rumpled nose. "Fuck your black heart," he said.

"What?" the detective asked, his brows frowning in sudden interest. Daniel glared back, silent.

The questioning ended abruptly. Daniel's lawyer left, promising to contact him soon. The detective with the rumpled nose helped escort Daniel to his cell. As the guard drew back the door, someone hit Daniel in the ear, dropping him to the concrete floor. The guard carried him inside.

When the throbbing stopped, Daniel pulled himself up to the cell window, and stared through the glass at the stars. He would not be convicted of this crime because he didn't do it. But the stink of the accusation might hover over him. He banished the worry with a single thought. Ten minutes. The jogger had tortured her. When the idiots who were investigating the crime stopped congratulating themselves and released him— they would have to release him!— he would seek retribution. He would avenge her.

Then, alone in his cell, the realization of what had happened seized him, and took his breath away. For a few minutes his anguish was unbearable. Alone, without an audience, he wept hot, bitter tears.

The long hours came creeping across the cold cement floor. He tried to sleep, but ugly images crawled behind his closed eyes. Instead, he sat on the cot, staring at the black window pane. After a while, he found that he was too exhausted to cry. Grief gave way to a numb depression.

He searched back over the past week, wondering where the lesson was. Surely there was a plan, a reason for the string of events. Like dominoes, each event had triggered a subsequent event, and the final heavy domino had dropped on Rayleen, crushing her.

Perhaps it was silly to view her as an innocent, but there it was. She was a confused young lady. She was afraid that love did not exist in the world, and she spent her energy proving she was right, all the while wishing that she was wrong.

Still, she hurt no one with her lifestyle, and she'd had a great bursting entrepreneurial talent that amazed him. When he started his own business, he'd imagined himself clever enough to carve an empire, reinvesting his profits until he'd reinvented private investigation. Beer dreams. She was the real deal, and he knew the difference.

And she could be kind. He recalled Rayleen with her party guests, attentive to everyone, acknowledging everyone.

She was also vulnerable. Maybe a world numbed by violence tolerated atrocities, or perhaps it simply couldn't prevent them. Either way, there would always be victims. Rayleen was open to attack, and Daniel couldn't protect her, not without violating her himself. He could have demanded that she stay with him, that she submit to his protection, but how different would the cure be from the disease?

His thoughts did not ease a sickening sense of guilt.

The morning hours ticked past. A comedy played itself out down the hall. One prisoner gibbered incoherent phrases, bits of senseless English. Another prisoner tried to shout him down. "Shut up! Shut the fuck up!" The detention center was a noisy rumble of a building. The staff worked through the night, and the serenity of the prisoners was not their concern. Daniel welcomed the muttering and the shouts, his only diversion.

Through the early morning hours, Daniel sat with his back against the wall, his neck stiff with fatigue. He dozed for a few minutes at a time, but there would be no real sleep. He entertained the possibility that he might be convicted of Rayleen's murder. It was the stuff of movies, but he was tired, and his mind would not function on a logical level. Ugly consequences slipped into his dreams, ending with the sudden snap of the neck, head erect, his burning eyes open in the dark. When the sun came, he stopped dozing.

Breakfast was a scoop of eggs, a piece of toast, and a dry slice of ham. He poked at the food, and put it aside. His throat was raw, and he couldn't swallow.

By mid-morning, his head pounded, and his eyes had swollen nearly shut. He didn't notice the guard that came to let him out until he heard the cell door lock.

"You can go," he said.

Daniel squinted at the guard. "What's the story?"

The guard pointed down the hall, and stepped back.

The detective who had interrogated him was at the cell gate to greet him. "You got in touch with the women's shelter?" he asked.

250

The detective's eyes narrowed. He gave Daniel a faint smile. "They never heard of you."

Daniel stopped. "Did you talk to my sister? Penny Bain?"

The detective shook his head. "No. Spoke with the shelter representative, though. The victim stayed there for a night. She was referred by a woman, not your sister."

"Christine?"

"I don't remember the name. We checked it out. She never heard of you."

Daniel swayed in place, trying to avoid the glare from a window above the cell gate. "Then you found the breaking and entering report?"

The detective nodded. "The officer remembered you very well. He said you were a smart-assed prick."

"Yeah, I'm a bad guy," Daniel whispered. "So why am I getting out?"

"Don't have enough evidence to charge you. Yet. We will. You're in the hot seat, there's no doubt about that."

"What about Jeremy Booth?"

"Oh yes. The 'stalking jogger,' right? You didn't know anything about the murder, and then suddenly, you knew who committed it."

Daniel sagged as he stood. "Listen, I need a shower. Either take me home, or put me back in the cell. Either way, fuck yourself." As he said the words, his head began to throb again. They'd hit him once already, hadn't they?

The detective laughed in his face. "I'm going to love watching you fall for this, Bain. You're a nasty motherfucker, and you're going down."

"Take me home," Daniel said.

The detective stepped aside and pointed at a window down the hall. "You can get your personal things there. There's a phone at the entrance if you want to call a cab."

Daniel nodded, choking back the bile. He was angry, but the detective wasn't worth the consequences of losing his temper.

Cab service was slow. While he waited, Daniel tried to plan. He would drive to Boulder after he slept for an hour or two. The morning sun reminded him that he had not run with Thomas. Again. How many days was it? He went back to the payphone. He needed to talk to Thomas. His friend was a pastor. He needed to hear the voice of spiritual authority on the death of young girls.

Thomas answered the call. "It's me," Daniel said, rushing his words to include an excuse. "I missed the workout this morning, but I had a hell of a reason. I really need to talk to you. . ."

A sound in the background at Thomas's end startled him. A sob? "It doesn't matter," Thomas said. "I wasn't there either." He sounded angry, distracted.

"Is this a bad time?" Daniel asked.

"Yes, actually, it is."

"Okay," Daniel said, thinking to hang up. Then he stopped. Thomas sounded genuinely angry. He couldn't afford to lose another friend. "I'll let you go," he said, "but I really couldn't make it today. I was in jail."

Thomas was speaking. ". . .so I have to go now. We're battling a personal tragedy here."

"What's wrong, friend?" Daniel asked.

Pause. "They found my daughter. The one who ran away."

Daniel started to congratulate him, but clearly, there was no celebration in his voice. He waited.

Thomas started to speak again. His voice cracked. "They found her dead. They killed my daughter. My little Rayleen."

"I'm coming over," Daniel said. He hung up the phone.

Outside, the bright morning sun blinded him. He sat down on the curb to wait for the cab. He knew what the phone call meant. He had another piece of a puzzle, a full picture, still without meaning, without sense. He shut it out. He couldn't think beyond the cab that had not yet arrived.

A car passed. A dog barked in the distance. The morning air felt nice on his face. His back hurt. His throat was sore. Stretching felt good, his legs splayed out in front of the curb. He held these things close, bits of sensory detail, a talisman against the truth that he would not confront.

Rayleen was the daughter of his best friend.

Too many coincidences.

It simply could not be.

Thomas met him at the door and let him in. The pastor spoke softly, not wanting to disturb his wife. "The doctor gave her some medicine to get her through the night, but it didn't work very well," he said. "Neither one of us slept much. She's quiet right now." He shook his head.

"When is the funeral?" Daniel blurted.

"The day after tomorrow. The people from the battered women's shelter asked to help with the service, and I told them yes. They want to. . ." He turned suddenly. "There's something I have to tell you about my daughter."

"I have to talk to you too," Daniel said. He sat down at the kitchen table, a small Formica oval, careful not to bang his head on the overhead light. Thomas sat too, his back erect, his hands folded on the table. His face was unreadable. "How can I help you?" he asked, a touch of weary irony in his voice.

"I meant, I have to talk to you about your daughter," Daniel said.

253

"Ahhh," Thomas said. Daniel stared. How could he not have heard his echo in her voice? How could he have not seen the resemblance? Thomas had told him everything about his daughter. Surely he'd mentioned her name. Why hadn't he remembered?

Thomas was speaking. "She led. . .an unfortunate lifestyle. She. . ." he paused.

"I know."

"No you don't," Thomas said, shaking his head. "It was so unexpected. She allowed herself to be photographed. . .for pornography."

Daniel nodded miserably. "I know, Thomas."

"You can't imagine. Her mother is. . .shattered. You counsel people with serious problems, and it's so easy to distance yourself. Then your own daughter. . .and you can't possibly know. You tell people that you understand, but until it happens to you. . ."

"I know," Daniel repeated. "I knew her."

Thomas was still speaking. ". . .every imaginable pose. I won't be able to scrub those pictures from my mind. And worst of all, I still see her as a little girl. She was so happy, so bright. . ."

"She was extremely intelligent," Daniel agreed.

"They think they know who did it. They had him in custody."

"No!" Daniel said, flushing with anger. "They had me in custody! The guy who did it lives in Boulder. That is, I think a guy in Boulder. . ."

"What are you talking about?" Thomas was clearly irritated.

"I spent the night in jail," Daniel said. "It was bull shit."

"I'm sorry you're having trouble with the law," Thomas said. "Today just isn't a good day to talk about it. My daughter is dead." His voice had gone cold.

"Didn't they tell you who they had in custody?"

"I didn't want to know," Thomas said. "He did. . .terrible things to her." His eyes were red welts, and his voice was cracking again.

"I'm trying to tell you that I knew your daughter," Daniel repeated. "They arrested me last night. I spent some time with her the last week or so. A stalker was after her, someone who had seen her web site. . ." Thomas stared, his mouth open. "Rayleen was afraid, and she stayed with me. I even put her in the women's shelter one night. My sister does volunteer work for them. . ."

"You knew my Rayleen?" Thomas said. It was an accusation, not a question.

"Yes!" Daniel said, his voice rising. He was near tears. Frustration and grief threatened his self-control. "We were friends. She helped me with that case I was working on. . ."

"How did you meet?"

Daniel stopped. There was no compromising the answer. He stared into Thomas's eyes. "I saw her web site."

"Let me get this straight. You saw her on that web site, and you met her. And this last week, the girl who was with you, that was my daughter?"

Daniel nodded.

"Get out." The words sounded calm, but a firestorm raged behind Thomas's red eyes, and his hands had begun to shake.

"I didn't kill your daughter," Daniel said.

"I believe you. Now get the hell out of my house."

Daniel stood. "I know some things about your daughter," he said. "Good things. Things you ought to know. . ."

"For the love of God, get out of my house!" He grimaced, eyes squeezed shut against the tears, and his hands gripped the edge of the table, lifting it, and then slamming it down against the floor.

Daniel held his hands up, palms facing Thomas. "I'm going."

When Daniel reached his apartment, he grabbed the map to Jeremy Booth's home and headed for the bank. He checked his balance, wondering if the IRS had already frozen his account. Reassured that the money was there, he pulled out a thousand dollars, and took it to the car. He hid it under the driver's side seat, tucked into a spring where a hole had worn through the upholstery.

The drive to Boulder was flat and gray, with fields of stubble and patches of dirty snow that lulled him. He had to bite his lips to stay awake. Large black birds lined the intersections, riding the tops of the telephone poles. They reminded him of vultures, waiting for dinner to die.

What if Jeremy Booth wasn't the jogger? He would apologize, and head home. Then he would go back to Rayleen's disc and find the bastard who killed her. He wouldn't sleep until he'd solved the mystery. He would never sleep again, if need be. Anger ripped through him as he drove. He cursed a red light, cursed other drivers, and by the time he reached Jeremy Booth's house, he had wound himself into a frenzy.

Booth's house was in poor repair. The yard was badly kept. A small wooden arch centered a garden of weeds. The paint had worn away, and the top of the arch was broken, so it tilted to the side. The porch had a row of clay pots filled with dead plants. The sun was setting and lights were off in the house. Perhaps he wasn't home. Daniel waited, trying not to fall asleep.

And if Jeremy Smith was the jogger?

Daniel did not explore the thought. He wasn't interested in knowing where it might lead. Knowing the truth was an end in itself. What came after wouldn't matter.

Or would it? Was he lying to himself? Did he intend to hurt Booth? A piece of music slipped into his head, a phrase from his subconscious. An oldie, he realized after finding the lyric on his lips. "My boyfriend's back, and there's going to be trouble. . ." He laughed, a sound stripped of mirth, steeped in pain.

There was nothing to be gained by hiding the truth. It would be just fine with him if the jogger recognized him and took a swing. Then he could dish out a fair portion of vengeance. But mostly, he wanted the jogger to look him in the eye and know that retribution would follow. Let the courts have him. Daniel wanted him to know that justice would prevail.

When the sun set, Daniel decided to try the door. Perhaps Booth was sitting inside in the dark. There was a risk involved. He could imagine the door opening suddenly, and a gun barrel firing. He knocked anyway. There was no sound inside. He rang the doorbell. He could hear the bell. No answer.

He returned to the car. He was not going back to Fort Collins, not without finding out what he needed to know. In the meantime, he would visit Derek Ryan. Derek's apartment was only a few blocks away. He would see what he had to say about Jeremy Booth. He would look Derek in the eyes and see if there was a connection beyond a confounding serendipity.

His head ached. He needed sleep. He parked outside Derek's apartment and headed for the door, shambling into the street without looking. The scream of tires told him how close he'd come— a car lurched to a stop inches from his knees. The driver rolled down his window and began shouting, but Daniel was already gone, dodging bicycles and leaping to the curb.

At the apartment, Daniel hammered on the door. It opened, just a little. Derek had a chain fastened. He stared out at Daniel. "What do you want?" he asked.

"I need to ask you about your roommate."

"I live alone." Derek started to close the door.

"Your roommate in college. I think he was involved in a crime. I'm wondering what it has to do with you and your father."

Derek kept staring. "Why do you keep bothering me?"

"The young woman who was with me when I came here the first time? She was murdered. I believe the killer was Jeremy Booth. I want to know why all of this is happening."

Derek undid the latch. He opened the door, and stepped back. "I don't know anything that would help you. I don't know what you mean when you ask why 'all of this' is happening. All of what?"

Daniel walked in, leaving the door open behind him. "I was hired by your father to find 'Jesus.' What he wanted was his son. You were the man my wife left me for the night she died. Meanwhile, I'm spending time with a girl from a porn web site, and she's being stalked. Unknown to me, she is the runaway daughter of my best friend, also the minister of my church. The stalker kills the girl just after you confront your father. Your old college roommate might be the murderer."

"I can't follow any of that," Derek said, staring at Daniel, obviously concerned. "Are you ill?" He took a step closer to Daniel.

"No." Daniel backed against the wall. "I need to know. Did your father orchestrate any of this?"

Derek shook his head. "Seriously, how could he?"

"When was the last time you saw Jeremy Booth?"

"I haven't seen him since college." Derek took another step. "We weren't close. He was confused in his faith, and we had disagreements. . ."

The sound of the door stopped them both. A man stepped inside, closing the door behind him. He was in his early thirties, younger-looking than Derek. He had a mustache. Dressed in street clothes, he looked a little soft. His chin had started to double, and he had a paunch. He also had a gun.

"Jeremy?" Derek asked.

"Back up," Booth said, waving Derek over to the wall. Then he smiled at Daniel, a painful, twisted smile, part rictus, part irony; the smile of a man who almost never smiled. "I sat watching you from my living room window," he told Daniel. "I didn't want to settle this at my house. I would still prefer to handle this without involving my name. I have other work to do. How did you enjoy your stay in jail?"

Daniel didn't answer.

Booth held the gun out, pointing it at Daniel's chest. "You're not very talkative when the odds are against you," he said. He glanced back and forth at his two captives. "Ironic, finding you two together, isn't it?" He grinned. "You know who he is, don't you Derek? You know who his wife was?"

Daniel rubbed his eyes. "Why did you kill Rayleen?" he asked. "She harmed no one."

Jeremy aimed the gun at Daniel's head. "You shut up. Anything you say would be a lie. You work for the Prince of Liars. Don't speak."

"Do you mean Mordecai?" Daniel asked. Derek turned suddenly, staring at Daniel. Jeremy looked confused.

"If you stand against the Prince of Liars, then don't take this path," Derek told Jeremy.

"Shut up," Jeremy said, pointing the gun at Derek. "I'm doing the work of Jesus. . ."

"You mean him?" Daniel asked, pointing a thumb at Derek. The gun came back, aimed at his face. "I'm sorry," he said, starting to laugh, his control slipping away. "This is just too funny. Derek is Jesus, or maybe not. His dad is Joseph, or Longinus, or the Prince of Liars. Or were you talking about Satan? Jeremy here is doing God's work, or maybe. . ." his voice darkened, "maybe he's a fucking psycho who likes to kill young girls."

Someone pounded on the door. "Police. Open up."

Jeremy froze.

"They got you, asshole," Daniel said, laughing softly.

Jeremy sighted down the barrel. "I'm just here tracking a killer," he said.

Derek Ryan shot forward, deliberately moving in front of Daniel. The door burst open. Jeremy's gun fired, and men in uniform came tumbling into the room. More shots followed. Daniel fell back, banging his head against the wall. Derek spun, shoved into the mantle by a uniformed officer who was trying to cover him. The impact knocked the picture from the mantle, shattering the glass on the floor. Jeremy Booth waved his pistol in the air, and an officer snatched it from him. The room was full of policemen. One officer turned Daniel to the wall and began frisking him. He looked up. There was a bullet hole in the wall just a foot above him.

No more than five seconds had passed.

When Daniel turned again, he saw Jeremy Booth on the floor, his shirt soaked in his own blood. Derek Ryan stood by the mantle, rubbing his head. He hadn't been shot.

The detective with the rumpled nose who'd questioned Daniel strolled into the room, flanked by two other detectives. There were both Fort Collins Police and Boulder Police on the premises. The detective walked straight up to Daniel.

"Well, Bain," he said. "You come out of it without a scratch. Lucky for you we were following Booth."

An officer kneeling by Booth's side looked up. "He's gone," he said.

"Are you sure?"

"Oh yeah," the officer said. "His chest is a mess." He pulled the microphone from his belt radio. "We're secure here," he said. "Suspect down. . ."

"Well, your friend Mr. Booth is dead," the detective sighed. "Another lucky break for you. I'm willing to bet you were involved in the girl's murder, but I'm going to have a tough time proving it with him dead."

Daniel scowled. "Bull shit. You knew I'd try to confront him. You let me do your work for you. You weren't following Booth, you were following me. Who needs a warrant when you have a dupe?"

"Fuck you," the detective smiled.

Over the detective's shoulder, Daniel watched Derek Ryan walk to his old roommate, kneel, and lay a hand on Booth's cheek. One of the officers took Derek by the shoulder, trying to steer him away, but Derek would not be moved. "Let me be, please," he said. He whispered something, and put his hand on Booth's forehead.

Daniel had a clear view of what happened next. As the weeks passed, he would replay the memory, trying to understand. Jeremy Booth shuddered, a convulsion. Then he sat up, a sudden thrashing movement, his eyes open, white with horror. He took a huge breath, and screamed. Blood ran from his mouth, and spilled into his lap. Derek still knelt beside him, his hand still on his head.

"Get those paramedics in here now!" an officer shouted into his radio. Jeremy continued to thrash and scream on the floor. Derek slid his hand down, brushing Booth's cheek, and let go.

"What the hell is going on?" the detective shouted. The room erupted in a cascade of words, nearly drowned out by the piercing screams of Jeremy Booth, back from the dead.

XXXIV

TO: Daniel Bain

FROM: Rayleen

SUBJECT: Sorry

Dear Daniel,

Okay, so I'm driving home, and I start crying for no reason at all. And I'm wondering if I'm PMS-ing, or what. I started talking to you, like you were in the car with me, and I'm so pissed at you, I'm shouting! That's when I realized I missed you.

You probably hate me after last night. I was SUCH A BITCH. Sorry. Not the "fuck-you-very-much" sorry I gave you, but the real thing.

I need a few days to think things over. I was very content with the way I had the world figured out, and you've put a glitch in that, and I'm not very happy about it. Being with you has made me realize that I've missed something in my life, and that scares the absolute shit out of me.

For one thing, you remind me of my father. I think he'd actually like you. And that has got me thinking about calling my family, and that's another thing I'm angry at you for.

I know we never talked about us, and it seems silly as I write it, because I don't know if you think there's an "us," and even if you do, there's only been an "us" for a week or so.

And you're kind of old, you know? So I don't want you to get your hopes up. And I don't want you to get my hopes up. But please say we'll be friends for a long, long time, okay? I hate this, I really do, but I think I need you, and I want you to be around.

Anyway, about last night— sorry. Sorry, sorry, sorry!

There. That's all you get. Love, Rayleen

XXXV

When he got home, he checked his e-mail. The letter from Rayleen came up, and he realized that she had written him one last time before dying. He gave thought to not opening the e-mail. He could save it. It would be one last piece of her, not yet encountered, a piece of her alive, long after her death. Then he thought, no, the letter might be nothing more than a goodby. He clicked and began to read.

When he finished, he cried. He was tired, spent, and the letter was the last straw. He read it again and again, and then tumbled into bed.

Sometime in the night, he woke up to use the bathroom. His eyes had crusted over and his head ached. He put himself back to bed immediately. He slept until morning, when the first phone call came. After that, there was no rest at all.

The resurrection incident made great copy, and the story went nationwide immediately. An ex-minister, retired in his early thirties to "rewrite gospel," confronts a murderer. When the police shoot the intruder, killing him, the ex-minister "lays on hands" and brings a corpse back from the dead.

Booth's reprieve was short-lived. He "died again" on the operating table just after midnight. The chief surgeon told reporters, "That he died is no surprise. What I can't figure out is why he was alive." Police rounds had blown a hole the size of a grapefruit in his chest. Half of his internal organs were damaged or destroyed.

Derek Ryan's personae helped to sell the story. He was elusive, secretive, answering reporter's questions with questions of his own, quick to credit God for Booth's miraculous resurrection. "Grace is God's gift to mankind," he said, "no matter what the sin." Certain comparisons to a fisherman from Galilee were inevitable. Some religious leaders acknowledged the "miracle." Others decried the press's lack of skepticism.

As for Jeremy Booth, a search of his apartment yielded a wealth of information, but no answers. The police found computer journals, full of long, rambling threats against Rayleen, Daniel, his professors at the theology college, every supervisor at every job he'd ever held, even the register man at the nearby Seven-Eleven. Initial reports would only say that Booth was a "deeply disturbed individual." Commentators criticized the inability to spot and deter potential murderers. Why didn't anyone stop Booth before he began killing? Legislation was proposed, and a bill known as the "Booth Bill" drew some attention in the House of Representatives before dying in committee.

Rayleen became the poor-little-rich-girl, a runaway who fell into a life of sex and drugs, and paid the ultimate price. For some, she was an object lesson in the perils of immorality.

The local women's movement made enthusiastic use of her murder, calling her a "victim in life, a victim in death." Men had used her, forcing her natural entrepreneurial talents into a field that degraded her.

The tabloids would retell her death for months to come, lingering over a single detail; the burned eyes. Her final agony was being used to entertain the inquisitive public.

For Daniel, there were phone calls. Reporters for both the print and broadcast media were relentless. And there was a call from Winthrop, informing him that Mordecai Ryan had passed on in the night. Daniel was reminded of the old legend. Longinus could rest only when Christ had returned.

Daniel called Penny early in the morning to ask about the funeral. "I heard that your shelter is helping to organize Rayleen's service. Where and when?" Penny seemed withdrawn, evasive. "Are you all right?" he asked.

"Fine." A single, clipped word.

"I don't know if you know this," Daniel said, "but the cops had me in jail overnight. They thought I might have had something to do with Rayleen's murder. I told them to call the women's shelter, but the detective said he was told that I didn't bring her there."

"Technically, you didn't."

He sighed. "Not personally, but I brought her to you."

"I have to ask you this. Did you have anything to do with her death?"

Daniel held the receiver away from his head and stared at it. "Are you kidding me?" he said at last. "Of course not. She was my friend. Did you seriously think I killed her? Jesus, Penny! This is me!"

"All right, I believe you." She sounded like Thomas, offering cold reassurance.

"Is that why you're so reluctant to give me information about the services?" he asked. "Because you think I killed her?"

"No," she said. "But I don't think it's a good idea for you to go there."

"I'm sorry to hear that. Why?"

Pause. "I don't think it's appropriate."

"Again, I'm sorry to hear that. But I will be at the service. Sorry to have upset you." He hung up the phone.

He went into the bathroom, and stared into the mirror. He stepped back, surprised. His reflection looked tired and angry, but determined. It was him, perhaps a slimmer him than he was expecting, little older, by a year or two. Had he been on the case for just a few weeks?

He had changed. His circumstances were the same, perhaps worse. He still lived in a studio apartment. He was still broke. The police didn't like him. His sister and her friends wanted nothing to do with him. His best friend wasn't speaking to him. He'd spent the last week with a nineteen year-old porn model, and she was dead.

But it didn't feel like rock bottom. It felt uncertain, shifting, changing, but ripe with possibility. He closed his eyes, and gave thanks. She had given his life a jump start, and he would not squander it.

The phone rang again. It was his mother. "Penny called me. She's very upset."

"I'm sorry to hear that."

"I don't want you to go to the service tomorrow, Daniel."

"It's not negotiable, Mom." He smiled. "Don't do this. You hate confrontations. Don't get caught in the middle of this."

"I can't help it. I don't want you two to fight."

"I won't fight with her, Mom," he said. "But I won't stay away from the funeral."

"But we're supposed to be family!" she wailed.

"We are. But I'm also Daniel. My friend Rayleen is dead. I'm going to celebrate her memory."

"We're supposed to get along. It's not right." Her voice was tired now.

"We'll be fine," Daniel said. "We can argue and still love each other. Now, you've done your best. Let me go. I'll talk to you soon." When she hung up, Daniel unplugged the phone.

◆ ◆ ◆

The service was held the following afternoon. Media vans lined the street, and cars from Colorado and other neighboring states were squeezed together as if they'd been shoved into the curb sideways. Daniel parked four blocks away and walked toward the chapel, past the winter trees, over broken old sidewalks. The homes along the way were tired frame houses, built in the forties and fifties. Some of them were well-kept. Others let time strip them, warp them, and cover them in weeds.

He was nervous. He had been to a funeral where he was not welcome, and he was heading to another one. As before, he would do what he thought he ought to. This time, though, he would not apologize for himself. He had a right to be there.

The sun had already begun its arc down, hovering over the rim of the mountains to the west. It was clear and cold. He could taste ice in the air. People were singing up ahead. He saw women holding signs. "Take Back the Streets!" one cried. From whom? "Never Again!" said another. Daniel snorted. A pipe dream, at least in the world he knew, a world of frightened humans, not noticing those around them, trying not to be noticed themselves. Fractured, fragmented souls holding the narratives of their lives together by threads and memories. Imperfect people, imagining perfection in others, lying about who they were, giving themselves the perfect story.

Packed together, always afraid, most would protect themselves, creating boundaries with their words. A few would hide in their little rooms and plot, hoping to shock the world into noticing them. Men like Jeremy Booth. And there would be victims.

Penny, Christine, and a half dozen women met him on the chapel lawn. "You're not wanted here," one announced. She was tall, willowy, with flat, straight hair down to the small of her back. Her voice was layered with a hundred angers, and Daniel was the focus of all of them. A photographer stopped, and began snapping pictures. The tall woman stood closer, going nose to nose with Daniel, helping to frame the shot.

"I understand that you're uncomfortable with me here," he said, "and I'm sorry. But I'm here to say goodby to a friend." He tried to move around, but his sister blocked his way.

"I can't believe you're doing this!" she hissed. "I don't understand you!"

"I'll take you at your word," he said, "and try to explain it to you. I'm saying goodby to a friend. If this was just about you, I'd stay away, Penny. Right or wrong, I'd stay away. But it's not about you. It's about my friend Rayleen." He moved again, and two of the women moved with him. Penny stood still.

"I have a right to be here," he said. "You don't have to like it." They were shouting at him now, demanding that he leave. Reporters trotting over, microphones extended, looking for an angle, a hook to hang a story on, a way to give the death meaning. Daniel stood still. Across the lawn, he saw Thomas and his wife. Their attention had been drawn by the commotion, and they had stopped to watch. Daniel's eyes locked on Thomas's, and Daniel shrugged. Do you want me to leave? She was your daughter. . .

Thomas looked down, and grimaced. The struggle was obvious. Daniel started to back away. On his left, a trio of young people, two girls and a boy in their late teens, came up to brace him. They were dressed in an odd assortment of designer jeans and second-hand sweaters and vests. They carried pamphlets, and the boy held a sign proclaiming "The New Millennium of the Spirit." "We can all get along together," one girl said, her eyebrow ring punctuating her serious eyes. "We all belong to one another. Even this man." Daniel groaned.

Christine pushed her way next to him. "You're hurting your sister!" she said. Her eyes were rimmed red with tears. It was an emotional morning.

Daniel leaned close, his hands behind him. "I really want to like you, Christine," he said. "You treat Penny like she deserves to be treated. But that doesn't give you a license to treat me like shit." She started to squall, and he cut her short. "I have a right to be here."

A pair of policeman came over to maintain order, and on cue, the willowy woman began shouting again, this time with her hands clasped in front of her, shrinking from Daniel, as if he would strike her. And in the back of his mind was the urge to do just that, the urge to slap her self-righteous, camera-conscious face.

One of the policemen was the officer who had come to his apartment after the first break-in. They recognized each other, Daniel with a wry smile, and the officer with a stone glare. "Making friends again, I see," he said.

"He doesn't belong here! How can you let him be here?" The willowy woman railed at Daniel's obvious transgression.

"He's all right officer," said the girl with the pierced brow.

Reporters clustered around the swelling spiral of people on the chapel lawn, shoving microphones into the faces of anyone with an opinion. It was becoming difficult to hear. Those being interviewed had to shout to state their positions. One officer was jostled from behind by a young girl in an ankle-length dress and down vest. He turned angrily, calling to his partner, who grabbed the girl from behind, a rough move that angered some of the women in the crowd. Some of them began chanting, "No More Violence! No More Violence!" Officers called for backup while the women with signs screamed at point-blank range. The pamphlet-carriers started to join in, but stopped, realizing that the words were not an echo of their message, but a battle cry. They began singing instead, accompanied by people from the crowd who had joined hands.

Daniel slipped around behind the officers and the wall of chanters, unnoticed for just a moment. By the time shouts warned the crowd— "He's over there!" — he had already started up the walk to the chapel. A few quick steps, and he was inside.

The chapel interior was bright. Light streamed in from floor-to-ceiling windows, tumbling over dozens of flower arrangements. Thomas was seated in the second row with his wife. Neither one would meet his gaze. Daniel walked to the closed casket. No one would stop him, not inside the chapel.

He wouldn't stay long. He had already been a disruption. He hadn't done anything wrong. His involvement in the circus outside was an accident of circumstance. Nevertheless, he was a focus of attention, and this was supposed to be a day to remember Rayleen. He would say goodby and leave, and let the various factions battle over the meaning of the service.

He put his hand on the dark wood casket. A few family members stood to the side, paying him no notice. He was grateful. "You have a lot of advocates here," he whispered. "I thought you'd like a friend too." The thought made him smile.

A memory came to him. They were dining at a Perkins, the first night they'd met. She put her head down on the table, and then glanced up at him, planning to ask if she could stay with him for the night. A simple moment. But what did it mean? She was a child cradling her head in her arms. She was a woman, flirting with him. She was frightened. She was brave. She was being manipulative, and she was being cute. It would have taken him forever to get to know her. And it would have been fun to try.

The smell of flowers was everywhere. People talked in whispers, like soft rain at the window. It was a quiet moment, and he let it happen.

He wasn't sure if what he'd felt was love, but given time, it surely could have been. And he would love someone again, he was certain now. He started to speak, but it felt wrong. She wasn't here. She was gone. He touched the casket, and left.

The next day he attended a second funeral. Mordecai Ryan's ceremony was muted, dark, and nearly unattended. Derek Ryan was in New York, filming appearances for television news shows, and was unable to be there. Daniel recalled the rewritten gospel passage, demanding that a follower leave his father unburied. Derek was, at the very least, consistent.

The weather had changed again. Hard rain turned the ground to mud. A half-dozen people endured the short service, huddled under umbrellas. Winthrop was absent, and Daniel did not recognize any of the others. The wind picked up near the end, driving the rain in waves through the air. A bouquet of flowers placed on the casket blew off twice— the second time they were left in the mud while the speaker finished the eulogy.

Why had he come? Daniel liked Mordecai Ryan a little, but only in the way that one might like a well-drawn villain in a book or a movie he liked him from a distance. Up close, the old man had been dry rot, inside and out. He was a manipulator and a liar. But Daniel knew that his own life had changed when the old man hired him. And it bothered Daniel that any life would pass without notice.

Mordecai Ryan was an enigma. Derek's most recent web posting was the parable of the wheat and the weeds, but Mordecai was neither one, or more correctly, he was both. He was a smuggler, a Nazi collaborator, scholar, a preacher, a father, a tyrant, and possibly a saint. He was a part of Daniel's story now. Acknowledging the old man was a part of acknowledging himself. He stood in the rain, paying his respect in the conventional way. Later, while drinking a beer, he thought of Mordecai Ryan again, and offered a silent toast.

It was the parable of the wheat and weeds that stuck in his mind. Something about Derek's last Internet post bothered him, and for a day or two, he was unable to find the reason for his unease. It was while cleaning his desk from two week's clutter that it came to him.

The answer was in the academic piece that Derek Ryan wrote when he was in college. Derek found the title in his notes. The work was hard to find, but the college library got him a copy through the intra-library loan program. *"Obscuring the Message: Authorial Intrusion in the Four Gospels"* was a dense read, laced with references to previous Biblical criticism. Still, the prose was clear enough, and Daniel found what he was looking for.

The curly-haired police detective sat in the booth, hunched over his beer, looking everywhere but into Daniel's eyes. He'd bumped into Daniel at the grocery store ("Let me buy you a beer. Really, I insist"), and Daniel found himself sipping a micro-brew in one of the hangouts on South College Avenue. The students were out in

273

force, celebrating finals and the end of the semester. Music battled the shouts and laughter for attention. It was a good place to hold a careful conversation.

"So let me get all of this straight. . ."

"Are we on the record?"

"No, we're just two guys having a beer," the detective insisted. He ran a finger along his rumpled nose and sniffed. "I just want to get the story right in my head. For myself. You don't mind, do you?"

"Yes, I do mind, but if you have more questions, I'm willing to answer them. This time."

The detective pulled out a file card with some notes scribbled in pencil. "So you never met Ms. Rogers until the week before the murder?"

"No."

"But she was the daughter of a friend of yours?" The detective shouted over the music.

"You already know that." A young couple passed by the booth, laughing. The girl bumped the lip of the table with her hip, spilling foam down the side of Daniel's beer glass.

"Bear with me. You're hired to find Jesus, who turns out to be the man who took your wife from you. The Jesus-guy's roommate is the psycho who kills the daughter of your best friend, someone you just met. The IRS freezes your accounts because the man who hired you is a career criminal. He's also the father of the man you're hired to find. And the one person who sets the whole mess rolling down the alley like a shit-ball after a set of pins is you. Am I right?"

"I guess so," Daniel admitted. "If I hadn't met Rayleen, there would've been no connections." All the dominoes tumbled from a single moment, the moment he'd first gone to Boulder, the moment Rayleen ran from her house, spotted his car, and climbed in to escape Jeremy Booth.

"Too many coincidences, huh?" The detective sipped his beer, his eyes suddenly locked on Daniel.

"Like you bumping into me tonight," Daniel said. "So I'm guessing you think Rayleen's death was some kind of conspiracy?"

"I know it was," the detective said. "There's no such thing as a coincidence. I don't know what the motive was. Money is a good guess, knowing human nature. If I knew for sure what everyone stood to gain, I'd have you all figured out."

Daniel pushed his beer away. "Am I being recorded? I worry about tape editing."

"I'm not wearing a wire," the detective scowled. "And this place is too noisy to pick up anything. You can talk to me, one-on-one. I just want to know. I want to know the truth."

The truth, Daniel thought.

"You can tell me. The case is considered closed."

The DJ in the bar put on some old techno. The thump of the bass drilled into Daniel's temples. The detective wasn't going to believe him, because believing him meant believing in serendipity, and that wasn't in the man's character. "Okay, here's the deal," Daniel said. He leaned forward, as if to deliver a secret. "I don't think God was behind this."

"Right. Thanks for that. What about the conspiracy?"

"If there was a conspiracy, everything had to have come from me. I had to be the lynch-pin, the trigger, the mastermind. And I have special knowledge on that matter. I don't know what Jeremy Booth was thinking. I don't know what old man Ryan was thinking. But I know what I was thinking, and I wasn't involved in a conspiracy."

The detective snorted. "Somebody got away with something, you can bet on that." He leaned in closer, his hands flat out on the table. "But the curiosity is killing me. Come on, tell me. What really happened?" His eyes had narrowed. A half-smile showed his teeth. He looked like a cat ready to spring.

"Why detective, you're scaring me a little."

"You have some reason to be scared?"

"Yes, I think I do. You're the asshole who hit me from behind at the jail, aren't you?"

The detective blinked. The smile was gone. His face was flat and empty. There was no way to read him.

"There was no conspiracy, Detective. It was all one huge coincidence."

"Yeah, right. What are the odds?"

"You tell me." Daniel paused. "What are the odds that a police detective would wrap up a case that involved the torture of an innocent girl by buying the suspect a beer and listening to techno just days before Christmas? What are the odds? Tell me, what's your part in the conspiracy?"

Daniel slid out of the booth and put his jacket on. "Let me answer my own question for you, Detective. The odds are one-in-one, because that's what happened. Every event looks funny if you look at it from the wrong end of the telescope."

"What the fuck does that mean?"

"Figure it out. You're the sleuth."

"So what are you saying? You think Derek Becker is the Messiah?"

Daniel smiled and said, "Actually, I know the answer to that one." Then he turned and left.

At first, Daniel wondered. Might Derek Ryan really be the Second Coming of Christ? An increasing number of people were anxious to believe, anxious to follow Derek's well-publicized path. Mordecai's son had become very powerful in a short period of time, making enemies in the process. The Bishop in Denver was said to be considering a meeting. At the same time, a movement to denounce the new light of the spiritual world was spreading, spearheaded by some members of the Council of Churches. In politics as in religion, the call for obedience required administrators, executors, leaders. Derek Ryan was a player now. Daniel wished him luck.

But was he the Messiah? Daniel had an answer, one supplied by Derek himself. In his writings, Derek argued that the gospel writers couldn't resist weaving their own opinions and hopes into the text of the Passion Gospels, hiding the true Christ behind the fabric of their words.

On the ride from Boulder to Ft. Collins, Derek repeated the notion when he explained the rewritten Gospels on his web page. "I think of it as returning to the original Word...Somewhere, the message got lost."

According to Derek's paper, one sure sign of authorial intrusion was apocalyptic referencing. Jesus was direct and compelling, but Derek's Jesus didn't threaten his followers with the end of the world.

Yet Derek himself offered up a rewritten version of the parable of the wheat and weeds, the most apocalyptic of all the parables. Even Derek Ryan couldn't resist the urge to threaten. It wasn't enough to say, "Obey." It had to be, "Obey, or else."

Derek's actions could be measured and judged by his own standards. His rewritten Gospel was laced with the very things he argued against. The "new" Gospel was false, and so was Derek Becker.

Daniel had no proof, but he'd spotted a contradiction, and that was enough. In his mind, the mystery was solved.

On the other hand, if Derek was just a man, then events had been the result of random chance. There was no hand of God. There was no conspiracy. There was only chance.

That possibility frightened Daniel at first. His mind rebelled at the thought of helplessness in the face of chaos. He preferred conspiracy or providence. At least someone was in charge. At least someone pulled the strings.

Daniel believed that he'd wanted the truth. Wasn't that what he'd said, again and again? He knew the facts. But the truth? What he really wanted was a story, something to tie the loose ends into a neat bundle. He didn't want the truth, he wanted a tale to make sense of what had happened.

But no tale could do that.

As the days passed, Daniel kept his routine, running, lifting and doing computer work to pay the bills. He contacted some of the larger investigation firms, dropping off business cards, offering to do contract work, a move that yielded a few extra jobs. He also placed a few well-chosen ads, targeting collections as his niche. Business was good, despite bad economic news. Even the latest downturn on Wall Street and the collapse of the Euro-dollar hadn't hurt his business. He could envision a time when he would have to either cut back and take only the higher paying jobs or add an assistant.

He was sleeping better, enough to keep regular hours. He would never get used to sleeping alone, he decided, but he would take his time solving that particular problem.

The IRS had frozen his bank account and refused to release it—guilty until proven innocent when dealing with those folks. Luckily, his rent had been paid ahead, and he had cash tucked in the upholstery of his car. The little amount the IRS had confiscated wouldn't mean much down the road. His lawyer seemed certain that Daniel would win his case eventually.

Daniel avoided Thanksgiving dinner at his mother's house. It was too soon after the funeral to see anyone. He was secretly thankful not to have to lie about the dryness of the turkey his mother had surely burned. By Christmas, though, his sister and Christine would probably be ready to see him again. And he would stay in touch because his family was a part of his story (though he was certain that future chapters would find him less willing to tolerate Christine's rude behavior and more apt to demand civility and respect from them all).

Soon after the funeral, he saw Rayleen in a dream. She stood at a distance, silhouetted by a blinding sun, wearing a white cotton nightgown, ankle-length with frills and lace, the kind of nightgown she would never have worn. Daniel stepped to the side, blocking the sun with his hand, and saw that she was standing in his mother's yard. Weeds had overrun the lawn; huge green and brown growths with stalks like trunks. Smaller weeds twisted through the chain-link and pulled down the fence, swallowing it in old leaves.

The weeds became a forest, blotting the sun. He could see more clearly now, but the lush growth blocked his view of the girl. It had been Rayleen, he was certain of it. He knew her smile, even in the twilight. He crept forward, winding through the trees, but lost sight of her completely in the lengthening shadows.

He pushed through the underbrush, through the sick, sweet smell of weed pollen. She'd been right there in front of him, hadn't she? The bark of an older oak had a curious shape where a branch had torn free and scarred over. The lip of the bark looked like a face. Had he been fooled? And where was his mother's house?

He looked down. A window shutter sat half-buried in the mud where rainwater trickled past the roots of a pine. I'm dreaming, he thought. He sat down in the dark wood, stretching his legs into the weeds until they became bed sheets.

He tried to go back to sleep, to find her again in another dream. He dreamed of yard work instead, pushing a mower through his mother's dead lawn.

XXXVI

Soon after the funeral, he saw Rayleen in a dream. She stood at a distance, silhouetted by a blinding sun, wearing a white cotton nightgown, ankle-length with frills and lace, the kind of nightgown she would never have worn. Daniel stepped to the side, blocking the sun with his hand, and saw that she stood in his mother's yard. Weeds had overrun the lawn; huge green and brown growths with stalks like trunks. Smaller weeds twisted through the chain-link and pulled down the fence, swallowing it in old leaves.

The weeds became a forest, blotting the sun. He could see more clearly now, but the lush growth blocked his view of the girl. It had been Rayleen, he was certain of it. He knew her smile, even in the twilight. He crept forward, winding through the trees, but lost sight of her completely in the lengthening shadows.

He pushed through the underbrush, through the sick, sweet smell of weed pollen. She'd been right there in front of him, hadn't she? The bark of an older oak had a curious shape where a branch had torn free and scarred over. The lip of the bark looked like a face. Had he been fooled? And where was his mother's house?

He looked down. A window shutter sat half-buried in the mud where rainwater trickled past the roots of a pine. I'm dreaming, he thought. He sat down in the dark wood, stretching his legs into the weeds until they became bed sheets.

He tried to go back to sleep, to find her again in another dream. He dreamed of yard work instead, pushing a mower through his mother's dead lawn.

XXXVII

When Daniel moved to a larger apartment, he came across the video tapes he'd purchased from Rayleen. He threw the two he'd already watched into the trash and put the unopened tapes into a box for safe-keeping.

Later that same day, he fished the two discarded tapes back out of the trash and added them to the box.

As each dark morning came, Daniel wondered if Thomas would join him for a run in the Oval. He continued to hope. One morning in early December, he passed by a black Saturn with dealer plates. The man climbing from the driver's side door was tall and clean-shaven. It took a moment to recognize him.

Daniel smiled. "Are you here to run?"

Thomas took off his coat, revealing a new jogging suit. He pitched the coat into the car and locked the door.

"New car," Daniel said. "Nice."

Thomas nodded and began to stretch. Daniel joined him, puffing vapor into the dark morning air. When Thomas was ready, they jogged into the Oval.

"I'm glad you're here," Daniel said.

"Me too," he answered. His face was rigid with a smile. "It's been an exciting time for me, this last week. Our denomination is exploring the possibility of affiliating itself with the New Spiritual Movement."

"What's that?"

"We're in a rebirth, Daniel. A time of spiritual renewal. This country was built on a special relationship with God, and we've turned away. Until now. Now, there's a feeling of hope, a sense that we're coming home."

"It sounds like your crisis of faith is over," Daniel said. Thomas flinched, and Daniel wished he could take the sentence back. Thomas might have taken it as a taunt. "I hadn't heard of any new spiritual movement. . ."

"No, the New Spiritual Movement. That's the name of the church."

"Oh." Daniel frowned. "Say, that wouldn't have anything to do with Derek Becker, would it?"

"You've met him," Thomas said. His voice was careful, cautious. "What do you think of him?"

"Please don't ask," Daniel said. They were moving quickly, and his breath came hard. "To tell you the truth, I don't give a damn about Derek Becker. I wanted to talk to you about Rayleen."

Thomas ran stiff-necked, his jaw jutting forward.

"We can just run if you'd prefer."

Thomas scowled. He pounded ahead, picking up the pace. "I'm still angry with you," he said at last. "She was nineteen, Daniel."

Daniel listened.

"I thought I might not be so angry, but seeing you. . ." He clenched his fists in frustration. "I might be angry with you for a long time."

"That's okay. We're here to run. Being pissed off isn't a bad thing when you're facing a couple of miles in the cold." Thomas gave a grudging nod.

They continued at a furious pace. Daniel was much lighter than he had been before, and weeks of running had kept him in excellent shape. But before long, Thomas pulled ahead, as he always had, and when they finished, Daniel was a half-lap behind, struggling to breathe.

The weeks of separation hadn't cost Thomas a step. "Great run," Daniel gasped. "You didn't lose anything. . ."

"I lost a daughter," he said. Silence. There was no proper answer.

Thomas kicked the curb with his running shoes. "I won't be able to run with you very often." Thomas stared at the dark morning sky. "My schedule is funny right now. The realignment means a tremendous amount of work. . ."

Daniel smiled. "This didn't work for you, did it?"

Thomas glared at him. "I thought I could do it," he said. "I wanted to forgive you." He sighed. "A good Christian man should be able. . ."

"You are a good man," Daniel said. "But you're wrong. Perhaps you aren't able to forgive me because there's nothing to forgive. I didn't do anything wrong. Rayleen and I were friends. She was a lovely young woman. She touched my life."

"Don't tell me you loved her," Thomas growled.

"Why not? I'd be talking to her father, the man who raised her, the man who held her when she got her shots, the man who cleaned her up when she scraped her knees. Who else would understand how special she was?"

Thomas winced.

"Maybe I didn't know her well enough to love her," Daniel continued. "But I could have loved her if I'd had time. She deserved to be loved. Hell, you raised her."

"I didn't raise her that way!" he cried. "Not the way she ended up. It's killing her mother just knowing what she did."

"She was good, Thomas. Being confused doesn't mean she was bad."

Thomas waved him off. "Please, I can't discuss this now," he said. "Besides, I came here for you. I thought of you often over the last few weeks. I've prayed that after everything, you would find your way to God. You're one of a few people blessed with the chance to meet the one we look to for hope. . ."

Daniel shook his head. "I don't believe."

"I don't understand that!" Thomas exclaimed. The anguish in his voice was real. "You were at the center of this. . .this mess. How can you not believe that it was part of a plan?"

"I can live with not understanding everything that happens to me."

"But can you bear a world without God? Doesn't it frighten you?"

"A world without God doesn't frighten me, Thomas. What frightens me is a God who would create a world where big fish eat little fish. I'll take a chaotic universe over cruelty by design."

Thomas closed his eyes. When he opened them again, his face had hardened. "I'll pray for you."

"Don't go yet," Daniel said. "I want you to know that she loved you. She said that you and I were a lot alike. I think that was part of the attraction."

Thomas didn't move.

"Some day, I want to tell you what I knew about her. And I want to hear what you know. You know the stories. You were her father. I want to hear everything about her. We'll sit down over a bottle of wine, and talk. She won't fade away if we talk about her. . ." He stopped. His words sounded hollow, because he was selling, trying to convince Thomas, and because dredging for memories wouldn't bring her back.

It was an old temptation, and he resisted it. It would be so easy to spend his future archiving her memory. It was the same old pattern, hiding from life, playing up the broken heart. But she had already marked his life, and he was a different man now. "Maybe it's the wrong time," he finished glumly. "Someday. It would be good to talk about her. I'll wait until the pain's gone."

"The pain will never be gone."

Daniel nodded. "Maybe so. But I will hope for the day." The sun was coming up over the rooftops now. Who knew what weather the day would bring? The air was stiff with cold, but the sky was clear. "It was nice running with you today, Thomas." He felt a sudden sadness. His words felt like a goodby.

"And with you," Thomas mumbled. They bowed in awkward deference to a past friendship and parted ways.

Months later, when Daniel called the church, he learned that Thomas had transferred to the west coast. The new pastor told him that Thomas and his wife were doing very well, that they loved the northern California climate. Daniel asked for a forwarding address. He wrote it down and put it in his wallet, where he kept it as a symbol of hope, bittersweet with faint potential.

Afterword

The idea of harvesting the real words of Jesus from the Gospels came from "The Five Gospels: The Search for the Authentic Words of Jesus" by Robert W. Funk, Roy W. Hoover, and the Jesus Seminar. (Polebridge Press, from Scribner, 1993). I want to thank the Jesus Seminar for the notion, and their kind permission to use it as a starting point.

Fort Collins residents will recognize real landmarks next to imaginary ones. "The Apocalypse Parable" is a novel, so I played fast and loose with the geography. The characters in the novel are completely fictional.

A special thanks to Polish artist Waldek Kaminski who crafted an unnervingly accurate portrayal of Daniel Bain's dream.

And finally, thanks to my publisher Charles Kaine, who not only went out on a limb for this novel, he took a saw with him and hacked away at the only escape route…

Anyone who wishes to correspond about the themes or resolution of "The Apocalypse Parable" can reach me at bkaufman@verinet.com.